...on lives in the Forest of Dea...
... with her lovely husband and Bengal cat, Ziggy.

'I'm a hopeless romantic, self-confessed chocaholic and lover of strong coffee. For me, life is all about family, friends and writing.

At the weekend, I can be found either in the garden weeding, or with a paint brush in my hand - house renovation and upcycling furniture is another passion of mine! Oh, and I do enjoy the occasional glass of White Grenache ...'

Linn's novels have been short-listed in the UK's Festival of Romance and the eFestival of Words Book Awards. Linn won the 2013 UK Festival of Romance: Innovation in Romantic Fiction award.

Linn writes chick lit, cosy mystery/romances, romcoms and women's contemporary fiction– *written from the heart, for the heart*!

@LinnBHalton

facebook.com/LinnBHaltonAuthor

www.linnbhalton.co.uk

Also by Linn B. Halton

Falling: The Complete Angels Among Us
A Cottage in the Country

LINN B. HALTON

the Secrets of Villa Rosso

A division of HarperCollins*Publishers*

www.harpercollins.co.uk

Harper*Impulse* an imprint of
HarperCollins*Publishers*
The News Building
1 London Bridge Street
London SE1 9GF

www.harpercollins.co.uk

This paperback edition 2017

First published in Great Britain in ebook format by
HarperCollins*Publishers* 2017

A catalogue record for this book
is available from the British Library

ISBN: 9780008261283

When you have an idea that is like a tiny seed in the back of your head, you dash off some words knowing that one day the story will begin to make itself known to you. That 'one day' turned out to be three years later.

I have to thank my lovely husband, Lawrence, for being instrumental in helping me to find the perfect setting in which to unravel Ellie's tale. Once I had that, the words just flowed until I found myself writing *The End*.

Over the years we have always found the Italian people to be so very warm and welcoming. The scenery is out of this world and I can still close my eyes and spirit myself away to some memorable evenings dining al fresco, accompanied by the sounds of the singing cicadas.

Love you always and forever.

OUR NINETEENTH WEDDING ANNIVERSARY

Chapter 1

Staring back at me from the crystal ball cradled within my hands is the mirror image of a foetus. Then I realise it isn't one but two little beings facing each other. The picture is so unexpected that my arms begin to tremble and I almost drop the heavy sphere. Their umbilical cords are still attached and my eyes seek out every little detail, wondering why this is being shown to me. The little faces suddenly become animated and I can see their mouths moving as they talk to each other. Surreal doesn't even begin to describe the feeling that overcomes me and I barely register that I'm no longer alone, until a familiar voice breaks the silence.

'Oh, Ellie, you've found my crystal ball! It doesn't work; no one has ever seen anything in it. I was told it belonged to a famous medium, but it's going to end up being a very expensive ornament.' My boss and best friend's voice reflects amusement as our eyes meet. Stunned, I have to compose myself before I can return her casual smile and make light of the moment.

Livvie is completely unaware of the images I'm holding within my hands. As I look away from her I glance down once more. It's only then that I notice that the two little babies are actually divided, within the globe, by a glass wall. A significant detail I nearly missed, which makes my heart race. I feel as if I'm being given a message, but I have no idea at all what it means. Or maybe I'm a desperate woman in search of peace and normality, looking for answers to a problem which has become almost too much to bear.

I replace the globe on the aged, wooden stand and a sudden chill sends a tremor through me. Livvie is already making her way back out through the house to the patio, where the party is in full swing. I follow in her footsteps, angry with myself and wondering why on earth I'd picked the damned thing up in the first place. Had it been calling out to me?

'There you are. I've missed you.' Josh wraps a comforting arm around my waist and passes me a cocktail. 'The ice has already begun to melt; you said you'd only be a minute. You nearly missed your own toast. To us, darling!'

He holds his glass aloft and everyone steps forward to chink glasses.

'To Josh and Ellie on their nineteenth wedding anniversary. You guys remind us all that true love really does last forever.'

Livvie's toast is from the heart and maybe for a moment she's wondering if she'll ever find a Mr Right. I suspect the thought is only a fleeting one, though.

I look up at Josh, trying hard to stop my face from reflecting the rush of emotions those pale-grey eyes always stir within me. That familiar tousled, brown hair frames the face I know so well, partly obscuring the birthmark on his cheek. I call it his 'kiss from an angel' and that always makes him smile.

All I ever longed for was to love and be loved, and when Livvie introduced me to Josh, one tiny moment in time changed my whole life forever. He was, and is, my Prince Charming. I remember it as if it were only yesterday, wondering how nineteen years could have passed by at such a frightening speed and deposited us here. Where did all those days go? And why did my wonderful life have to be turned upside down?

IN THE BEGINNING

Chapter 2

The first time I found myself face to face with Josh it ignited a spark that put everything else in the shade. More important, even, than the moment we first said 'I love you' to each other, because at that point we already knew in our hearts it was a done deal. We just hadn't spoken the words out loud, as if it was tempting fate and something might happen to spoil our happiness. By then we were living together, but our first trip to Paris took our relationship to a whole new level.

~

'Ellie, head for that one.' Josh tilted his head and I followed his gaze. Then I sprinted ahead. Pulling open the taxi door I threw my bag in first and leapt in after it, sliding across the back seat to make room for Josh. He bundled in behind me, forcing the large holdall onto our laps.

We started to laugh, nervous relief taking over as the driver waited patiently to hear our destination.

'English?' Josh enquired, hopefully,

'*Non*. A leetle, meybee.' The driver shrugged his shoulders.

'*Désolé, j'ai l'adresse quelque part.*' It was a brave attempt on Josh's part and I gave him an encouraging smile.

After much fumbling in pockets, Josh finally held up his hand, thrusting a piece of paper bearing the address of our hotel across to the driver, who nodded. Settling back in our seats, the car sped along avenues and over crossroads, cutting down side streets. We stared in awe at the tantalising glimpses of Parisian life, seen up close for the first time. The driver's hand seemed to be constantly on the horn as he kept up a low mumble of complaint. When he dropped us off we had no idea how much he was asking for and Josh had bravely stuffed a note into his hand. The driver's face broke out into a small smile and we guessed that Josh had given him a big tip. He rammed the car into gear and sped away in haste, no doubt worried Josh would change his mind.

Standing on the kerb outside that hotel, Josh pulled me into his arms and lifted me high into the air. Spinning me around until my head became dizzy, I knew I was completely safe in his grasp.

'We're here! I love you so much, Ellie, and we're going to have a fabulous time.'

As I looked down at his face I could see an expression of pure joy. Nothing could dent or spoil the exhilaration of being in the city of lovers.

When we unlocked the door to our room, the acrid smell of fresh paint and new carpet was unexpected. The room had been cleansed of any memories and was like a blank page in a book that had been waiting for us to begin writing a new chapter in it. Did Paris realise that something very special was about to happen?

The ornately carved French doors opened out onto a tiny balcony. They were open to air the room and the summer breeze was playing with the curtains, wafting them gently back and forth. As the deliciously cool air circulated around the room, it carried with it the tantalising smell of freshly baked bread from the hotel kitchens below. I can clearly recall the murmur of distant traffic and voices trilling in the background. It served to remind us how decadent it was to be lying in bed making love on that warm summer's afternoon.

Even now, all these years later, I can still close my eyes and recapture the magic of those passionate and thrilling days together in Paris. The smell of summer had been heady and the playful breeze had made my skin cool to the touch, a pleasant sensation after the warmth our bodies had created. I clearly remember looking at Josh as he lay sprawled across the bed diagonally, looking deliciously sexy. I wanted to squeal with joy, 'You're mine and I'm yours!'

It was the moment when I knew I had nothing to fear. I could trust Josh with everything – my heart, my innermost thoughts – the real me that I often kept hidden. In return he was prepared to lay bare his own emotions. That was when I knew beyond any shadow of a doubt that we were soul mates.

However, that was a time when I truly believed you could have only one soul mate. I was young and naive, assuming that those blessed with that one-in-a-million connection had been chosen and it was destiny. Nothing could hinder the plan that life had laid out for me and that was the first glimpse of my future. A surge of power coursed through me, as if nothing could touch us because it was meant to be. Together we were one, cocooned by the strength of our love.

~

The balcony looked out over the Cimetière de Montmartre. It sounds grim, but walking among the graves and tomb-stones later that day we didn't sense death, but the perpetuity of life. A reminder that we each add something to future generations who share the same genes. It signalled a prelude to new beginnings and the knowledge that we would both have a hand in shaping our future.

Life was heady and intoxicating as each new, shared discovery served to confirm that we were made for each other. Moving in together had been a big step in the eyes of our respective families, but for us it was simply the next step.

And afternoon love in that wonderful little room in Paris, fresh and crisp from the refurbishment, gave an air of newness to everything. Like a dream, time seemed to slow down and each second became meaningful, rather than merely one brief moment ticking by.

Always foot-weary, we were glad to go back to the hotel to avoid the midday sun, arms full of sun-ripened fruit, croissants and French pastries. Decadent food for decadent afternoons.

Our walks took us to the artists' quarter of Montmartre, where we watched the painters effortlessly recreating every imaginable scene. From a beautiful vista of lush meadows filled with wheat and poppies, to a drawing of a peasant enjoying a rustic meal outside a humble dwelling. The sights, sounds and smells were an experience in themselves as we walked along arm in arm.

We mocked each other as we struggled to speak the language with an air of confidence. Our poor attempts to imitate that smooth, low and amazingly sexy French drawl were met with raised eyebrows that made us laugh even more. The people we met warmed to us, as they do to all young couples who are so obviously in love.

Vivid in my memory, still, is the evening we walked from the hotel up to the Basilique du Sacré-Cœur. Churches had always fascinated me, but I wasn't sure whether Josh would understand that. As our pace slowed and the incline started to bite on our already tired calf muscles, there was a tangible feeling of something magical around us. Whether it was the dark, velvety-blue sky with a mass of twinkling stars surrounding us like a cloak, as we climbed higher and higher, I don't know. Or perhaps we were simply falling under the spell of Paris. The imposing building with its huge domes that rose up before us was a stark white contrast against the heavenly background. Nothing else existed that night.

When we finally reached the church I had to place my hand on the stonework to reassure myself it was real. There were very few people around; most were at home preparing dinner, or sitting in restaurants waiting to be served. As we entered the church itself a small group of people came hurrying towards us.

'Bonsoir,' they chorused as we passed them and continued on inside. It was deserted and serenely tranquil.

'When a church is empty the space feels holy, truly hallowed ground. It isn't tainted by the negativity of people, or the games they play and the lies they tell. It feels different, as if it has a life of its own; a shrine to the devotion and love of the craftsmen who toiled to bring the vision alive.

Can you feel it too?' I'd held my breath, as if it was a test I needed Josh to pass.

Embarrassed and wishing I hadn't blurted out my thoughts, I'd turned to face him. He was looking up at the tall, vaulted ceiling, his head tipped back. He made no move to speak and we stood side by side, entranced as we took in the grandeur and magnificence of the building.

'It has to be a church wedding. It feels right,' he said suddenly, turning slightly to look down into my eyes.

'A church wedding?' I repeated, my heart pounding so loudly, the colour started to rise in my cheeks.

'I love you and I know nothing will ever come between us. But I'd forgotten about the sense of history and tradition churches hold within their walls. That's what I want for us on our wedding day.'

I was stunned and could not speak. We were both overwhelmed by a mystical sense of presence, endorsement and destiny. Josh amazed me. Not only did he understand, but he was prepared to open himself up, despite the very natural feeling of vulnerability I saw reflected in his eyes. We'd hugged each other so tightly it hurt, relishing what we knew was a special moment.

Touring the building in a comfortable silence, we stopped to read the inscriptions on the plaques and carved stone memorials. It seemed fitting to offer up our silence as a mark of respect to those who had gone before. We didn't break it until we were, once more, outside under the inky blackness of the late-evening sky.

'Food, wine and music I think!' Josh had exclaimed, squeezing my hand lovingly. 'The world is ours.'

I laughed, stealing a moment to glimpse back over my shoulder and grab one final glance at the Sacré-Cœur. I knew I was imprinting the moment on my mind forever.

'It looks like a wedding cake,' I whispered.

'It's a sign,' Josh laughed, then covered my face in soft little kisses.

'It looks unreal and yet we're here, up close.'

'Well, I'm glad you made me take the climb.' He began humming an old French song we'd heard earlier in the day. He started to sway, grabbing my hand and raising it above my head to twirl me around. And then he dropped down onto one knee and, with a tremor in his voice, he said the words. 'Marry me, Ellie.'

Paris had worked its magic and if you can't be lovers in Paris, then you have no romance in your soul. But I also knew that Paris had taken us to her heart because she, too, recognised when fate had chosen two people to be together for eternity. But that was back when life was simpler, much simpler.

Chapter 3

Our wedding day was perfect. In between showers of warm, summer rain it was a day made for happiness. Our friends and family were overjoyed to celebrate with us and no one really wanted the party to end. As Josh and I circulated, whenever we brushed past each other we linked fingers for the briefest of moments, eyes seeking each other out with a smile that came from the heart. Discreetly mouthing 'I love you' to each other, before moving on to receive congratulations and hugs from those around us. How strange that on your wedding day you spend most of the time with other people, grabbing as many tantalising moments together as you can before being pulled away. But the happiness was tangible and infectious, reminding everyone that life, when it's good, is very good.

However, the path of life isn't smooth and tragedy was to come our way. My first pregnancy ended in miscarriage in the fifth month. The grief was overwhelming, but drew us closer together in a way that few can truly understand unless they have suffered a similar loss. It was a time of mourning and that was difficult, not least because we needed it to be private. Those close to us were not allowed inside the tight little box we created around our emotions. To the world we stayed strong, but alone we were distraught and trying desperately to mend our broken hearts.

Marrying so young I'd barely finished my internship with a large interior design company, Westings Interiors, before Josh swept me off my feet. I had taken a little time off after the miscarriage, but quickly settled back into my work routine and put all thoughts of having a baby aside. Then the unexpected news that I was pregnant again came out of the blue. It seemed that fate was smiling upon us once more and as we didn't want to take any risks. I gave up work when I was at the twenty-week stage. I don't think either of us relaxed until the moment we finally held Hettie in our arms.

Two years later we welcomed our youngest daughter, Rosie, into the world and she was the bonus that made our little family complete. Whilst nothing would replace the baby we had lost, our lives were rich and full because of our loving daughters. We thanked God every single day for the joy they brought us. We commiserated with each other just as regularly over the sleepless nights and the angst that comes with being a parent. But we managed to survive all of that and our love has grown because of the things we've been through together. We've weathered our little storms well and hope that it was more by judgement than sheer luck that the girls have turned out so well.

Josh hasn't been just a husband and a lover, but a friend and confidante. I've always shared things with him rather than my mother, when she was alive, or girlfriends. I realised, of course, that was unusual and maybe even a little hurtful to some people, at times. But that reflected the true nature of our relationship. It has given me a growing sense of unease over the years, because it set us apart from every other couple we knew.

We became introvertly self-sufficient, each giving the other everything they needed. When those around us came to me to pour out their hearts and trust me with their biggest fears, I couldn't do the same in return. I've seen a number of very good friends though a difficult divorce, close-family deaths and child-rearing woes. However, I'm conscious that there is a line I have drawn about what I'm prepared to share. Does anyone notice that I hold back and do they realise that Josh is my number-one friend, above all others? Does that make me any less of a friend to them?

I sometimes feel like a complete fraud, as if I should say, 'You don't know everything about me, does that matter to you?' They think they know me, of course, but the simple truth is that they only see what I allow them to see. I find that most people are grateful to have someone who will listen to them; someone who cares enough to hear what they are saying and feel their pain. Often, all they need is a hug, or to let loose that inner turmoil by finally hearing themselves uttering the words. Once shared, it's a form of release and they are suddenly free to move on. I'm a listener, a hugger and a shoulder to cry on.

But my shoulder to cry on is Josh, because the truth is that I don't need anyone else. Since that fateful day ... it's not that I love him any less than I did, it's more complicated than that. Naturally he senses, and has done for a while, that something has changed in me, but he can't verbalise it. I'm too afraid to break my silence, partly because I'm not sure I could explain what is happening to me. I don't really understand it myself, but I do know that I now fear I am losing my grip on reality. Or rather, what is real as opposed to what exists solely in my mind.

But I'm talking about before all of that happened; the years when life was somehow more straightforward, despite what fate had to throw at us. We knew some of the knocks we would experience in life would be hard to take, but youth gives one a feeling of invincibility. It's only as you grow older that you begin to see things differently. Worry begins to hover around you, like a threatening rain cloud on an otherwise bright and sunny day.

For our seventh wedding anniversary we had a party

and it also marked the end of the first month in our new, much bigger, home.

'Beware the seven-year itch, my friend. It comes to us all,' Nathan, Josh's boss had joked, slapping him on the back. 'It suddenly hits you that you're in for the long haul and that mortgage begins to feel like an increasingly heavy burden. The family grows, you need more space and then you find the home of your dreams. Now you get to spend the rest of your life paying it off. You realise that freedom is something you took for granted in the dim and distant past.'

His wife, the lovely Liz, had pulled a face.

'So kind of you to share your utterly depressing thoughts, Nathan.' Her eyes had flashed him a look of amusement, but I noticed a worrying trace of disapproval lurking behind her smile. 'We're lucky we've survived; many don't. Yes, it's hard bringing up a family and it's only natural there are times when we all long to take a break from everyday life. But if you were still single now, you'd be way out of control.' Was there a hint of reluctant acceptance in her softly spoken words?

'Ah, behind every successful man there is a woman,' Josh spoke up, conscious that the silly banter was in danger of getting out of hand.

Nathan had downed the remainder of his drink in one. 'I thought the saying was that behind every successful man is a woman, and behind her is his wife.'

Everyone had laughed at that point, because we were all unaware at the time of the cracks in what had seemed like a very solid relationship. But within a year of that conversation, their marriage was over and Nathan began the first in a string of disastrous hook-ups. As for us, Hettie was five years old by then, and Rosie had just turned three. We had joined in that conversation good-naturedly, too tired from disturbed nights and the strains of the house move to read any more into it. Rosie had way too much energy to sleep for more than a couple of hours at a stretch. She was this endless bundle of activity, stopping only when she was exhausted. Often she would fall asleep in the middle of eating a meal, or suddenly curl up on the floor, toy in hand. Who had the energy to even have an itch, we wondered? Certainly not us. I had no idea if Josh worried about it, but we continued to sail through each anniversary and our love was strong and unwavering. The only worry in my mind was what would I do if I ever lost Josh? What if one of us died prematurely? I knew it worried him too, but we chose to never voice those concerns.

Life was ruled by the usual day-to-day family highs and lows, as we negotiated our way through temper tantrums and growing pains. Rosie had just started nursery school and she loved it, blossoming in an environment of play activity and making new friends. By then Josh had been promoted and was running the entire IT section. His week was busy and he often worked long hours, but weekends were family time.

I lost touch with most of my work colleagues as the years continued to fly by, but one of the other interns, Olivia Bradley, remained my one very close friend. Our lives were, and are still, so very different, but that's partly why my friendship with Livvie works so well. I think we can see in each other the life we didn't choose, if that makes any sense. There, but for the grace of God, go I. It helps to reaffirm that the individual paths we chose were ultimately the right ones for us.

Livvie thinks children and marriage are overrated. She now lives in a pristinely perfect, designer home, which is spread over three levels and clings to the side of a valley. A few times over the years she's come to stay for the weekend, but I always feel awkward as it's hard to keep the house quiet with a constant throng of girls parading through it. Livvie went on to have a single, but exciting, life and now runs her own interior-design company named Bradley's Design Creative. She works very closely with a building company in which she has a part share. If a client wants their house remodelled before the interior is redesigned, then Livvie oversees the whole project. Of course, I probably flatter myself thinking that Livvie had the life I would have had if I hadn't met Josh. Would I have been that successful? I doubt it. But when I told her I was thinking of returning to work she had immediately offered me a job.

'You must come and work for me, Ellie,' she'd cooed down the phone and I envied her that calm, sultry, yet professional, voice. I was used to being a drill sergeant at home and having to talk just that little bit higher and louder than two noisy girls, and a husband with a distinctly tenor voice. I'd readjusted my pitch and tone in an attempt to bolster my flagging confidence.

'I don't know, Livvie, it's very kind of you but I'm going to need some time to rediscover the, um, other side of me. I'm not sure what I have to offer. I've probably forgotten everything I learnt. It feels like a lifetime ago.'

'Nonsense. Your eye for a good design is instinctive; that's not something that can be learnt. Plus, both of the girls are at school now, so how else will you fill your day? What you have is life experience and common sense. That's in short supply at the moment, believe me. Some of the people I employ might have really good credentials, but give them a problem and it's instantly a crisis. I'm looking for someone with a cool head, who can make decisions and think outside the box. I've seen the way you boss that family of yours around and keep them on track, Ellie. Those are precisely the skills I need. You would be doing me a favour.'

I realised that was exactly why Livvie had made such a success of her business, because she was a people person.

She understood what made people tick and utilised their skills in the best possible way. I knew her well enough to trust that she wouldn't put me into a situation where I would feel I was totally out of my depth. And she was right; being at work gave me a sense of completeness and I loved it from day one. I eased myself into working three days a week, as the liaison point between the designer, clients and contractors. The job itself was perfect for me and Josh and the girls were very supportive. Within two years the business suddenly took off in a new direction when Livvie started taking on hotel refurbishment projects. As the team beneath her expanded, her time was very much focused on suppliers, staff turnover and recruitment.

Then, one fateful day, a phone call neither of us expected caused Livvie to change her plans.

REWIND ONE YEAR AND FIVE DAYS

You can't un-see what you've seen and you can't un-say what you've said ... you can only try to limit the damage.

Chapter 4

Livvie is due to fly out to Italy to check out a new supplier she's keen to use. They specialise in a wide range of well-designed, artisan goods and it looks like a promising proposition. They approached her recently, offering big price incentives to become one of her regular suppliers. If she likes their set-up and everything is as good up close as it is in the brochure, this could be the start of a fast-growing relationship. As she prepares to leave the office her mobile kicks into life and I can see by the look on her face that it isn't good news.

'My mother's had a fall. That was her neighbour, letting me know that the ambulance is taking Mum to the accident and emergency centre. I can't believe it. I'm not sure what to do.'

Her eyes search mine as her head tries to process the information. I'm used to dealing with family emergencies, but for Livvie this is a first. Her father died when she was quite small; too young to have any memories attached to it, whether good or bad. This was something for which she wasn't prepared, as Livvie's life is all about work. Domestic traumas usually come in the form of something breaking down. She has a phone full of contacts ready to sort whatever issue threatens to interrupt her working day. Okay, it's often at a premium, but if it isn't important to the running of her business, then it isn't a good use of her time. It's merely an annoying inconvenience.

'Drop everything. Just head off to the hospital.'

She looks at me quite blankly, as if what's happening hasn't quite sunk in. 'But it's too late to cancel the trip ... the flights—'

Her face tells me exactly what she's asking me to do and we both know there simply isn't anyone else who can do it.

'I'll go in your place. You can ring me later and talk me through what I need to know before the meeting. Family comes first, Livvie, and your mum needs you to show her that.'

She's nodding her head, but it takes her a few moments to swing into action. Grabbing a pile of papers from inside her briefcase, she thrusts them into my hands. Livvie looks shell-shocked and I wonder if she's going to have a panic attack or something. I've never seen her look so unsure of herself.

'Thank you, Ellie. But what about the girls?'

Life with a thirteen and a fifteen-year-old is all about routine and making lists so no one forgets their homework, or ballet class, or gymnastics, or that must-go-to party.

'I'll arrange for our neighbour, Dawn, to pick the girls up from school and stay with them until Josh arrives home. It will be fine. Just go, and drive carefully.' I try to ignore the image of Hettie having a strop and muttering under her breath that at the grand old age of fifteen it's about time we stopped treating her like a baby. But there's also Rosie to consider and that two-year age difference is awkward. It causes a lot of friction between them and that's why I need Dawn to be around, even if it's only to keep the peace.

I give Livvie a hug and I can feel the turmoil and confusion like a ball whirling around her. It's the reason why our lives are so different; Livvie was born with a business head and I was born with the ability to cope with family emergencies. Emotion is an annoyance to Livvie, but it's at the heart of my existence. If I had received that phone call I would already have been in the car without a moment's hesitation.

'I hate hospitals. I think I'm allergic to them.'

'I know, but your mum needs you right now, Livvie. You can do this, really you can. And don't worry about what's happening here. Things aren't going to fall apart overnight.'

I'm anxious on her behalf, hardly giving a thought to

the offer I've made so easily, as if it is nothing. Once I'm on my way home it hits me with full force. Livvie is heading into a situation for which she isn't prepared and I, too, am about to find myself exploring unknown territory, alone. Heck, I'm not even sure I have the necessary experience to handle this on my own.

~

'Thanks, Dawn, I feel like I'm going off on a jolly,' I admit. Inside my head, though, there's a battle between guilt and self-doubt raging war against each other. I realise I hadn't given any thought at all to how the girls will react when they find out I'm going away. Josh was understandably surprised when I rang him, but when I explained the situation he put me at ease. He waved away my concern about landing him with the girls and having to make arrangements at short notice. Sitting right alongside that sensation of fear lying in the pit of my stomach was a tinge of excitement and I wondered if he had heard that reflected in my voice.

'Josh will be home by four-thirty. To say thank you, how about you and Rich coming over for dinner on Saturday evening? Tell Rich I'll make his favourite risotto.' The chatter is a way of calming my nerves, which are beginning to pump adrenalin around my body at an alarming rate. I have everything crossed that the travel agent has managed to sort out the change of name for the tickets. But I know that Livvie will be on the case and she always manages to make things happen. She's not the sort to sit and hold anyone's hand. Instead she'll opt to wait outside and her phone won't leave her hand.

'You don't have to do that, it's not often you ask for a favour and now Will's at university I've told you, I'm free any time. Besides, the girls are fun to be around. I learn a lot.' She chuckles and I don't even want to think about the useless bits of information and gossip she overhears from my two.

'You're a great neighbour! The best, have I ever mentioned that before?' I laugh lightly, as I continue packing the suitcase in front of me.

'Once or twice, usually when you want something,' she banters. 'Have a ball! How often do you get to have an experience like this?'

'Well, it is work, Dawn,' I reflect, soberly. 'There wasn't anyone else to step in at such short notice. Livvie knew it, and I knew it, too. It's not as if I was chosen to represent her on this trip.'

'You know, Ellie, you don't give yourself enough credit at times. I bet you do as much working part-time as most manage to fit into a full working week. Livvie is very lucky to have someone to rely on at a time like this.'

I hadn't looked at it like that. Livvie is simply the sister I never had and this isn't only about work, but friendship as well. As I wave Dawn goodbye, it's already too late to stop what has been put in motion. But my conscience is telling me that this is about doing a good deed, or maybe paying Livvie back for putting her trust in me when I returned to work. I pushed away the fleeting thought that maybe I was grasping at a chance to have an adventure, or even to prove to everyone that I too can be that consummate professional. It isn't something I've ever yearned for because my life already feels complete. I work first and foremost to benefit the family and bring in a little extra money, and secondly because it keeps me busy when the girls aren't around. Or maybe this is fate and I'm simply a pawn, being moved from one square to another – who knows?

~

'I'm at Heathrow and about to go in search of a cup of coffee.' I try to keep my words even and light, which is an enormous effort given that my stomach is now churning with nerves. The last few hours have been quite stressful, but the moment I arrive at the check-in desk relief washes over me, calming me down. Part one of my journey is now ticked off on Livvie's itinerary and I haven't fallen at the first hurdle. Livvie would have taken this in her stride, of course, but I'm not used to travelling on my own.

'I'm just glad to hear your voice. I miss you – we miss you. The girls want to have a quick word, but don't hang up afterwards.' I can hear the anxiety in Josh's voice and the reluctance with which he hands over the phone is tangible. Going away for a couple of days on a course is one thing, but flying off to another country is something else entirely. The concern is running like an undertone beneath his words.

The girls start babbling with excitement, both of them throwing questions at the phone and talking over each other. They are clearly impressed and maybe even a little shocked by my behaviour. I mean, this is their mum, the person who is always there because that's my real job.

'Slow down, girls. I don't have a lot of detail other than I'm heading for a villa just outside the town of Castrovillari. It's in southern Italy, you know, the bit that looks like a big boot. I have no idea how hot it's going to be when I get there and, no, I don't think there's going to be a swimming pool.'

Then it's on to the mundane things, as Rosie has misplaced one of her school books. Then Hettie wants to know whether I'd be back in time to ferry her to and fro for a friend's birthday party on Friday evening. When Josh finally wrestles the phone out of their hands his voice is in sharp contrast to the girls' bubbling enthusiasm about my adventure.

'Mum can't worry about Friday evening, Hettie, I'll sort that. Listen, Ellie, I just want you to be aware of what's going on around you. Travelling alone isn't ideal, darling, so please take extra special care of yourself.' He's emotional and I feel sad that there hadn't been time to give him a goodbye hug.

'Yes, boss! I'll be careful, but everything has been arranged so all I have to do is sit back and be driven around. Three days and I'll be back home. I'm counting the hours.'

'Me, too, darling. Have you heard anything from Livvie?'

'It's not good news. Her mother has broken her arm and fractured a bone at the top of her leg. They are going to operate on her arm, but the other fracture will have to heal over time. Livvie is panicking. I don't quite know what she's going to do, as she's freaking out just having to make hospital visits. It's all very worrying, as she's no nurse, that's for sure. And her house is so impractical for an invalid.'

'She's a capable and successful business woman, Ellie. I'm sure she'll figure out a solution. In the meantime, you've done everything you can and I might add that I'm feeling I've been relegated to second place.' I can hear the concern creeping into his words, even though he's trying to disguise it with humour.

'It all happened so quickly. I'm sorry there wasn't any other solution, darling. A lot hangs on this deal and it could take away a few problems. So much is mass produced these days and looks like what it is, rather bland and cheaply turned out. This is quality stuff at very affordable prices. Unique pieces that could elevate the finished look of any design, because they can't be found anywhere else. Anyway, we won't know for sure until I've seen it all first-hand. It's going to be very late when I reach Lamezia airport and finally arrive at the villa. I'll text you when I'm there – promise.'

'I appreciate that it's going to be tiring. Travel always is. But I won't go to sleep until I know you are safe, Ellie, no matter how late it is. And don't forget to lock your bedroom door before you go to bed.'

I stifle a laugh. I'm going to be staying in a beautiful and elegant villa in the middle of rolling Italian countryside. If Josh and the girls were by my side the thought of that would be heaven. Instead I bid him goodnight, wondering what exactly lies ahead of me. As strange and vulnerable as I'm feeling about this trip, there's an undercurrent of excitement and anticipation bubbling up inside of me. This is a taste of the other life, the road I chose not to travel because my heart is happiest when my family are close.

But, like the forbidden fruit, a taste is tantalising and I feel a sense of both apprehension and adventure. What harm can it do to step into someone else's shoes if it's only for a few days?

Chapter 5

The Città di Lamezia Terme airport is bewildering, not least because I already feel completely drained. And that's before joining the long queue for passport control. Although the flight left Heathrow at just before five this evening, there was a stopover at Rome Fiumicino airport with an hour-and-twenty-minute wait. Now, at least, I'm about to begin the last leg of the journey. By the time I locate the driver holding up a card with Livvie's name on it, it's nearly midnight. There's little point in trying to explain I'm her representative, so I just point to the card and nod by way of acknowledgement.

I settle back into the rear seat, grateful to be starting the last leg of the journey. Livvie's schedule confirms it's going to be an hour and a half's drive. Having established the fact that the driver doesn't speak any English, there is little chance of striking up a conversation. My Italian consists of three words, *ciao*, *per favore* and *grazie*, but in my defence I've had no time at all to prepare for this trip. Tiredness is now making my eyes blurry and my head is throbbing, so I swallow two painkillers with a mouthful of water, hoping relief will kick in quickly.

A business trip is nothing at all like going on a family holiday, where the main concern is ensuring no one wanders off. All I usually do is rely upon Josh's direction and focus on keeping everyone happy. Here, alone, looking out into the gloomy darkness I feel totally disorientated.

Once we're away from the terminal the car speeds along a little too fast for comfort. We seem to be on a motorway, as there are several lanes, by the look of it. However, it's dark and everything is flashing by so quickly that my brain is refusing to take in any of the detail. What if we have an accident? How would I cope, with no grasp of the language and no real idea of where I am? Even the air smells different, a perfume of tantalising scents that leave me feeling uncomfortably vulnerable. I gulp down a lump that rises up in my throat. Already I'm feeling homesick and I know that I have to get a grip on my emotions. This is business and Livvie obviously thinks I'm capable of being her eyes and ears. So I have to work on my self-belief and stop undermining my ability to cope with the unknown. I shift around in the seat, hoping I'm out of view of the driver's rear mirror. I close my eyes to concentrate on my breathing.

Gradually my short, shallow breaths became longer and deeper, slowing my racing heartbeat. I focus on the dashboard clock and then, quite suddenly, my head jolts forward. I realise I've been asleep and the driver has turned in his seat to look at me. The car is at a standstill.

'Villa Rosso,' he nods.

'Ah, *grazie. Grazie.*' As I speak it raises a tired smile. I even manage a sense of intonation and he looks back at me, eyebrows slightly raised in surprise. Then he rolls off an entire sentence which means absolutely nothing to me and I wish I'd just said the anticipated 'thank you' in English.

To my relief the passenger door opens and an older man offers his hand to help me out.

Standing, I see that the driver has already unloaded my luggage and given it to another member of the hotel staff. I pull out the ten-euro note I stuffed into my jacket pocket earlier and give it to the driver, who looks surprised, but pleased. He says something I don't catch and I nod my appreciation to him, then turn and follow my new companion.

The old building looms up in the darkness. The lights from several ground-floor windows flood out, illuminating only one small corner of what seems to be quite a vast terrace. I'm bewildered by the strangest sensation that comes over me without warning. I've never seen this place before, how could I? But I feel that same sense of well-being that I have when I arrive home after a difficult day. Cosy, familiar and safe.

Suspecting that the other guests have been asleep for quite a while, all I want to do now is to drop into bed. I'm conscious of several staff hovering, but am quickly whisked away and handed a key that looks like it would unlock a castle.

As the door to my room on the first floor swings open, once more I utter '*grazie*' and will my legs to carry me inside. Grabbing my phone I text Josh, telling him I've arrived safely but am totally exhausted. Within minutes my weary head is touching the pillow and I sink into a deep, untroubled sleep.

~

When my ear begins to buzz it takes me a moment or two to realise where I am and what's happening. I must have pushed my phone up under the pillow during the night. Reaching for it, I see it's the alarm I set on the flight over. I had visions of waking up to find it was late morning and I'd totally messed up before I'd even begun.

I sit up, leaning back against the old, carved wooden headboard and take in my surroundings for the first time. The room is spacious and surprisingly modern. Whitewashed walls, dark-stained floors and furnished in a distinctly minimalist way. This is no dusty old villa that time forgot, that's for sure. The style of the room is in keeping with the reception area I briefly visited in the early hours of this morning. It's like something out of a glossy magazine and that's the last thing I expected. However, it bodes well for this visit, as clearly whoever is running the business has their feet firmly planted in today's marketplace.

The exposed chestnut beams overhead are commanding, so high above the bed. Two beautifully upholstered chairs, a small coffee table and a large wooden armoire seem almost lost in the vast space. Similarly styled bedside tables with oversized lamps complete the decor without making it feel fussy.

The bedding is crisp and white, only the drapes at the large window add a splash of colour, with rich purple, mauve and a thread of silver running through them. It was so dark when I arrived that I didn't think to close them and now the early morning sun is beginning to filter in through the window.

The overtly contemporary styling is rather sophisticated and that's a real surprise. I really was expecting to be transported back in time, but even the ensuite is of the same standard. There are no in-room facilities, so all I have is bottled water. But I'm content to wander over and sit in one of the armchairs while I read Livvie's itinerary again and her hand-written notes, to bring me up to speed.

Max Jackson manages Villa Rosso and aside from being a hotel, the main business of the estate is the olive groves and oil refinery plant. In recent years it has also been involved in a new cooperative exporting textiles, metalwork, carved wooden items and ceramics, in celebration of the local artisan craftsmanship. And that's why Livvie was coming here, to meet Max in person. Being escorted on a tour of some of the individual workshops, which are a part of the new business set-up would allow her to gauge if this operation was really viable as a new source. The worst-case scenario is that we'll struggle to find enough items to fill a container to ship over to the UK. Or that they won't be organised well enough to guarantee they could meet deadlines, which would be a total disaster. We want variety and for some items we will also need quantity. When we are refurbishing a hotel with a hundred rooms they all have to reflect the same style. My phone pings and then pings again and the first is a message from Josh.

Love you, honey. Miss you. No pressure, but if you get time to ring me for a quick chat this morning it would be lovely to hear your voice. Everything is fine here. Jx

The other ping is an email from Livvie.

Morning
Hope you slept well. Sorry it was such a late arrival time, it wouldn't have bothered me but I realise it was really throwing you in at the deep end.

Mum is having an operation to pin the bone in her arm later today. Did I tell you I'm squeamish? Even the thought of it makes my stomach heave!

Right – work. Max is easy to deal with, he doesn't play games and there's no issue over getting a good price if we buy a container load at a time. I'm guessing he's probably the only English-speaking person you will come into contact with on your trip. He will escort you everywhere, so don't worry about that. Your job is to suss out whether what's on offer will fit into our new hotel refurbishment schemes. If it's a big hotel we are kitting out, but it's clear they couldn't scale up to meet our order, then we know we can only look at them as a supplier for our bespoke service. But if there aren't enough items that jump out at you as being what we're looking for, then it will make it too costly; even if, as Max has suggested, we could share part of a container with another client. Sorry I'm waffling but I'm so tired my brain feels like cotton wool.

If you send me photos of what you think is right for us and it starts to look promising, then this trip will have been worthwhile. What I also need is your view on whether the operation is robust enough. The last thing we want is to place large orders and then suffer constant delays because there are weak links in their chain. I really appreciate the sacrifice on your part, my lovely friend. I know you – bet you are already homesick!

Anyway, enjoy the sun. It's pouring with rain here and I'm off to the hospital. Shudder. Even the smell as I enter the building makes me want to turn and run away. And have some fun!

Hugs,

Livvie

PS Don't forget to send me pics of the villa. I'm really gutted not to be experiencing it first-hand.

Poor Livvie, or maybe I should be reserving my sympathy for her mother. As I begin typing a reply there's a tap on the door. With no further hesitation a smiling young woman steps inside, a breakfast tray balanced on one upturned hand.

'Good morning, Mrs Maddison, I hope you slept well.'

My jaw drops, as the last thing I expected was to be greeted by a young Englishwoman. She's probably in her early twenties; her dark hair has vivid blue streaks running through it, clearly visible even though it's neatly tied back in a ponytail.

'You're English, this is a surprise.' The words are out of my mouth before I engage my brain. She turns to smile at me, one eyebrow raised. I feel the need to explain myself.

'Sorry, my boss just emailed me to say the manager here is probably going to be the only English-speaking person I'm likely to meet.'

She laughs.

'I'm Bella and your boss is almost correct. Some of our hotel staff can speak a few words of English, but I gather you're here to tour some of the outworkers' locations. Mr Johnson will be escorting you, so there's no need to worry. Everyone calls him Max, by the way.'

'Thank goodness. I had to switch places with my boss at the last minute and so I had no time to prepare. It feels wrong, and a bit rude, not being able to speak at least a little of the language. Ironically I can speak French quite well and a little German, but this is my first trip to Italy. Have you lived here a long time?'

As we talk, Bella's hands busily uncover several plates with a range of fruits, cheeses and pastries. The aroma from the coffee pot makes my mouth salivate.

'I came here for my gap year, mainly to please my mother. She's Italian and my father is a Londoner. We've always spoken mainly English at home, so I thought what better way to brush up on my Italian than to come and live here for a year? It put me in her good books for a while; we don't always see eye to eye.'

We exchange sympathetic glances.

'For a while?'

She gives me a broad smile, accompanied by a hearty laugh. 'When the year was up the family asked me to stay and so here I am. My mother wasn't impressed as she had high hopes for me. She says I'm not ambitious enough, but in an ironic twist of fate I've fallen under the spell of the Italian way of life. Anyway, Max thought you'd want to have a quiet breakfast and says he'll be at your disposal any time after ten this morning. Just let reception know when you are ready.'

'Thank you, I will. I'm hoping I'll pick up a few Italian words over the next couple of days.'

'*Dove c'è una volontà, c'è un modo.*'

I look at Bella blankly and she immediately interprets it for me.

'Where there's a will, there's a way – more, or less. But doesn't it sound better in Italian?'

'You're right. It's just hard not being able to pick up any clues. You could have been saying anything to me.'

We exchange friendly smiles.

'Max will do everything to make your visit pleasant and enjoyable. He's a lovely man and very personable. I don't know what the locals would do without him. If there's anything you need, you only have to ask.'

'Thank you, but right now that coffee is calling to me.'

'I'll leave you to enjoy it, then. Have a good day.' As the door is about to close Bella says, 'That's buona giornata.'

'*Grazie*, Bella.' I think I just said thank you, beautiful!

Right, coffee first and the next task is to ring Josh, tell him how much I'm missing him and say good morning to my girls before my big adventure begins.

Chapter 6

I dress with care, knowing that first impressions are everything when it comes to appearing confident and professional. Slipping into my favourite little black dress, teamed with a lightweight white linen cropped-sleeve jacket, I'm not unhappy with the image staring back at me. A little makeup, a quick brush of my shoulder-length dark-blonde hair and I'm done. Oh, I nearly forgot about earrings. I dive into my bag to rescue my jewellery pouch and settle on the single pearls. They were an anniversary present from Josh and as I slip them on it adds a little sparkle to my eyes. He says I'm beautiful; it's not true, of course, and what I see is a face that looks rather plain, with dark-blue eyes that aren't of the piercing variety. Just, well, ordinary.

One last check that I have everything I need, before I slip on my flat leather pumps and my work persona is ready to go. It allows me to push those nagging little domestic worries to one side and remember that there's a big wide world out there. I can rise to any challenge and I know that. But this is a first for me and everything has happened so quickly. I haven't had time to transition between the two worlds; that leap from the domestic to the business world is a big one. And yet the moment I stepped out of the car last night it was almost like a home-coming. Perhaps one of my internal wires isn't working and is giving me a false reading. That thought is a worrying one, as everyone I meet will be expecting an experienced business woman who knows exactly what she's doing.

I grab the large, gate-keeper-style key and lock the door, then walk across to the ornate metal balustrade and peer down over the reception area. The white-washed walls and dark wooden beams throughout add a sense of space and height to the vaulted ceiling. The central light is an art form, with a cascade of cleverly intertwined metal leaves highlighted with enamelling in shades of white, silver and grey. As I slowly descend the elegant staircase I reflect that it's the sort of piece Livvie would love to get her hands on at almost any price.

There's no one around and the clock on the wall confirms it's only just after nine-thirty. It's quite cool inside. I'm longing to feel the morning sunshine on my skin, so I head straight for the door.

Stepping over the threshold all of my senses start reacting at the same time. But it's the commanding view that forces my feet forward, traversing the aged sandstone paving of the exterior terrace. The closer I get to the edge of the flat expanse, the more the vista in front of me seems to open up. As I glimpse beyond the small islands of tall trees that flank the edge of the paved area, there is nothing to restrict the eye. Only the mountains, way in the distance, stand as a backdrop, like a curtain. Camera in hand I snap away, knowing how hard it will be to get a perspective on this seemingly never-ending scene. Directly ahead the land slopes away to infinity, ending in a mere shimmer before it slips over the distant horizon. The fertile plain is studded with vast swathes of olive trees. Further away the dotted landscape is interspersed with neat rows of planting that are tiny by comparison, but could well be fruit trees rather than bushes.

It isn't just the sunshine and the electric-blue sky, but the musical calls of the countryside that reach out to me. A chorus of low-level sounds play like a soft melody in the background. It's breathtakingly beautiful and I feel like I'm watching a re-run of a favourite film. I could stand here for a long time simply taking in the detail and with each sweep of my eyes noticing something new.

Spinning around I look back at the villa, taking in the rustic beauty of the stonework and the pale orange-red hue of the sun-bleached roof tiles. This is, quite simply, unreal. It's a little piece of heaven and so far removed from my daily life that it's hard to believe this is on the same planet. The sheer scale of the landscape literally steals your breath away. I'm a mere speck, small and insignificant in the grand scheme nature is presenting to me. But rather bizarrely, it doesn't feel alien in anyway at all. The vastness isn't over-whelming, but strangely comforting.

I walk back to a cluster of wooden tables surrounding a small fountain and take a seat. As I dive into my bag to extract some sunglasses, I hear a polite cough and look up at the face staring down at me.

'Mrs Maddison? I'm Max, Max Johnson. Welcome to Villa Rosso.'

I stand, automatically plastering a pleasant smile on my surprised face as recognition kicks in. I know this man. I mean, I've met him before. At least I think I have, but there's nothing similar reflected back at me, only a warm smile. The sort of smile that radiates from mysteriously deep, hazel eyes. We shake hands. He's younger than I expected, probably in his early forties and tall. Six-foot something, that's for sure, because I feel he's towering over me.

'I'm sorry to disturb you. I just wanted you to know that I'm here at your disposal whenever you are ready to begin. Would you like me to fetch you a coffee so you can sit for a while and enjoy the view?'

Although I knew he was British, his tan and elegant demeanour lend an air of cosmopolitan sophistication. I would not have been at all surprised if he had been Italian. He's hovering politely and I still haven't answered him.

'No, really, I was just killing time and trying to absorb the stunning scenery. It's heady stuff.'

Those serious eyes search my face and he nods, approvingly. Is it approval of my appreciation or, as his eyes settle on me, is he—

'What is that constant sound, like a chirping?'

'Tree crickets, *la cicada*. You'll gradually get used to it until it becomes almost unnoticeable. I trust that the last-minute change of plans hasn't inconvenienced you too much? It was quite a surprise when Olivia Bradley called to say something had cropped up and you would be taking her place. Anyway, it's a pleasure to meet you, Mrs Maddison.'

'It's Ellie, you can call me Ellie.' Why did I just repeat my own name? That wasn't cool, and you shouldn't have shortened it. You should have taken a lead from Olivia.

'Which is short for—?'

'Elouise. My mother was the only person who ever called me that, but she died a few years ago.' Too much information, Ellie. Concentrate. I swallow hard, mentally berating myself, and take a deep breath to clear my head as I stand. 'Let's make a start, then.'

Max holds open the car door as I settle myself into the passenger seat of what looks like an almost brand-new

Alfa Romeo in a tasteful charcoal metallic finish. He insists on taking my small satchel and places it in the back, then clicks the door shut. While he's walking around to the driver's side my brain is working overtime, trying to establish why I'm so convinced I've met him before. Is this business famous enough for him to have been featured on TV, or maybe I've seen his face in a cookery magazine talking about the benefits of olive oil. Or maybe he just has one of those handsome, beguiling faces that sort of looks like someone famous and inspires a sense of instant recognition.

As Max slips into the driver's seat a waft of something with a hint of bergamot tickles my nose. It's fresh and citrusy, immediately masking that slightly overpowering smell of new leather. Instinctively, I reach out to touch his arm and make a comment, when I abruptly pull myself back, rather sharply. How totally embarrassing! I hope I succeeded in making the gesture look as if I was simply putting my hand up to smoothe down my hair.

What is going on with me? Why does this man whom, it seems, really is just a stranger to me, feel so familiar?

'Our first stop is a small family business whose land abuts our own. Olivia said she was very interested in ceramics and I think you'll be pleasantly surprised by the quality and designs on offer.'

His eyes check out my seat belt before he starts the

engine and, with a warm smile, he turns his gaze back towards the road ahead.

We are both content to travel in silence. As my eyes scan the open countryside, the car purrs along, heading towards the sloping planes of that wonderful vista. Up close some of that unidentifiable greenery turns out to be swathes of grape vines and citrus trees, divided into neat little plots. Every now and again I catch a glimpse of farm workers, mostly elderly men and women, with skin the colour of tanned leather. We pass a group of younger workers with baskets full of lemons, the women wearing colourful scarves and shouting back and forth to each other. Most wave to Max as we pass by.

'Villa Rosso's land extends to the east. The processing plant is on the other side of trees that you can see at the foot of the mountains. Castrovillari is situated at the base of the Monte Pollino, the Parco Nazionale. From here almost as far as you can see it's mostly small parcels of land owned by families who have worked the soil for generations.'

'Do they manage to make a living? It must be hard to sustain a family if this is their only income.'

Max nods, his face quite sombre.

'It's never been easy for them. But everyone is still suffering from what we call the black year, the harvest of 2014. Unusual weather patterns, lack of water and a proliferation of insects and bacterial blight saw the average yield cut by half. We've also been battling with unusually large flocks of starlings destroying the fruits, although mercifully that hasn't affected everyone.'

'But doesn't that simply mean that the cost of olive oil rises?'

'I wish it worked like that, but not all countries were affected in the same way, so some gained while we suffered. And as for any price increases, very little filters down to the poor farmers. That's why we're trying so hard to grow this artisan crafts cooperative. The local market is small, as the vast majority of the workers here lead very simple lives. You can see for yourself how rustic their farm dwellings are. When they're not working the old women are found gossiping in doorways, complaining about the menfolk. It falls on deaf ears and the old men relax nearby in the shade, playing cards.' He turns to look at me, giving a wry smile. 'But the daily fight against poverty and the need to feed their families is a worry that never goes away. The wealthier families, like the Ormannis, employ as many local people as they can but they, too, are affected by a bad harvest and the vagaries of nature. That's why diversification is essential at every level, although olive production will always be at the heart and soul of the business. But the real problem is the exodus of the younger generation to the cities, where they can usually earn a lot more money and enjoy all the benefits of modern living. As any farmer will tell you, working the land is, at times, heart-breaking.'

Max looks resigned, but the deep lines between his eyebrows are furrowed. The tension he feels for a situation that must seem like an endless battle against a nameless enemy, is etched on his face. His profile shows a firm jaw line, rigidly set. I wonder what is going through his mind at this precise moment.

'And here we are.'

The track we're on is bumpy and for the last hundred yards, or so, the car has been literally crawling along.

Max parks up in front of a series of large sheds, similar to outbuildings seen on farms in the UK. But whereas we'd use them for cattle feed and machinery, I realise that for the owner this is a huge investment in a business venture that's a considerable gamble. It isn't just the locals who carry a heaven burden on their shoulders. Max, as their representative, knows exactly what these proud people stand to lose.

There's no ceremony – in fact Max escorts me inside the first shed as if it were in the grounds of Villa Rosso. He waves to two men wheeling large wooden trolleys with a collection of clay pots ready for the kiln. This appears to be a holding area and along the far wall five women of varying ages are busy packing boxes. From a young girl of indeterminate age, to a grandmother who must be in her nineties, they chatter as they work. The elderly woman looks up and smiles at Max, her toothless grin a happy one and the other women giggle, shyly.

Max steers me through a doorway into another shed, where seven or eight people are hand-painting designs onto a wide range of different pots.

We're attracting some curious glances, but no one approaches and I simply follow in Max's footsteps until he opens another door and ushers me inside. I suppose this is more like an office, although it's still only a wooden structure with a tin roof. But the floor-to-ceiling shelves hold an array of colourful and well-crafted ceramics that would grace any European showroom.

'I wasn't expecting such a departure from the old traditional styles,' I admit. 'Max, these wall tiles are amazing and the table lamps are exactly what we're looking for!'

For the first time since we set off, Max's forehead relaxes a little and he nods in appreciation.

'It's a big step for us to depart from the traditional designs people have come to associate with Italian majolica. We are focusing on a different clientele and market, hoping to give interior designers the quality and statement pieces they are looking for, at a very competitive price.'

'Can I take some photos to send to Olivia?'

'Of course. Take your time. I'll go and do the rounds as they're all holding their breath, wondering what the English lady will think.'

The pressure isn't just one-sided, but I suspect they have nothing to worry about. This is exactly what Livvie was hoping to find. I snap away quite happily until Max returns, stealing a glance at his watch.

'We should go shortly, as I want to show you around our next stop before we head back for lunch.'

'Can I purchase a few things to take back as presents?'

'Of course.' I follow Max through to the packing area and select a couple of items for the girls and something for Dawn. At first the elderly Italian woman refuses to take the notes I offer, but I insist and she nods her head in gratitude.

I make an effort to smile at everyone I pass who looks our way, as we retrace our steps.

'The tension is palpable. Can one order make that much of a difference?'

'More than you probably realise. This is a fairly new venture still and we have a long way to go to get a full order book. A deal with your company could kick-start this initiative and give us the cash injection we need to expand. A lot is riding on your visit and there's no point in pretending otherwise.'

'Can't you use a middleman? Someone with contacts already in place?'

Max shakes his head.

'Not all of the operations are as large, or advanced, as

this one. In order to offer people like Olivia the deal they are looking for we need to keep non-production costs to the minimum. It's one less link in the chain taking a cut out of the profits and this is diversity for survival of the whole. Besides, I seriously doubt we'd consistently be able to meet the sort of production levels required to fill global orders, because of the investment levels required. So we are going for the niche, interior design market. If you want two hundred table lamps, that's not a problem. But if you wanted five thousand—'

'Ah, now I understand. Where are we going next?'

I try to sound upbeat, despite feeling the pressure beginning to mount.

'Our biggest producer of textiles. I think you'll be impressed by the set-up. It's actually attached to one of the local churches.'

Max opens the car door as I slide into the seat. A young woman calls out to him, holding something up and Max strides across, placing his hand on her shoulder and taking the item with his other hand.

When he returns he hands me a chilled bottle. 'Here, this is for you.'

'What is Gassossa Neri, exactly?' I ask, wondering if it's some sort of locally distilled alcohol that will take off the top of my head.

'It's good to drink, just carbonated sugar water, really.

It's old school, hard to find these days, so treasured amongst the older people as it was the soft drink of their childhood. Notice that I wasn't offered one.' He drops the corners of his mouth in an exaggerated fashion.

'What a nice gesture.'

Max holds out his hand, pulling a bottle opener from the side pocket of the door.

'Enjoy. It seems you are making quite an impression.' Flipping the lid, he hands it back to me and I can't resist taking a long sip and letting out an appreciative sigh of satisfaction.

As he kicks the engine into life he starts laughing and it's a heart-warming sound.

Chapter 7

'You sound different.' Josh's words are tinged with sadness, or maybe it's simply loneliness. Suddenly finding ourselves apart, and in different countries, is something neither of us would ever have expected.

'It's the distance and I'm, you know, wearing my business head.'

He yawns.

'Sorry, I didn't get much sleep last night. Rosie woke up in the early hours and had a little cry when she remembered you weren't here.'

Guilt washes over me as, suddenly, what I need more than anything is a hug from my girls.

'Did she settle back down?'

'She jumped into our bed and was soon snoring her head off. I really didn't mean to tell you about that. Everything is good this end, honestly. Dawn is being a star and brought over a homemade chicken pie.' I can feel he's annoyed with himself for mentioning Rosie and now he's trying to make light of it. But it's unlike Josh to sound so ... insecure and I wonder if something has happened that he feels he can't tell me. Or maybe it's just my imagination working overtime. He's tired and the girls can be a handful at times, especially if they aren't in the best of moods.

I'm lazing on a bed in an Italian villa. The breeze wafting in through the window carries the scent of oleander blossom and a hint of thyme from the tubs on the terrace. A conversation doesn't get any more surreal and I'm sure I'm worrying for the sake of it. The resulting smile on my face lifts my voice, even though my heart aches to think of the distance between us all.

'I know you are in safe hands. And tomorrow will fly by, then I'll be up early the next morning and on a plane home before you know it. It will be as if this never happened.'

'Funny you should say that, because it doesn't feel real. I keep expecting you to walk through the door, fling your coat on the chair and moan about the drizzly rain making your hair frizzy.'

He's joking with me and I appreciate the effort he's making.

'Did the girls do their homework?'

'Yes, all done. Rosie has a geography test tomorrow. Hettie had to write about a new skill she has acquired, recently. We spent the best part of an hour throwing suggestions around, including some quite inspiring ones, and then she ended up writing half a page about the time she helped you paint her bedroom walls.'

Aww, a sudden flashback makes my chest constrict.

'That's nice, but if my memory serves me right it was at least two years ago and she spent most of the time painting shapes and graffiti, while I followed behind her with the roller. Kids, eh?'

'I know. It's not the same when you aren't here and knowing that you're so far away is a little unsettling. You are the glue that holds us together, Ellie, and this has reminded us not to take you for granted. Anyway, enough about life in the Maddison household, how's Italy?'

'I can't even begin to describe it, Josh. It's so beautiful; and yet there's also a feeling of sadness, when you see how hard life is for the people who depend on the land to earn their living. Today I toured a ceramics workshop and then a textile business which was set up in a sprawling church annex. Everyone was nervous about my visit because they need buyers, or the money they've invested will be wasted. I think the owner of the villa has probably extended loans to some of the farmers who wanted to branch out and get involved with the cooperative. When you walk among the workers it's not just about appreciation of their skilled craftsmanship, but you get caught up in the emotional investment; their hopes and dreams.'

'Ellie, you are Livvie's eyes and ears out there but the ultimate business decision will be hers. It's out of your hands and you can't shoulder that responsibility. It's beginning to worry you already, isn't it? You need to develop a thicker skin, darling, or you'll never survive in the business world.'

Josh knows me better than I know myself.

'I hear what you are saying. I love you for understanding and not simply criticising me for being unduly sensitive. Livvie emailed early this morning but hasn't been in touch since. I've sent her about two dozen photos, but I guess it's unfair of me to expect her to respond quickly. I suspect her mum is back in the ward by now recovering from her op, so maybe I'll hear something after dinner. I would just feel much better being able to give Max an idea of Livvie's reaction, in case I'm getting it all wrong.'

'Well, you've done all you can for today and I'm proud of you. It's quite a thing to step into Livvie's expert shoes at such short notice. You are bound to feel a little intimidated. I know you will also be feeling a little out of your comfort zone. So try to relax, enjoy your meal and get a good night's sleep, honey. And don't stress about things. Love you and miss you. See you later, alligator.'

I smile at his parting words. That's our code – a pact we made after Josh's grandmother died. When the day arrives and we find ourselves facing the inevitable; we want to know for sure that love survives even death. We use that old, childhood saying, so we will never forget the only words that will leave us in no doubt whatsoever. 'In a while, crocodile.'

I'm left listening to static and a feeling of emptiness makes my stomach drop to the floor. The world has never felt quite as enormous as it does to me right now and I really wish Josh was here to wrap his arms around me. I know it's only tiredness so I lie back, throwing the phone onto the bed cover beside me. It's time for a nap before I shower and dress for dinner.

~

When I make my way into the dining room I'm surprised to see virtually all of the tables are full. Max immediately gives me a little wave and hurries over to escort me to a table. The dress code seems to be quite casual and I'm glad I kept it simple, as all of the tables are occupied by families.

'We're busy tonight,' Max explains. 'Once a month we have a dinner that honours the matriarch of the family. It's a tradition now, and our chef puts together a very special menu. But if it's not quite to your liking, then I can bring over the à la carte menu.'

A waiter hovers, pulling out a chair for me. I sit, feeling rather self-conscious as heads turn in our direction. Max is fussing with the table, moving a bowl of fresh flowers and giving one of the tall wine glasses a light polish, as if I'm someone of importance.

'I'm sure the special menu will be fine.' I glance at the list of dishes, not sure whether they are separate courses, or a selection from which you choose. Of course, everything is in Italian. 'I'm in your hands, Max.' I pass the printed menu back to him, smiling gratefully.

'It won't disappoint, I promise.' And with a broad smile he disappears in what I assume is the direction of the kitchen.

There are half a dozen staff members, including Bella, ferrying meals and taking away empty plates. Thankfully, there is quite a buzz in the room and now that I'm seated I'm no longer a source of distraction. Or perhaps the interest was more about Max than an Englishwoman travelling alone.

I can smell rich, sweet tomatoes and something tantalisingly spicy. A young waiter approaches the table bearing a bottle of wine. He holds up the label for me to inspect it and I nod my head, no idea at all if it's the finest wine I'm ever likely to drink, or a celebrated local vintage. Either way, when I'm invited to taste the rich, dark-red liquid it slips down easily. Dry and intensely fruity, my mouth is left with a zing of flavours and an aftertaste of cherries.

Each course is beautifully presented in small and

appealing portion sizes. Every dish is a first for me, bearing little or no resemblance at all to food I've eaten over the years in Italian restaurants back home. From the aperitivo, with Aperol Spritz, olives and crackers, to a mushroom dish with peppers and then, what Bella informs me is black pig fillet with strawberries. Each course is truly delicious.

Towards the end of the meal Max reappears as a willowy, older woman in a simple, yet elegant, silver-grey dress is clearing away the plate in front of me. He speaks to her in rapid Italian and she smiles, then nods, placing the plate back down on the table and extending her hand towards me.

'Trista Ormanni. You enjoy your visit 'ere, yes?'

The words are stilted and her cheeks colour slightly as she speaks.

'Yes, it's truly wonderful. And dinner was heavenly.'

I'm not sure she can understand what I'm saying, but my broad smile reflects the sentiments. She hurries away quickly, leaving us to chat.

'Trista is my fiancée's mother. All of the staff here are family members except Bella, whose mother was born just a few kilometres away. Now things have calmed down a little I wondered if you would like to join me for coffee out on the terrace? Unless you are tired and prefer to retire for the night.'

'No, that would be lovely, thank you.'

Max extends his hand to help me out of my seat. For a brief moment, as our hands touch, everything seems to stand still. I falter slightly and his grasp tightens.

'The wine seems to have gone to my head.' A laugh that ends up sounding more like a giggle doesn't really cover a moment of embarrassment. As he withdraws his hand and extends his arm in the direction of the door, he walks alongside me. His other arm is curled behind me at waist height, but without actually touching me. For some inexplicable reason I feel this is a walk I've done before. How ludicrous is that?

Outside, the balmy evening air is sweet, but there is an undercurrent of a rich woodland scent and a slightly musty, earthy smell. It's comforting, in a familiar way; like a smell from one's childhood. Except that I've never been to Italy before, or anywhere quite like this.

Max notices my reaction. 'Tonight the breeze carries with it the scent of the forests from the mountain slopes. Here, let me get your chair.'

One of the small tables on the terrace has been covered with a white linen table cloth and in the centre the glow from a large candle lantern sheds a soft flickering light.

'To the north we have the Pollino mountain range and to the south, La Sila. It's a difficult mix of terrain, but we are well served by the Calabrian ports of Reggio and Gioia Tauro.'

'How long has this been your home?'

Max shifts in his chair, his body language signalling hesitation. We aren't friends, just business acquaintances and I realise with dismay that I might have overstepped the mark when he was simply making polite conversation. Thankfully, the silence is interrupted by the arrival of coffee and a jovial-looking man who greets Max with a babble of Italian. Max replies and to my ear his mastery of the language makes him sound like a native inhabitant, a true son of Italy.

'*Grazie*, Gianni. *Sono il tuo stato introdotto per la signora* Maddison?'

A moth is attracted by the light from the candle and Max absentmindedly brushes it away, before it's drawn too close to the flame.

'*No, ho passato la giornata sopra presso la raffineria. Ci sono stati alcuni problemi, ma ora è fisso.*'

'*Bene, grazie.* My apologies, Ellie, this is Gianni, my fiancée's uncle. Gianni, this is Mrs Maddison. Gianni has been at the plant today, sorting out a problem that occurred during my absence.'

We shake hands and exchange polite smiles, before Gianni disappears back into the shadows of the villa. The light from the windows flood out onto the terrace, but everything beyond that is simply a series of dark shapes, lit only by a crescent moon and a heaven full of stars.

'Four years. I'm not even sure I could slot back into my old life if ever the opportunity arises.'

His reply to my previous question catches me by surprise. Clearly, his work is important to him. While I'm sure he misses his own family, it's plain that he's now a key member in the Ormanni family's business. Everyone seems to look towards him for direction, as if he's in sole charge.

He adds a little sugar to the coffee cup in front of him and then sinks back onto his chair. There's a sense of resignation in the movement.

'It's a complicated story and I don't want to bore you. I also don't want to spoil your relaxation time and I should be doing a much better job of being a host. I think you can tell that I don't often get the chance to sit down and have a conversation in my own language. It has become a novelty, as most of our guests at the villa are Italians enjoying a weekend retreat away from city life.'

Is he asking my permission to continue, or warning me off? There is a deep sadness in him, which I'd assumed was to do with his love for the people here and their plight. My instincts tell me not to pull back.

'I'm a good listener. And it's always easier talking to a stranger, isn't it? Is your fiancée bi-lingual?'

'Yes, Aletta speaks perfect English.' He pauses, and then glances across at me rather nervously. 'She went missing two years, three months ago.'

My coffee cup is halfway to my lips when Max speaks and immediately I set it back down.

'Oh, I'm so sorry, what a terrible thing to happen. I didn't mean to pry.'

Max looks apologetic and very uncomfortable.

'As I said, it's complicated.'

Whatever thoughts are running through his head, he's clearly unable to continue speaking and I finish drinking my coffee in silence. Standing, I gently bid him goodnight, but he doesn't raise his head. As I'm about to walk through the door into the villa he calls out to me.

'*Buona notte*, Ellie. Sleep well.'

The first thing I do when I return to my room is to check my phone for emails and messages, but there's nothing at all from Livvie. I text Josh to say a brief goodnight and prepare for bed.

Lying there I keep going over and over Max's words, searching for clues. I know people do sometimes disappear. I read the headlines in the papers and have skimmed stories that sound rather dubious, to say the least. But Max is just an ordinary guy and this old and established Italian family is so very traditional. How could their daughter simply disappear without trace? This is such a tight community in many ways, despite the size of the area. With so little going on, anything unusual is bound to become common knowledge. If this was a city, or even one of the larger towns, then it would be easier to understand.

Eventually I drift off, but my dreams are jumbled and I'm glad when dawn begins to break.

Chapter 8

As the rays of the early morning sunshine start to slant across the floor, a succession of pings has me scrabbling for my phone. Livvie is online and looking at the photos. I long to get up and swing open the window to let in the fresh air, but I'm anxious for information and can't wait.

Love these tiles; can you bring a sample back with you?

Looks great, just what I was hoping for – could you send me the dimensions?

Great defoot widesigns. Is that a church you're in???

I send her a quick email telling her that I'm very impressed by what I've seen so far and that Max is the perfect coordinator. I have no doubt that there is scope here for them to expand the operation once the orders come in. Labour isn't a problem, it's cash flow at the moment. I think that's more or less what she was expecting to hear, anyway. Max's professionalism and vision have already impressed her in the short time she's been talking to him.

Livvie's return email confirms as much. Then she goes on to tell me that her mum is doing well and is expected to be in hospital for at least a few days. Enough time, Livvie hopes, for her to sort out a nurse to do the day-to-day care and physio when she comes home. She sounds like she has switched back into organisational mode and is coping with the situation much better. But it is with relief that I read her final comment.

Looks like you've had a worthwhile trip, Ellie, and I'm so grateful to you. I know Josh and the kids will probably hate me for dragging you away from them, but secretly I think it might do you a little good. Nothing builds the confidence quicker than reminding yourself you can do anything, if you put your mind to it. Or, if you care enough about a friend to be there for her.

I'd be grateful if you could pass my thanks onto Max. Tell him that from what you've already shown me we should have no problem at all filling an order for our first container. I'm looking forward to developing a strong business relationship with Artigianato.

*Hugs, Ellie, and please do try to find time to soak up
some of that Italian sunshine. Enjoy a little relaxation
time. You deserve it, lady!*
Livvie xx

I mouth a silent *thank you*, sure that there must be some
patron saint linked to Castrovillari who is smiling down
on us all. My biggest fear was that I hadn't done justice to
the beautiful things I've seen and Livvie wouldn't feel as
enthused, being unable to witness them in person. I know
what Josh said, but isn't life better when what you do
benefits not just one person, but many? Business is all
about profit, I understand that, but this is news I know
will make a lot of people smile today. And I can't wait to
see the look on Max's face. After last night I might not
understand what's going on in his personal life, but if
anyone is in need of good news, it's him.

But Max doesn't put in an appearance at breakfast and
Bella informs me that he's been called to the refinery.

'Max sends his apologies, but the matter required his
urgent attention. He set off at five this morning and left a
message to say that he hopes to be back by eleven. He
suggested that after breakfast I give you a tour of the villa,
as we showcase many of the local crafts here. He thinks
there may be a few more things you'd like to photograph.'

'That's very kind, thank you, Bella. I haven't taken any

photos inside the villa in case it wasn't allowed. But I know my boss will love the chandelier above the staircase, in particular. I wasn't sure whether or not it was a local piece.'

Trista Ormanni approaches, looking wonderful in a simple cream linen skirt and top. She's a woman who catches your eye, her refined air reflecting her position and that of her family.

'Max 'eez away. Back soon. *Egli manda le sue scuse*—' She shrugs her shoulders and glances at Bella for help.

'He sends his apologies,' Bella translates. Trista seems satisfied and gives a smile of thanks, then nods in my direction before turning away.

'I should imagine Max appreciates having you around to translate when he's not here.'

Bella is brushing crumbs from the table.

'We don't get many British people here. Mostly Italians and a few Germans. Trista tries, but she struggles. She lost her husband, Stefano, a couple of years ago. To lose a soulmate must tear you apart and whenever I look at her I remember what she was like, you know, before he passed away. But it restores my faith in the existence of true love and the fact that it can last forever if you are lucky.' Bella grins.

'Oh, do I take that as implying your own path to true love hasn't been particularly smooth?'

'Let's just say I'm still looking. I'm off to cover the reception desk until ten, but after that we can do the tour, if that's convenient?'

'Perfect, see you in a little while.'

I finish my coffee and rise from the table, nodding to my fellow guests. Making my way out onto the terrace through the enormous glass-panelled doors, I feel happy and relaxed.

Already the bees are buzzing and the chirping of the tree crickets is like a backing track, low and incessant. Two butterflies are flitting in and out of the tubs, which are mainly filled with fragrant herbs. But it's the smell of the white, pink and red oleanders, with their lance-shaped, dark-green leaves that grab my attention. As I lean in to smell the white swirls it reminds me of apricots, but the pink and red ones give off more of a sweet, bubble gum scent. I walk across the terrace and a beautiful climbing rose dripping off some trellis work adds a distinctly floral boost to the air. You can literally close your eyes and still savour the southern Italian experience, as the gentle warmth of the morning sun accentuates the heady smells.

I head away from the terrace, descending a flight of stone steps leading down to a lower level and the first of the olive trees. These are very old trees with wide trunks and gnarled branches, from which the leaves and growing fruit hang like curtains. Mostly the sun is obscured, but here and there the foliage thins. Little shafts of sunlight appear to shimmer, as the breeze catches the leaves.

It's time to ring Josh, but I just wish he were here with me to enjoy this moment. The girls would be captivated by the ambience, but probably more eager to laze in the sun. But Josh would appreciate the sheer beauty of the scene in front of me. This is the very essence of southern Italy and something I feel privileged to enjoy.

Josh's voice is comforting, but when I hear how much he misses me, and then the sounds of the girls squabbling in the background, I have to gulp down the lump rising in my throat. The spell that has been cast over me is temporarily broken and all I want is to be back at home again. He touches briefly on a problem he has at work and it's clear he's under pressure, but there is nothing I can do to help. So instead I encourage him to talk about happier things, until he at least sounds brighter.

'I have to go, Josh, Bella is giving me a tour of the villa and I need to take some more photos to send to Livvie. Max is going to get that first order and it's looking promising for the future.'

'What did he say?'

'He isn't here at the moment, as there was a problem up at the processing plant, but he'll be back later this morning.'

Josh is suddenly very quiet, then mumbles, 'It won't delay your return, will it?'

'Of course not. The tickets are booked and I leave at four in the morning. The stopover is in Milan and it's a nine-hour wait unfortunately, but I'll land at Heathrow just after six in the evening.'

'That's later than I thought. The girls were hoping to see you before they went to bed.' It isn't only the girls who will be disappointed, he sounds totally deflated again.

'Sorry, I should have mentioned it before. Livvie was due to meet up with another supplier in Milan, so the delay wasn't a problem for her.'

'I'm being selfish, honey. I'll get over it. As they say, absence makes the heart grow fonder. I've never missed you so much, but then we've never been so far apart. Just concentrate on what you have to do; I can imagine how stressful it must be and how alien it must feel.'

I wish I could explain how comfortable I feel here, not alien at all, but I'm not sure Josh would understand in his present state of mind. 'See you later, alligator.'

He responds. 'In a while, crocodile.'

I don't feel strange here at all. What I feel is a weird sort of recognition. A sense of being at peace. I miss my family, naturally, but a part of me will be sad to leave this behind. As I retrace my steps I find that admission shocking. It's only when Bella appears in front of me that I snap out of my reverie.

Chapter 9

The tour of the villa is eye-opening as it's much bigger than I had realised. When you approach it from the terrace you see a cluster of three interlinking stone buildings, whose roofs are at differing heights. My room is more or less directly above the reception area and my window looks out across the front, southern elevation. The large building off to the side mostly comprises guests' rooms, but being at a ninety-degree angle to the main building the views look west, in the direction of the mountains. Between the two buildings is a smaller building, nestled into the corner and Bella informs me it's Trista's suite.

'Ooh, there's a wonderful chest in here you might like to see. I'm sure Trista won't mind if we go in.'

This part of the villa is very different to the rest, where everything has been carefully designed. Trista's room is a mix of the old and new. An ornate wooden table is covered with silver-framed photos and for the first time I get a glimpse of Trista's husband. Several are of their wedding day and they are young, happy and smiling fit to burst. I have no idea from the other photos if any of them include Aletta, as there are so many group photos taken over the years.

'Do you have children? Bella asks, noticing my interest.

'Yes, two. Hettie and Rosie. They're both teenagers. It's always chaotic in our house. Lots of noise.'

She smiles. 'I bet they're missing you. Where's home?'

'The Forest of Dean. It's on the Welsh border. It's a beautiful spot and we love exploring the nature trails.'

'Oh, I've never been, but I've heard of it.'

'I'll give you my number and if you go back home for a holiday and fancy a weekend away, give me a call. We have a spare bedroom and don't get many guests.'

'Thank you, I just might take you up on that. I'm overdue a return visit and that could be just the incentive I need to make it bearable!'

Bella stands in front of a wooden chest inlaid with panels of intricate metalwork.

'Lovely, isn't it? And it looks old.'

'Wow, that's gorgeous. I'm sure Olivia will love this. It's perfect for storing linen, or to use as a coffee table. Thank you, Bella.'

'That's Aletta,' Bella points to a photo of a beautiful young woman. Tall, slim and elegantly dressed. A young Audrey Hepburn springs to mind. I don't know quite what to say, so I point to the photo next to it.

'Is that Stefano Ormanni?'

She nods. 'Yes, it's all very sad, isn't it? To lose your daughter and your husband in such a short space of time is unimaginable. Life doesn't get much crueller than that. But Trista has Max to rely on and he's been her saviour. The son she never had.'

I flounder for something safe to say as a response, not wanting to pry.

'Only time can lessen the pain. You never really get over a loss like that, do you?'

Arrgghh, I shouldn't have made it a question.

'Trista will never get over it. She told me once that she feels her life is now about existing, rather than living. I didn't know what to say to her so I gave her a hug. There aren't many things that leave me speechless. But that was shortly after I arrived here and feelings were still running high. People were suspicious about Aletta's disappearance and it wasn't a good time.'

I make a show of taking a few snaps to avoid having to reply and then, thankfully, we move on to some of the rooms towards the rear of the main building. Bella has no idea how uncomfortable I feel and I'm glad the conversation about the family ends there. Is it wrong to be curious about someone else's tragedy?

The magnificent views of the mountains and the forest areas on the slopes looking north, which is the backdrop to the village of Castrovillari, soon have me clicking away once more. Too far away to see in any great detail, it's mostly the shapes and colours that dominate the horizon as far as the eye can see.

I continue snapping a few photos to show the girls on my return, in between shots of wall hangings, rugs, rustic metal-and-wood coffee tables, and various decorative items.

'This is such a good idea, Bella. What better setting in which to display what the cooperative has to offer than a stunning villa like this one?'

'That's Max, for you. He's constantly trying to think of ways to give the locals some return. The Ormannis weren't keen at first, treasuring some of the more old-fashioned family heirlooms that were a part of their heritage. He convinced them that updating the villa was essential and a part of that should be to make it a celebration of the way forward. When I arrived here the work was in full swing and tempers were a little frayed at times. But in the end everyone could see it was the right thing to do and now I do believe Trista genuinely loves it. In a way, I think it makes the past a little less painful, as so much of what is here now is new.'

I pretend to be occupied with taking some snaps of a rather large rug, but my head is trying to formulate a question. Bella smooths the cover on the bed, taking out a wrinkle.

'Is it possible to move on in such a situation?' It's an honest remark. How can any mother bear not knowing what happened to her only child?

I'm not sure what exactly Bella knows about Trista's daughter, maybe nothing, and I'm cross with myself for letting my curiosity get the better of me. But I'm going to spend several hours with Max again today and it would help to understand him a little more.

'Trista has had no choice but to accept what seems inevitable now, that she may never know for sure what happened. With every month that passes even clinging onto a slim hope now seems pointless. I feel so sorry for Max, too. Since Stefano's funeral Aletta's name is rarely mentioned and never by Trista or Max. Anyway, I think it's time we headed back downstairs, as he's probably waiting for you.'

I don't think Bella meant to cut off the conversation as such, but glancing at her wrist watch she's conscious of the time. However, I hate to take advantage of her willingness to chat to me about this, so in a way it's probably for the best.

'Thank you for the tour, Bella. I really appreciate it and I had no idea just how sprawling this place is; I've toured French chateaux that aren't as interesting, or commanding.'

'I feel lucky to be working here. My mother, however, will never forgive me.' The smile on her face says more than words could ever tell me. Here she feels free to be herself.

And I know that when I leave tomorrow a part of me will be very sorry to be saying goodbye.

~

'I must apologise for my absence, Ellie, but the matter was pressing. I'm sure we can make up some of the lost time and get you back here in time to rest up before dinner. I'm conscious that you have an early departure tomorrow and will want to retire promptly. I ... um—'

As Max holds the car door open I slip inside, then wait a few seconds as he walks around to the driver's door.

'I was wondering if you'd join me for dinner this evening?'

He seems hesitant, as if he's not sure it's the right thing to do.

'Well, as we have something to celebrate I think that would be very appropriate and a lovely way to end my visit.'

His head turns sharply and his brow lifts, taking in my words.

'You've spoken to Olivia?'

'Yes. She said to tell you that based on the photos I've sent her she will have absolutely no problem in filling the first container. And she said "first" container too, implying there will be others.'

Max slams his hands on the steering wheel as his body rocks back into the seat, the smile on his face quite possibly the biggest one I've seen so far. His eyes twinkle as he looks at me and grins.

'*Aiutati che Dio t'aiuta.*'

'Which means?'

'Quite literally, help yourself and God will help you. But I'm not forgetting the part you have played in this, Ellie. Sometimes He sends us a little help.'

'You seem relieved and yet, surely, this was only ever about seeking out the right clients? You already know the products are of a good quality.'

Max kicks the engine into life.

'I've come to learn that only a fool takes anything in this life for granted. Besides, it's slow-going, Ellie. The website isn't up and running yet, and how many buyers will take up the offer to come here in person? You are the first. But it's about much more than that, as the family are still not sure I'm taking things in the right direction. Some of the loans I've convinced them to make may never be repaid if we fail. If I fail.'

Today we head away from the plains, turning onto the main highway and I see that we are heading towards Castrovillari itself. But the view flying past my window goes unnoticed as my head is trying to unravel a puzzle. I realise that the pressure on Max is probably a little isolating.

To whom can he turn? But the biggest question on my mind is why does he stay?

~

Our first stop is very different to the places we visited yesterday. This is an ironworker's compound and it's on the edge of town. Large, wrought-iron gates lead us into a large parking area, surrounded on three sides by a one-storey stone outbuilding. This is an established business and immediately we pull up two men walk towards the car.

Max helps me out and one of the men steps forward, hand outstretched. They shake hands and then all eyes are on me.

'*Questa è la signora Maddison*. Ellie, this is Eduardo Camillucci and his son, Piero.'

Eduardo and I shake hands as he begins talking to me in rapid Italian. I then shake Piero's hand as Max says something to Eduardo, who nods vigorously. Unfortunately, the discovery that I can't speak Italian doesn't stop him talking to me and I give a sideways glance at Max, who simply smiles as if to say, 'Don't worry.'

It's the first time I've ever toured a workshop like this. Eduardo talks almost non-stop and Max patiently translates as I learn all about the Camillucci family. Eduardo has three sons, but two of them have already been lost to him. Max explains that moving to a city in the north is almost as devastating as losing a child to Eduardo and his wife. He follows in the tradition of his father and grandfather, but has to face up to the reality that the next generation are prepared to go in search of bigger things. Eduardo now has to ensure that the business makes enough money to keep their remaining son at home. But as I look around I realise that this isn't just where they conduct business. A part of the u-shaped stone building has smaller windows with shutters and is, in fact, their home. It's possibly big enough for three, but must have been very cramped when all of Eduardo's sons lived at home. And what of the one remaining son when it's time for him to settle down and have a family of his own?

We walk around for about an hour, as I snap away at the fine examples of sophisticated panels and a range of curls, rosettes, crowns, rims and ornamental elements for gates and handrails. But there are also stunning sculptures for the garden and finer metals used to create pieces like the leaf chandelier in the stairwell at the villa. Max explains that Eduardo and his son will make special pieces to order and guarantee a price that can't be beaten.

Max looks at his watch, no doubt thinking about the next part of our journey, but Eduardo immediately engages him in conversation that runs on for a few minutes. He turns to me, rather apologetically.

'Eduardo and his family insist we stay for lunch and we

will offend them if we refuse. I've explained that we have another appointment and he understands, but this is likely to take at least an hour. Are you happy to accept their hospitality?'

'Of course, please thank Eduardo and tell him I'd be delighted.'

Max smiles at me in appreciation. His eyes seem to linger, as if he's reluctant to look away and my pulse rate soars. We're sharing a moment and we both know it.

I quickly break the connection by looking at Eduardo and saying, *'Grazie.'*

It turns out to be a wonderful and relaxing hour, despite the language barrier. Eduardo's wife, Cristina, and her own mother busy themselves in the kitchen and present us with what looks like pink spaghetti. Max informs me it's pasta cooked in red wine, with parmesan cheese and black olives. It's certainly delicious and the accompanying wine, which Max declines, is very pleasant.

Bidding them goodbye I feel humbled by the warmth of their welcome and my heart is touched by what they are doing here. This is about the survival of a long tradition. Max's venture represents a lifeline for a simple family who have no idea how to market themselves beyond their own local community. What they do have is the commitment, skills and the working ethos to succeed, if they are given the chance.

Chapter 10

'Oh, Josh. I wish you could have been here today. I'm really getting to know these people, something that doesn't happen when you are merely a tourist. I had lunch with the Camillucci family after touring their workshop and this afternoon I visited a group of woodworkers. What was special was that they make the table tops for the metal frames made by Eduardo Camillucci and his son. I can hardly believe that in a little over twenty-four hours this will all be merely a memory.' I'm lying on my bed chatting to Josh on the mobile.

'It makes me happy that it's something you've enjoyed, but I'll admit that I feel lost here without you. I want you home again, by my side. Is that terribly selfish of me? I miss you too much, Ellie. Even the girls are only going through the motions until you get home. This hasn't changed anything, has it?'

His comment makes me feel flustered. Nothing has changed, why would it? Admittedly, I've had a series of experiences that have opened my eyes a little and I've seen a side of life that was previously unknown to me. But nothing has changed.

'I have no burning desire to start jetting off around the world, if that's what you mean. I miss you all too much for that. Besides, I'm the family-orientated one, right? It's Livvie who chose the cut and thrust of business life. She thrives on the excitement, but I'll be honest and say that I find it exhausting. And nerve-wracking at times.'

Josh laughs.

'Good to hear. I would be horrified if you came home all fired up and suddenly our life here was too mundane by comparison. But I would never want you to feel trapped, or that you'd made a sacrifice for us, Ellie. We love you too much for that.'

'You and the girls will always come first, Josh. You know that. In fact, this has made me realise how lucky we are with the life we have. Being able to provide for the girls is something we take for granted, but here it's very different. That's one of the things that makes me feel so sad.'

'It's a shame that even paradise has its drawbacks but I suppose nothing is ever perfect.'

My mobile phone buzzes and I see it's Livvie calling. 'Josh, I have to go, it's Livvie. Love you, hug the girls for me and I'll text you later.'

I press the connect button. 'Hi Livvie.'

'Hi Ellie, just a quick call to check that you are happy about the arrangements for tomorrow. Any concerns about the return journey?'

'Thanks, Livvie. I'm sure it will be fine. The only change is that Josh has decided to drive up to Heathrow to collect me, so you might want to cancel the seat on the coach. Our neighbour, Dawn, is going to look after the girls. How are things at your end?'

'Will do, and better, thanks. Mum is still taking some heavy-weight pain medication and isn't expecting to be discharged until early next week. Any movement is difficult at the moment and in a way I'm glad they are keeping her in for a while. Someone is going to come to the house to assess what we'll need to make her comfortable and I've arranged for the nurse to be here for that meeting. You know me, I have no idea at all what an invalid is likely to need. Anyway, I won't keep you and I hope you have something enjoyable planned for your last evening. Have you ventured into town?'

I know that Livvie would probably have hired a car and crammed in as much local sightseeing as possible.

'Max has invited me to dinner and today I did get some glimpses of Castrovillari, but there wasn't time to park and walk around. The heat is a little tiring and that's probably why people tend to start work early and nap after lunch. I've never slept in the day before and it feels rather decadent.'

'When in Rome, as they say,' she laughs, no doubt

thinking I've missed out on making the most of this trip. But I wouldn't change one single moment of it.

'I think I will leave a little bit of myself here when I leave,' I confess.

'Really?'

Why did I say that?

'I mean, the people are so welcoming and friendly they make you feel instantly at home. It touches your heart.'

'Well, just travel safely, Ellie. Keep all of your belongings close during that long stopover in Milan airport. There will be enough time to jump in a taxi and have a little tour around the city, but knowing you that's unlikely to happen.'

Now it's my turn to laugh.

'You are joking, of course! I have my Kindle and I also want to re-read the notes I've made for you about the trip. I'm sure the time will fly.'

'Well, enjoy your last supper.' Her throaty laughter is the last thing I hear before the line disconnects.

Suddenly there's a tap on the door and when I swing it open Max is standing there.

'I have a little surprise planned for dinner later. I thought it would be nice to take you into town. I've talked my favourite restaurant into opening up early for us, so that afterwards we can have a little walk around. I promise to have you back here well before nine o'clock. Is that okay with you?'

I feel flustered and know my face is colouring up.

'That's very kind of you, Max. It sounds perfect.'

He nods, pleased by my response. 'I'll see you in reception at five-thirty, then.'

A sudden buzz of excitement creeps over me as I head off to shower and wash my hair. I'm not sure the dress I brought to wear tonight is quite right for a dinner for two. I'd assumed I'd be eating alone and wanted to look like a well-travelled woman abroad. Max is always smart-casual and I so wish I'd packed something a bit more, well, relaxed. Instead, when I slip on the silky, olive green wrap-around dress I feel a little over-dressed. However, the contrast against the slight hint of a tan I've acquired gives me a glow I didn't have before and I will admit it is rather flattering. When I'm working it's usually black trousers and tops, and when I'm at home I live in jeans.

I guess I'm just a little nervous at the thought of spending a few hours with Max. There isn't much left to say that's business-related, that we haven't already covered. This is likely to get personal and I don't know if I can handle that with an appropriate level of detachment.

I can't help but admit that I feel drawn to him in some way, although I don't want to be, and I've tried my best to fight it. And it's not one-sided, because he's told me things that you wouldn't normally divulge to a mere business acquaintance. Explaining to me how important this visit is to the cooperative was dangerously honest of him. Not least because it isn't just about the quality of the merchandise, but also about the long-term viability of the supply chain. In a way, the least I know about the troubles here, the better for them, surely? I think he trusts me and can sense the empathy I have for these people. But I am curious about his personal situation, as my intuition is picking up on a hurt that runs very deep. The question I have to ask myself is why that should matter to me at all, given the circumstances. Or why Max feels he can be so relaxed and open in my company.

Chapter 11

Trista is there when I walk down to meet Max. I'm surprised to see that he's not as casually dressed as usual. He's wearing a smart white-cotton shirt and dark-grey trousers. He's so handsome, but his appeal is about much more than what the world can see. Beneath that he has a good heart. He smiles when he sees me and then turns to Trista, says about a dozen words before she raises her hand and nods in my direction. I notice she places her hand on his arm and gives it a gentle squeeze, before withdrawing it. As Max and I walk to the door I can feel her eyes on us, watching every step, and I suddenly feel very self-conscious. Does it upset her seeing Max with another woman? Reminding her that the person he should be walking out of the entrance to the villa with is her daughter.

Outside, Max appears unfazed and surprisingly relaxed. Once we set off a comfortable silence settles between us. Maybe I was over-thinking this and we can fill the time with idle chatter about the food and our surroundings. It's kind of him to go out of his way so that I can see the town up close and experience one of the local restaurants.

When we park, Max informs me it isn't far to the restaurant, which is called Il Giardino Di Ulivi. He doesn't interpret but it's easy enough to work out that it's The Garden of Olives. As we walk along the streets the huge mountain range in the background is visible at every twist and turn. The wide swathes of forest and the many canyons are easily identifiable and for the first time I get a real sense of the scale involved. And yet it seems like a very natural contrast, rather than a stark and overbearing shadow over a town that is divided into the old and the new. We reach a crossroads and head up a windy little road, until Max stops and I realise we have arrived.

The building has three floors, the outside is an aged, pale-yellow colour and blends into the street quite nicely. This restaurant has been here for a long time. There is a tiny courtyard at the front, separated from the street by intricate railings and a beautiful pair of wrought-iron gates that look familiar. An image of Eduardo immediately springs into my head. It wouldn't surprise me if Max is also a facilitator, putting people together for mutual benefit.

As we enter, the restaurant owner almost runs across to welcome Max and they hug, which surprises me, as it's the first time I've witnessed Max doing anything other than shaking hands.

A torrent of Italian fills the air, which lasts for a couple of minutes. I look on in fascination. These two have history and Max is very happy to be here. They turn to look at me.

'*E si ha una bella compagna così per la cena!*'

Max replies, then turns to me to add, 'This is Luca and he says I have a beautiful companion for dinner.'

I feel myself going red and smile back, then quickly turn away to look around the empty restaurant. It's mostly cream walls, with lots of exposed brick and rustic arches mounted on sturdy pillars. It's bigger than I was expecting and the property extends way back. There is a large serving hatch, through which a glimpse of the kitchen can be seen.

Max indicates for me to follow Luca and he escorts us to a table in the far corner. I was rather hoping we'd have a table at the front of the restaurant, where there is a window from which it's possible to see the mountain range. But Max looks very happy with Luca's choice. Max and Luca both move forward to pull out a chair for me and they exchange a little laughter and bantering, before Max allows Luca to do the honours.

Luca leaves us to peruse the menu and to my dismay it's all in Italian. I look up at Max and shrug my shoulders.

'Don't worry about it, it's merely for show. Luca will bring us what he feels we will enjoy eating. You've certainly made an impression on him and now he's going to show off a little. The food is always excellent, so just keep nodding and smiling. I promise that you are in for a real treat.'

And he was right, as we sampled a whole range of dishes. From the mushroom antipasto with chillies, to the roast lamb and three cheeses dish, caciocavallo grilled with green tomato mostardo, served alongside ricotta and pecorino with apple confit.

Max describes every ingredient in detail and all I have to do is savour each mouthful. After the meal we idle over coffee, but by then other dinner guests begin arriving.

Suddenly, the strains of Puccini's 'Nessun Dorma' fill the restaurant and for one moment Max closes his eyes.

When he opens them I can tell he wants to say something, but instead he clears his throat and looks away. As the aria continues and the music swells, it seems to tug at every emotion and I try not to let him see the unbidden tears it brings to my own eyes.

My heart seems to be saying 'I know you. I've known you. I feel what you feel.' Is it just the passion invoked by the music?

When I glance back at him, I see that Max is similarly moved and we continue to sit in silence, until the last note fades into nothingness. I notice we each have a hand lingering on the table, almost touching but not quite. Suddenly there is only the low buzz of background chatter to fill the silence and the spell is broken. Our eye contact is meaningful, our mouths say nothing. There's an air of awkwardness and I find myself needing to fill the void.

'I've heard it sung many times, but I have no idea how it translates. But that doesn't really matter, does it?' My voice is soft and almost apologetic.

Max's sadness when he looks back at me makes me hold my breath for a few moments. I want to wrap my arms around him and share his pain.

'No, you're right. The music is so powerful, that the words are of little importance. In each of us it will, no doubt, draw out a different range of emotions depending upon the life we have lived. I'm afraid for me it serves to highlight the fragility of life.'

And what did I feel? Wrenching sadness, to be pulled away from this place as I face the journey home. I want to go back to my life and the ones I love, so why then do I feel so much a part of this too? Am I tied to this place by a previous life? Does that sort of thing really exist? The flood of questions is like an onslaught.

Max suddenly stands, offering his hand and I'm happy to take it. As we touch it feels so very natural and I know that's wrong. I'm inches away from him and can feel the heat of his body. Our eyes meet for one brief second and then he leads me in the direction of the door, pausing only to wave to Luca. I follow suit, desperate to get out into the fresh air, because I feel so unsettled.

'I'm sorry. I spoilt the ending to a wonderful meal and I simply wanted to express my appreciation. I hope you will forgive me.'

What do I do? Do I say *yes* and we head back in silence? What is my heart telling me to do? Can I shrug off someone else's pain, when he's so obviously crying out for help? Max mistakes my silence for simple acceptance of his apology. He indicates with his hand, to steer me in the opposite direction to the way we came.

'Can we head back to the villa? Would you be too disappointed?'

He hesitates, his eyes searching my face.

'I was going to take you to see the Castello Aragonese, which is number one on every tourist's sightseeing list. Then on to meet Saint Julian, the patron saint of Castrovillari,' he muses, the sparkle back in his voice.

'Let's go back and sip wine on the terrace. I would like you to tell me about Aletta.'

His eyes are firmly fixed on mine, but I don't look away. A moment of understanding passes between us.

'As you wish.' Max turns on his heels and leads me back to the car.

Chapter 12

I twist the stem of the wine glass in front of me in my hands, nervously. In the candlelight, though, everything feels softer and subdued, less awkward. Settling back in my seat our eyes meet. Max raises his eyebrows and releases an involuntary sigh, then laughs at himself.

'This has nothing at all to do with business, Max. Whatever you tell me will never be repeated.'

'Do you believe in fate?'

'Of course. Do you?'

He nods. 'Yes, I always have done. This morning when you told me the good news I said God helps those who help themselves. What if the reason you're here has two purposes? You're a good listener and a person whose discretion I would trust without a doubt. And yet I hardly know you. Don't you think that's rather strange?'

He feels it too. This, whatever it is, isn't purely down to my imagination playing tricks, or because I'm a long way from home and feeling – what, vulnerable?

Unusually sensitive and emotional because I'm home-sick?

'What if Olivia was never meant to make this trip? Maybe everything really does happen for a reason.' I can't believe I've just whispered out loud the words that are in my head.

Max takes a mouthful of wine, savouring it before placing his glass back down onto the table. Then he rubs his hands over his eyes and lets out another sigh.

'You feel it too, that inexplicable link between us. It was there from the moment you arrived, wasn't it? You need to let me get my head around this. Everything is buried so deep it's not easy to drag it back up. I'm on the edge and I think, for whatever reason, you sense that. I hope those around me can't see the cracks, but they are very real. What if you tell me a little about yourself and your family first, while I gather my thoughts. I hardly know anything about you.'

It's my turn to take a mouthful of wine before I begin, wondering where to start and what to say.

'I found my soul mate, Josh, when I was only eighteen. He was a year older. I knew he was the one from the very first time I set eyes on him. Just like that.' I snap my fingers to emphasise the way it was at the time. Instant and without warning. 'We moved in together and married shortly after-wards. Life has had its ups and downs for sure. I miscarried our first baby, but we went on to have two wonderful daughters. Hettie is fifteen and Rosie is thirteen. I went back to work part-time for Olivia, who is also my best friend, when Rosie started school.

'Our life together revolves around work and family. I'm a very private person, not something I would admit to many people aside from Livvie, as I affectionately call her. People think they know me, but they don't. Only Josh. He knows me almost better than I know myself. He says I'm a worrier and he's right, I am, because sometimes I care a little too much about the people with whom I come into contact.

'My mother died a couple of years ago. I'm convinced it was of a broken heart after she discovered that my father was cheating on her. It turned out that he'd had a long-running affair and went on to marry his mistress, shortly after Mum died. We haven't talked since. There, that's more than most people I see every day at work know about me.'

Max looks relaxed, his face quite blank as he mulls over the quick analysis of my life.

'It hurts when you care that much, doesn't it?'

I nod, letting the silence indicate it's now Max's turn.

'If I'm honest it was probably a one-sided love at first sight when I met Aletta, but at the time I was so convinced it was mutual. At last, my search was over. My first true love, or so it seemed. She was beautiful, intelligent and vibrant. We met in London. Aletta was on holiday and I was attending a seminar at the Royal Institute of British Architects.'

He pauses to take another sip of his wine.

'You're a qualified architect?' It was the last thing I expected to hear.

'Yes, and project manager. I was beginning to make a name for myself after completing a rather prestigious build in London. Aletta and I kept in constant touch and I found myself with time on my hands, so I flew out to Italy for a holiday. At the time her father was recovering from his first stroke and one thing led to another. Aletta begged me to stay for a while, to help the family, as things were a little chaotic. Just until he was a little stronger, she said. I asked why her Uncle Gianni didn't step forward, but she said her father would never allow that. I thought it was some sort of feud between the brothers, but later found out Gianni had refused outright, saying he was out of his depth.

'He's my right-hand man now and I couldn't manage without him, but he would never take over control. Being the decision-maker isn't easy and it requires not just business acumen, but a mind that can quickly evaluate every situation. So I stayed and the months passed. Stefano and Trista started treating me like a son. It was a role I had no choice in accepting and I admit I was besotted with Aletta. After a while, though, I came to see that I could make a real difference here and it began to matter to me for a whole host of different reasons. I guess that's something you and I have in common.'

He pauses, his eye drawn by a cluster of fireflies, as one by one the lights in the restaurant are turned off. The door to the reception area opens and Bella walks towards us across the terrace. She hands Max a key and gives a nod in my direction.

'Sorry to interrupt. I've locked up and switched the reception phone through to Gianni. I'll say goodnight and sleep well.' She looks in my direction and gives me a smile, but there's a hint of curiosity behind those eyes. I'm glad it's only Bella who is on reception duty tonight. I wonder what Trista's reaction would have been, seeing us sitting here in the semi-gloom chatting and drinking together, like old friends.

Max accepts the keys. 'Thank you, Bella. You too.'

With fewer lights from the building, the stars above us are more noticeable. It feels magical, as if we are sitting here in a bubble and nothing else exists except for what we can see before us. I wonder whether Max will change his mind about revealing his story, using the interruption as an excuse.

'Did you think Aletta was the one?'

He drags his hand through his hair, a strand of silver grey illuminated by the candlelight draws my eye. I feel as if I've known his face forever, that somehow it's etched into my memory. The way it might feel if you don't see someone for many, many years and suddenly your paths cross once more. Instant recognition.

'I believe I did, but so much was happening in those early days. When I first arrived, the villa was a family residence. It was badly in need of renovation. It was my idea to expand the business and turn it into a hotel, so that it would strengthen their position. A safeguard, if you like, for years when the harvest was poor. Stefano had already identified that as the family's share in the olive oil industry grew, marketing was going to become increasingly important. Aletta had attended the University of Milan and graduated with a degree in marketing, sales and English. Oh, she was bright, but there was something different about her. Happy one minute, miserable the next. During the renovation work and the subsequent launch of the hotel, Aletta and I worked very closely together. But after that it was as if her interest in me waned. And then, suddenly, she became incredibly resentful of the way her family had accepted me.'

Max stops to pour a little more wine into our glasses.

'Stefano never thought to mentor her to take over at some point?'

He laughs.

'Aletta never intended to stay here, although the family weren't aware of that and it wasn't my place to share a confidence. She had her eyes firmly set on a career in

London, or Paris. Stefano would have been scandalised at what he would have perceived as a rejection of family loyalty and tradition. Just as her disappearance caused a scandal amongst some of her wider family and the older inhabitants of Castrovillari. In getting me to stay, Aletta had achieved her goal, but even then it hadn't made her happy. In a way I wasn't as surprised as I might have been when it happened.'

Is he trying to tell me that Aletta ran away, using Max to assuage her guilt about leaving?'

'We argued a lot, mainly because she was always finding excuses to go off on silly business jaunts, exploring vague, so-called opportunities. Few resulted in anything at all. The reality was that having begged me to stay, she was then free to do as she pleased without feeling guilty. Even though she knew her father's health was declining. I began to feel like the hired help to her, rather than her fiancé. Trista and Stefano were constantly pushing for us to get married and although I was beginning to have doubts, I just let them believe what they wanted to believe. I think I knew by then that there was no way I could turn my back on Villa Rosso, no matter what the future held for Aletta and me. It was a foolish thing to do, but I also accepted that it was my fate.'

He leans forward, hunched over in his seat, with his hands planted on the table either side of his wine glass. He looks desperate, tortured.

'Many men would have walked away, Max. Lots of relationships begin well and fizzle out, it happens. What did your own family think about what was happening?'

His eyes meet mine and in part-shadow they are filled with a deep despair.

'They didn't understand why I had walked away from everything my life had been, for a woman they had met only once. My mother said Aletta was cold, but at the time I was convinced they didn't understand her. She was different, exciting and charming, until I came to see that what she masked with smiles was really the ugliness of manipulation. By then it was too late, of course. They know very little about the detail, so at least I was spared that humiliation.'

An involuntary gasp escapes my lips. His tone is as cold as the words he's spoken.

'But you still refer to her as your fiancée.'

'I'm not saying that what happened was her intention from day one, but looking back it was clear she tired of me very quickly once I agreed to stay. As Trista became more and more concerned about Aletta's behaviour, we both tried to ensure that nothing reached Stefano's ears, as his declining health was the main concern. He doted on Aletta and it was tragic in a sadly pathetic way. Between us, Trista and I made sure he thought everything was fine. After the disappearance, the scandal rocked the whole community. Trista pleaded with me never to give up hope that Aletta would return. I'm simply honouring her wishes.'

I look at him, appalled. 'That must have been a nightmare. Stefano believing there would be a wedding at some point and feeling that at least the future of the family legacy was ensured. Then having to please Trista by acting as if Aletta could return at any time when, surely, hope must have waned with every passing day. But you could have left at any time and Trista must have realised that.'

Max nods, sitting back and taking a gulp of his wine.

'At first I couldn't leave because Aletta kept going off at a moment's notice, whenever and wherever she wanted. Trista was living from second to second, constantly fearing the worst for her ailing husband. After we lost contact with Aletta, if I'd walked away I would have been leaving a shell-shocked family to deal with the unthinkable. Even someone with a hardened heart might have had trouble with that decision.'

Instinctively I reach out across the table to him, but pull back before our hands can touch. It isn't my place to do anything other than listen. He continues.

'And then one day followed another. It was out of character for her to stay away so long, even for Aletta and her irrational behaviour. But this time there was no contact at all. We left voicemails every day and then, suddenly, the number we dialled was unobtainable. By then the police were involved and that's a time I try not to think about. Two months later her father passed away in his sleep and Trista told me he simply lost all hope.'

His head sinks down and he breathes out, one long, slow exhalation as his chest deflates.

'But surely that can't be it. There must have been an investigation? Someone, somewhere must know where she is?'

'For a while I was the focus of the police's attention. Trista was horrified, but it wasn't until they'd traced Aletta's flight and confirmed her arrival in London, that I was dismissed as a suspect. They succeeded in finding the hotel she stayed at and were able to establish some idea of where she had been from her credit card records. But the day her phone number was taken out of service was also the last day she used her card. After that, nothing. Nothing at all, but at least they know she didn't fly out from any of the London terminals. She's officially listed as a missing person to this day.'

'Do you think she's still in the UK?'

He shrugs, despondently.

'No one knows the answer to that and we probably never will. I'm never going to be able to prove for sure that I had nothing to do with her disappearance, to quieten those who are still suspicious. That thought will haunt me until the day I die.

'Look, it's getting late, Ellie, and I'm mindful that you have to get up in a couple of hours. This has helped, you know. Just finally putting the whole thing out there to someone who didn't start with their own preconceived idea of what really happened. It means a lot. No one ever talks about it now and they haven't since Stefano's funeral, out of respect for Trista. Maybe now I can begin to let it go and accept it's always going to be a story without a conclusion. It's devilishly hard moving forward when the ghosts of the past won't give you any peace, though.'

There's nothing at all I can say, so this time I reach out and place my hand on his. I let it linger for a few moments and then stand up.

'You deserve so much more than a tortured life, Max. Time is a great healer, though. Maybe you have to be patient for a while longer and then, one day, you can stop feeling responsible and start again somewhere else.'

Max stands too and we walk back towards the villa side by side. At the door he stops and turns to face me.

'I wish it was that simple. This is my home now. There are too many people reliant upon me to keep everything running smoothly. In a sad twist of irony I was made for this, to be here and shoulder this responsibility. It seems my path led me here for a reason. Life never was meant to be straightforward. Besides, you can't fight fate, can you? I've worked hard to win back the trust I lost from a handful of people. There are still a few who turn their backs on me and think I'm motivated by financial gain. They are unaware that I don't stand to inherit anything and the Ormanni business will be handed to Gianni and his family when Trista dies.'

I'm glad of the cover of darkness as a tear trickles down my face.

'But it seems so ... unfair. One sacrifice too far, Max. Trista must know that and I can't understand why she doesn't speak out on your behalf. I hope that some day you will be able to disconnect yourself from these memories and start afresh.'

'I may not be family by marriage, but I am family now.'

To my horror I realise that in Max's head he believes he owes this family the rest of his natural life. Aletta left them when she had tired of him and, because of that fact, some sort of ridiculous sense of indebtedness ties him to them forever. That's one of the saddest things I've ever heard.

'I hope you find a sense of peace, Max. And I hope fate brings you the happiness you deserve.'

'You are very kind, Ellie, and I'm grateful to you. God willing, our paths may cross again.'

We both know that's unlikely. This is a one-off trip for me and Livvie will be back at work as soon as her domestic arrangements are sorted. For some reason I don't want to move, even though we've lapsed into silence. And then I know why. Max puts his arms around me and holds me close for the briefest of moments. Time seems to stand still and my heart skips a beat.

He turns his head to whisper into my ear. 'Thank you for listening and for not judging me. Sleep well, Ellie Maddison, and travel back to your family safely. My only regret is that we didn't have more time together.'

Max releases me, then leans forward to hold open the door to the reception. I hurry forward without a backwards glance. My eyes are full of tears and my stomach is doing somersaults. The moment I close the door to my room I break down. I feel angry for a man who has a truly good heart, who simply found himself in the wrong place, at the wrong time. Or, from the perspective of the Ormanni family, the right place at precisely the right time. But isn't it wrong for one man to have to sacrifice the rest of his life for a tragedy that wasn't his fault?

I end up lying in bed, looking out at the inky-black sky, counting the stars in an attempt to stop my brain from buzzing. I can't seem to squeeze out my thoughts. How does someone disappear just like that? How can Trista simply accept what's happened? Can't she see that Max is trapped here and understand the cost of his very personal sacrifice?

The counting eventually slows down the questions until they subside and there's only one question left. Why did fate bring *me* here? Livvie wouldn't have been drawn into Max's situation, that's for sure. I realise that tiredness means nothing is making sense any more. As I drift into a disturbed sleep it's Max's face I see, accompanied by an overwhelming sense of well-being. I know you, Max, we've met before. I just don't know where, or when, how, or why. Or whether there's another reason for all of this.

Chapter 13

Leaving the villa behind without seeing Max one last time is the hardest thing I've ever done. But I'm only a guest, not a friend or family member. Max cannot be seen to do anything that could be misinterpreted, in any way. It would be inappropriate and unprofessional, but that doesn't stop me wishing it could be different. As I stand by the passenger door of the taxi I take one last look up at the facade of the villa in total disbelief that this is it. My adventure is over and my fate is simply to accept that fact. But understanding Max's agony tears at my heart. I long for him to suddenly appear, just to say one final goodbye, but I know he simply can't do that. Gianni waves me off, the few words he mutters are unrecognisable to me.

~

By the time the first leg of my journey is over, Italy already begins to feel like something out of a dream. The sort where you wake up half-convinced what happened was real and the other half of you knowing it isn't. I manage to reason with myself that it's in my nature to worry too much about other people's sadness, even when there's nothing I can actually do to help. If the police can't solve the mystery of Aletta's disappearance, then no one can help Max.

But what about this connection I feel? Not just to Max, but to a place I didn't know existed until a few days ago?

With a long stopover ahead of me at Milano Linate airport, I saunter around the duty- free area to pass a little time. I manage to pick up a few things for the girls, in addition to the little decorative pots I purchased on my trip to the pottery. The book section catches my eye and I start browsing the titles. Then I spot it. It's not a book I'd normally be drawn to, but the title jumps out at me. *When The Past Catches Up With You – A True Story of Past Life Regression* by Alison Lang. Could this explain what's been happening to me?

The young man serving me chatters away quite pleasantly in English.

'I hope you had a good trip. Something to read on the plane?' He enquires, picking up the book to scan it and adding it to the other items in the carrier bag. There's a lilt in his voice that's familiar.

'It's been an experience of a lifetime. Pity I have such a

long wait for my next flight.' I feel rather self-conscious, almost wanting to explain away my choice of reading material. 'Is that an Irish accent hiding away there?' I muse, and he smiles.

'Well, I've lived all over but, yes, Ireland is home. But it's been a very long time since I was there.'

'You must miss it,' I reflect, thinking longingly of my own home.

'After a while you get used to it. Italy has been home to me for quite a few years now and I love the lifestyle. Who wouldn't want to live here and enjoy the sunshine?'

As the payment processes I nod my head. 'I was thinking the exact same thing.'

He smiles at me, good-naturedly.

'Well, have a great flight home and I hope your wait passes quickly.'

As I pick up the carrier bag something tells me I'm not going to be bored, that's for sure.

Walking back through to the seating area, already a sense of normality is returning and I pull out my mobile to check for messages. It's just after eight in the morning and all around me the airport is already buzzing. There's a missed call from Josh and I hit redial.

'Hey stranger, nice of you to return my call.' Josh is wide awake and I realise he's probably sorting out the girls' breakfasts.

'Thought it was about time I checked in.' It feels so good to hear his voice and know that after the craziness of the last few days things will soon be back to normal. When I get home this will all be behind me. 'It's just after eight and I now have a long wait ahead of me. The flight lands at six o'clock this evening.'

'And I'll be waiting at the airport, ready to grab those bags and whisk my woman away from the temptations of a more glamorous lifestyle.'

'Glamorous? Hardly. I already feel crumpled and I hope I can find a reasonably comfortable seat to while away the time. I'm surrounded by people talking so fast I can't even catch the odd word, let alone understand anything I over-hear. And my stomach is rumbling, so I have to go in search of something to eat. It's a bit bewildering here, to be honest.'

'Poor you, but hey, you did it. You stepped into Livvie's shoes like a true professional and I never doubted that for a moment. Tell the truth, Ellie, is it the tantalising world you thought it would be? You know, being out there on your own, totally free and independent?'

He's worried I've had fun and will want to do it again.

'Don't worry; I survived, but only just. This isn't me, and it never was. There's a reason why Livvie is good at what she does and why I'm good at being a wife and a mum. So we exchanged roles for a little while, but I suspect we will both be very glad to slip back into our respective routines. I enjoy having a foot in both worlds, but to tell the truth, I feel exhausted already, as I didn't get much sleep last night.'

A stab of guilt hits me square in the stomach, which suddenly begins to churn. Do I have anything to feel guilty about? I've done nothing wrong, just lent a listening ear to someone in distress. You wanted to reach out to Max, Ellie, my inner voice reminds me. You can't deny that. But reaching out isn't being unfaithful, it's being compassionate.

I almost miss Josh's words as my inner voice threatens to take over.

'Italy failed to charm you, then. I'm relieved to hear it. Now, I simply want you back home where you belong.'

I laugh, awkwardly. Italy did charm me. The word *belong* echoes around inside my head. Where do I belong? I snap out of my little daydream and say a quick goodbye.

'In a while, crocodile,' I reply automatically to Josh's words. It takes me back to that first time we had to spend a night apart. He was on a course and I was at home with two very noisy young children, missing him like mad. My heart constricts at the memory.

His final words, 'Be safe,' travel down the line before we disconnect.

For a brief moment something akin to panic threatens to overtake me. I look around, feeling disorientated and scared, then realise I'm simply homesick. So I walk around in search of somewhere pleasant to sit and read, while I grab some breakfast. Several of the larger restaurants aren't open for breakfast, but the Aroma Café looks perfect.

Juggling a tray holding a slice of panettone and a large coffee, I head straight for a small corner table. Somewhere I can hopefully sit, read and people-watch for an hour or two, at the very least. It's going to be a long day.

Chapter 14

'Mum, where's my new school jumper? It's not in my wardrobe.' Rosie's voice drifts down the stairs and seeks me out as I sip my coffee. I was so tired when Josh and I eventually arrived home, late last night. I slept soundly; the sort of sleep that leaves you feeling as if you can't quite wake up properly. The day is beginning to drip-feed into my pores and I saunter up the stairs, coffee in hand, to find out why Rosie is panicking.

'What's wrong? It was there the other day. I remember hanging it up for you,' I add, calmly.

'But it's not here now! Mum, has Hettie borrowed it?' Her eyes blaze, ready to accuse, and I shake my head.

'I don't know, I wasn't here. Remember? Hettie is in the bathroom. I'll check with her in a moment,' I reply. It's funny that here we are, once more, and it feels like I never left. What happened was merely a dream, a little interlude that is totally unrelated to real life.

Rosie opens and shuts cupboard doors, rifling through

the tightly packed garments in search of the missing item.

'You really need to sort out your clothes, Rosie. There's so much in here that you never wear, darling. It would make finding things a lot easier.' I add, gently. I can feel she's about to explode, the novelty of having her mum home already a thing of the past. I swallow the remainder of my extra-strong coffee in a few gulps, set down the cup and help sort through the rails.

'Here it is!' Almost instantly I rescue it from its hiding place between her cuddly fake fur jacket and her dressing down. 'It was pushed to the back, but in the same place as when I hung it up before I left. You must have pulled your jacket out and it became squashed towards the back of the cupboard. I think you owe your sister an apology when she surfaces.'

Rosie spins around, gives me a quick hug and dashes into the ensuite.

'Thanks Mum, you're a star,' she shouts over her shoulder.

I begin tidying some of the things she pulled out in her search. As I close the wardrobe doors I catch sight of myself in the mirrored front and run my hands through my hair. I looked tired, drawn, even, and I realise I failed to take off my mascara properly in my haste to drop into bed last night. Tiredness meant a quick slosh of water over the basin and the merest slick of moisturising cream before sliding between the sheets. I wipe away the black residue pooling beneath both eyes, like wayward eyeliner, with a tissue. I notice that I still look the same; nothing has changed, even though inside I feel a little different. Jet-lagged maybe. Yes, it's definitely jet-lag.

'You've welcome,' I shout back, over the noise of the shower. In my head I'm thinking about what Josh said as he cuddled into my back last night.

'At last. I was getting worried,' he'd murmured. His hand had brushed against my thigh, gently moving upwards, to curl around my waist. 'Glad you're home.'

He'd pressed his body against mine and his skin had been cool to the touch. Within seconds his breathing became slow and rhythmic, relief that I was safely home, allowing him to relax once more.

I assumed he had fallen asleep, when his hand had moved up, exploring. I'd turned over and laughed quietly at him.

'Go to sleep, I'm shattered. You must be tired, too, you're fighting it – I can tell!'

'Okay, I give in. Was the trip a success?' He'd pulled me closer against his chest. There was a sudden waft of shower gel and deodorant, a weird mix of citrus and something with a smoky quality to it.

'Fine, nerve-wracking, but fine,' I'd spoken softly, not wanting to awaken the girls, or rouse Josh from his semi-sleepy state.

'Thought you'd run away,' his voice had been barely

audible as his breathing became more laboured. Run away? A chill strikes at my heart, wondering if Josh has picked up on the mess of emotions running through my head. Can he sense that something in me has changed in a way even I can't understand?

'Never,' I'd replied so softly I doubt he would have heard it, even if he hadn't been gently snoring.

But I lay there for a long time afterwards and all I could think about were those mysterious, twinkling hazel eyes and the touch that had been like an electric shock. I know you, Max, but how can I? As my own breathing deepened, the thoughts swirling around in my head were refusing to leave me alone. I snuggled closer to my loving husband, not sure if it was for comfort, or out of guilt. I only knew that I could never do anything to put what we have together at risk.

Rosie reappears, disturbing my thoughts, to give me a quick hug before we make our way downstairs.

'It is nice to have you home again. Did Dad tell you I missed you?'

Before I have time to answer we've sauntered into the kitchen and that one simple act makes me feel that every-thing in my world is as it should be. Whatever I need to make me happy is here, right now.

'Tea or coffee, ladeez?' Josh sports his best smile. Hettie points in the direction of the jug of orange juice, her mouth full of toast and marmalade.

'I'm starving,' Rosie says, grabbing some toast and taking a big bite. 'You home today, Mum?'

I nod, swallowing to clear a mouthful of food and thinking how wonderful something simple like buttered toast can taste. 'I'm back in tomorrow. Livvie left a message and now the new contract is in place, she wants me to choose the pieces for the first consignment.'

'Wow, Mum, good for you! Another job title to add to the list.' Hettie makes it sound grand, but it's common sense for me to place the first order, having seen the goods first–hand.

'Will this mean a pay rise?' Josh enquires cheekily, but no doubt thinking about the fact that my car isn't going to last forever. With over a hundred thousand miles on the clock, it's past its best and we could look forward to a future of unknown garage bills.

I raise my eyebrows at him and he receives the message loud and clear. I can only take this one step at a time and my future depends upon what is happening in Livvie's life. I'm happy with the way things are, if I'm honest, although a little extra income would be nice. As for the future, well, who knows? Maybe one day I could be a clone of Livvie's, jetting here, there and everywhere. I almost laugh out loud at the ridiculousness of that transient thought.

'Time to go, girls. And by the look of it, I think Mum

should head back to bed. You look shattered, Ellie. Cute, but shattered.'

Both Hettie and Rosie roll their eyes as they jump up to grab bags and coats.

'Bye, Mum. It really is nice to have you home.' Rosie kisses my cheek and gives me a bear hug. Hettie is much more reserved, leaning in for a quick kiss before turning away, but unable to hide the big smile on her face. It's not easy being fifteen years old and having raging hormones while trying to remain fashionably aloof.

'Is it nice to have me home, Hettie?'

Another roll of the eyes. 'Okay, I missed you. You don't have to be so needy.'

I'm not even sure that's English, but it will do.

'Have a good day, people.'

'See you later, alligator.' Josh homes in for a lingering kiss and a hug. 'Get some rest. That's an order.'

'In a while, crocodile.'

The silence after they've left is heavy. One moment the room is full of life and the next it's so quiet the silence almost has a vibration, a silent noise level.

I walk over to my handbag and pull out the book I bought at the airport. I'm halfway through it, but I've marked two sections with a torn strip from a flyer. I flip it open on the first marker and read the paragraph I high-lighted in the coffee shop.

Have you experienced a sense of déjà vu, a recurring dream that plays out like a story? Or are obsessed with a place, time in history, or person, for no obvious reason? Even unexplained phobias and pain that seem not to have an identifiable cause can be due to a link to a past life.

Something stirs in the pit of my stomach. Unease, maybe, rather than a fear of the unknown. But isn't that thought rather chilling? Now I'm home everything seems to have slotted back into place rather nicely. I had an interlude where anxiety took my emotions on a rollercoaster ride. Max's story is little short of a tragedy for all involved, but that's the whole point. It's a tragedy for those involved – and that doesn't include me. This innate instinct I have to be empathetic to other people's problems went into overdrive for a while there, that's all.

But after showering and dressing I'm still feeling a little disjointed about the whole thing. What I need is another person's perspective and I grab my phone and dial.

'Aunt Clare, it's Ellie. How are you?'

'Not as well as you. Are you pink and glowing, or just sickeningly lightly bronzed?'

Of course Josh would have phoned and told her where I was as she's the only one he's ever been comfortable talking with when I'm not around. She took Mum's place without realising she was filling her sister's shoes. Our loss hit Josh as hard as it did the girls and me. Mum was our rock and we knew life was never going to be quite the same again. Aunt Clare is reliable, discreet and a great listener. But she also has this unique way of looking at things and that's so totally opposite to my mum. I find myself laughing.

'What's funny?'

'I just realised that we can't sidestep what's passed on in our genes. And, yes, I do have a bit of a sun-kissed glow. But it was work and I was inside more than I was outside enjoying the sunshine. I was wondering if we could meet up for coffee and a chat.'

'Well, I'm just on my way out as I have to pick up some dry-cleaning. If you are home all day I could pop round this afternoon after I've finished my errands.'

'Perfect, you're a star! It will be nice to catch up. And I wanted your opinion on something.'

'Ooh, now I'm intrigued.'

'Well, I think you might be surprised. Looking forward to it, bye.' Actually, surprised might be a bit of an understatement.

Chapter 15

'Wow, that's not quite what I was expecting to talk about. Past-life regression, you say? Can't say I've ever given it any thought and I certainly don't know anyone who has ventured down that road. How do they do it? Hypnotherapy, I assume?'

I toy with the cake on the plate in front of me as Aunt Clare doesn't shift her gaze from my face. This isn't an easy topic to raise, that's for sure.

'It's just that I'm reading this book and finding it very interesting. Who knows what happened in the past, or if this sort of thing is real? But a lot of what I've read so far seems to make a lot of sense. You know, the unexplained things that happen in life.'

Aunt Clare downs her fork. 'Really? Sense, you say? Give me an example.'

I shift around on my chair, feeling decidedly uncomfortable.

'Have you ever been somewhere for the first time and

experienced an unexpected and, maybe even an unwelcome, sense of familiarity?'

Now Aunt Clare is staring at me without blinking.

'What on earth happened in Italy? I think this is something you need to share, lovely, as clearly it's set you on edge. It's not like you to go all new-age on me. You know what I'm like. If I can't see or touch it, then it ain't real to me. But that doesn't mean to say I don't have a healthy dose of respect for people who do believe in the esoteric.'

'Isn't that a bit like having your cake and eating it? I mean, either you believe or you don't.'

Aunt Clare shrugs her shoulders as another cube of cake disappears into her mouth.

'If it were that simple it wouldn't be one of the most fiercely debated topics of all time, now would it?'

I push away the plate in front of me, my appetite having suddenly disappeared. I can't mention Max, or his situation. Not that there's anything to hide, of course, but what he told me was in confidence.

'Let me approach this from a different angle. When a person goes somewhere for the first time everything is an unknown. The scenery, the people and the way they live their lives. It takes a while to adjust, especially when what you are experiencing bears no resemblance whatsoever to your own day-to-day life.'

I stop, trying to judge whether she's still with me.

'Agreed.' More cake disappears.

'I'd never even heard of the Italian town of Castrovillari until Livvie's plans suddenly changed and I ended up taking her place. Up until that point all she'd mentioned was that she was due to fly out to southern Italy.'

Aunt Clare places her fork down on the empty plate. 'Nothing strange there, I've never heard of it, either.'

'But from the moment I arrived everything seemed, well, vaguely familiar.'

I'm beginning to feel exasperated as I'm trying to put the impossible into words.

Aunt Clare's face looks blank and then she starts speaking. 'Blues skies, tall trees, colourful shrubs; a few mountains, obviously. Am I right?'

I nod.

'You need to travel more, lovely. That could describe hundreds of holiday destinations around the world. I know this wasn't a holiday, but it's the same feeling. That foreign, exciting and yet-to-be discovered adventure.'

'Did you miss the *vaguely familiar* bit I do believe I mentioned?'

She frowns. 'As in vaguely familiar from the last time you went abroad? Wasn't that Spain, the year before last?'

The image of Max's face appears in my head.

'No. I mean Castrovillari itself.'

'You recognised the villa? Perhaps you've seen something similar in a TV ad during the holiday season.'

I sigh. 'No, I've never seen the actual villa before. But it welcomed me, as if I was going back to a place that I didn't instantly recognise, because I hadn't been there for a very long time. It was welcoming me back and giving me a sense of belonging. I didn't feel like a stranger in a foreign place at all.'

Did I really just say that out loud? Aunt Clare shoots me a concerned look.

'Then I'm not really surprised you're reading ... what is that, oh, a true story of past-life regression. Which came first, your experience or reading the book?'

'Aunt Clare!'

She holds up her hands. 'Sorry, I am trying to take this seriously, really I am. But I've never heard you talking like this before, Ellie. Talking in riddles—'

'There were people there who my instincts were telling me I knew well, not just some vague look-alike feeling that you can't quite put your finger on. The connection was real and I know I sound totally mad saying that. You're the only person I can talk to about this, but when I started reading this book it made me feel worse. I seem to be suffering from the classic symptoms of something it refers to as triggered recall.' It's mostly true, except for the word 'people' substitute the name Max.

'If you want my honest opinion, then I don't think it's madness, it's just unusual. Most of us have experienced that "I've done this before" feeling. But what you are saying, if I'm interpreting you correctly, is that you sensed that your feelings ran a little deeper on this occasion. Perhaps we do have multiple lives, who knows? Personally I think that's a rather depressing thought. I sort of hoped the place we went to after this life was easier to contend with. I think I will have earned a rest after the life I've had.'

We stare at each other uneasily. She's right, of course. That's the hope, but what of the reality?

'It doesn't mention parallel universes, does it? I seem to remember reading about that when I was going through my arrogant teen years. I was convinced I wasn't really a part of the family as I had this constant desire not to conform. And you know what your mum was like, as near to darned perfect as you can get. Having established it was unlikely I was from a parallel universe, I reluctantly accepted it was time to do the smart thing and dampen down my outlandish behaviour,' she confesses with a smile.

At last! Whacky, but then that's Aunt Clare. She has this amazing talent for thinking outside the box and considering the alternatives. She's also what I affectionately refer to as unshockable, although I'm not even sure that's a real word.

'Is there a point to all this?' The frown is back.

'Only that I'm wondering why me, I suppose. It just leaves me feeling as if I've walked away leaving things up in the air. Like a task only half-completed.'

She catches my eye and we both burst out laughing.

'Please don't mention this to anyone, promise! I'm sure I'll get over it and shake off the feeling,' I say.

'Don't worry; no one would believe me, anyway.'

So Aunt Clare isn't dismissing this out of hand.

'I wonder what Mum's reaction would have been? Something along the lines of, "Darling, are you coming down with something?" I think.'

Aunt Clare smiles. 'Sleep on it, Ellie. Some of the real mysteries of life aren't meant to be solved. I'll always have a sceptical side to me, but that doesn't stop me believing in some sort of divine intervention that throws us a clue here and there along life's path. Now whether we choose to act upon those pointers is entirely another matter. But I rather suspect you were just a little bit outside your comfort zone. Stress can do funny things, you know. It can upset the balance of the body and mind, and then all sorts of signals get messed up. I don't think you need to worry about past lives or hidden meanings here.'

'I really needed to hear that, thank you. My moment of meltdown is over and you are right, I was way outside my comfort zone. You know me, I'm a worrier and I guess some sort of reaction was normal.'

'No one in our family has ever been normal, lovely. Uniquely interesting is the term I prefer to use.'

The saying 'a problem shared is a problem halved' holds a lot of truth. After Aunt Clare left I went straight onto the internet and read a few articles about the effects when stress hormones are released. Seems a chemical reaction can cause all sorts of weird things to happen. The thing is, I'm convinced it wasn't merely my vivid imagination. What I experienced was real, it just didn't mean anything. The sense of relief is intense and I immediately hide the book away at the back of the bookcase, so I'm not tempted to pick it up again. It's probably very good for people who are having real experiences, but a little worrying for someone in full-on panic mode.

Chapter 16

'She's back,' Livvie hurries across the office to give me a welcome-home hug.

'What have I missed?'

Livvie frowns. 'Not much. Oh, you mean at home. I'm off the hook and I've hired this amazing woman who seems to be a nurse and a wonderful companion for my mother, all rolled into one. It isn't cheap, but my conscience is heaving a huge sigh of relief.'

I look at Livvie and shake my head. 'You are a lost cause, Livvie. I worry about you. If all you have is your work, then you'll end up being little more than a robot. People are what make our lives bearable and you can't treat them like an inconvenience.'

There aren't many people to whom you can say something like that and know it will have absolutely no effect whatsoever. Livvie is one of them.

'Sickness isn't dignified and it isn't pretty. I'm being a dutiful daughter and saving her the horrors of having to put up with my inept attempts to see her through the healing process. That's a good thing, isn't it?'

I give up. 'I suppose so, when you put it like that. But I hope you will grab a moment here and there to sit with her and just talk. You know, like mothers and daughters tend to do.'

Livvie throws back her head and laughs. 'You mean *normal* mothers and daughters. I don't think that applies here. Anyway, enough personal drivel. Max has been on the phone and confirmed that the new website is up and running at last. The full inventory is on there and he said to mention that there will be quite a few things you haven't already seen. I think you need to check it out before you pull that first order together.'

Livvie doesn't waste time, that's for sure. A slight unease passed over me when she mentioned Max's name, but it was fleeting, thank goodness. A part of me is relieved that Livvie didn't start asking questions about my visit, but that's not who she is and it's all about work, work, work. This is probably the first and only time I appreciate her single-minded approach – usually I find it bizarrely detached. But then that's at the heart of the difference in our personalities and makeup. I don't do emotional detachment.

'I'll start working on that right away.'

'I've left a list of the upcoming projects on your desk to

give you some idea of the volume required when you are ordering. It wasn't all bedside visits while you were gone and I've just signed a contract for the refurbishment of a large, very modern-day manor house in Sussex. Big budget, huge house. I'll leave you to do your thing.'

With that, Livvie walks away from me, her mind already on the next task to hand. Then she stops and looks back at me. 'Oh, and congratulations. You are now the Assistant Buyer with a nice little pay rise coming your way.'

As I turn on my heels I can't stop a little smile of satisfaction from creeping over my face. I can't wait to tell Josh and, in a way, I feel that this is his reward for an interlude that I still find curiously puzzling.

~

'Mum, we need to go shopping. Everything I have is either too small or a throwback to last year.' Hettie's voice reflects that particular brand of despair that only a teenager can feel when choosing something to wear. Virtually the entire contents of her wardrobe is in a heap on her bed, discarded with less than a moment's consideration.

'Awful. Did I wear that, seriously? Mum, how could you possibly have let me buy this?'

This is one of my least-favourite motherly moments. Josh is driving Hettie to the party and unless she wants to be fashionably late, which apparently isn't fashionable any more, they have to leave in the next ten minutes.

'I mean, Mum, I'm in serious trouble here. I can't go. I simply can't go.'

The face that spins around in my direction pulls at my heart strings. I guess someone special is going to be there and Hettie wants to stand out from the crowd.

Rosie saunters in, looking at the state of the bed in horror. 'Hmm. It's not fair and I can't see why I can't go, too.'

'It's a party for my friends, not yours, Rosie. You're too young.'

'Okay, girls. Rosie you have homework to do, so off you go. Hettie, honey, how do you want to look? Isn't there something here we can salvage? Why don't you take a look in my wardrobe?'

Hettie looks at me as if I've lost my mind.

'I don't want to look like someone's mother. I assume you are joking, Mum.'

I sigh. The Hettie of just six months ago would never have been so rude, or thoughtless. Or self-centred. Or so insecure. My heart squishes up as I so badly want to help her leave the house feeling special. And grown up.

'Josh, we might be a few minutes' late. Grab a coffee or something.' I shout down to our waiting taxi driver. 'Hettie, grab your iPad.'

We Google fashion for fifteen-year-olds and staring back at us is a mass of photos with virtually every young model and celebrity you could name, if you watch E! News. Which Ellie does, more than I think is good for her.

'Okay, Ellie, is there a look here that catches your eye?'

She scrolls down, suddenly going very quiet. And down. And down.

'I quite like this look. Not too dressy. That's legit.'

'Legit?'

'Cool, in your terms, Mum. Could we put something together like that? I mean, there isn't much here,' she turns to the mountain on the bed.

'Well, to me it looks like a plain white baggy t-shirt with a crushed velvet, spaghetti strap dress over the top.'

'Can you please speak in a language I can understand? What's a spaghetti strap?'

I shake my head. I'm not sure even I could dive into my wardrobe and find anything at all in crushed velvet.

'Now this, we could do!' I point to a sylph-like model wearing what to my eye is a jersey top with cut-outs. It's been blinged-up with chunky jewellery and teamed with a pair of tight black leggings. 'What do you think?'

Hettie looks at me in surprise. 'You can do that? Like, now?'

'I'll grab my scissors.'

It doesn't take long for Hettie to pick a top from my

149

wardrobe that takes her fancy. The fabric has a sheen to it, giving the pale grey an interesting lustre.

'You can cut into it, just like that?'

I begin chopping out irregular shapes. First exposing just the tops of her shoulders, then random areas down each sleeve. Finally, I cut a slash about an inch down from the neckline, hoping it's high enough not to show inappropriate cleavage. For once Hettie is smiling. Ironically, Rosie comes to the rescue in the jewellery department as she's a lover of bling, much to Hettie's usual disdain. But tonight's different and Rosie blushes when Hettie stoops to give her a kiss on her cheek by way of a reward.

When we walk into the kitchen and Josh's head swivels around in surprise, his jaw drops a little.

'Wow. I mean, I thought you'd be a while. You look amazing, Hettie.'

As she does a twirl and then heads for the downstairs shower room to check herself out in the mirror, Josh saunters up to me.

'Is that appropriate for a fifteen-year-old these days? She looks rather grown up.'

He peers at me, questioningly.

'It's legit, darling. Your daughter is growing into a beautiful young woman, so you are going to have to get used to it.'

I leave him to it and head off to the study to download the photos from my camera. With Rosie in her room doing her homework, I have a couple of hours' peace and quiet to enjoy. I don't intend to waste it.

Chapter 17

Aunt Clare calls to ask how I'm doing and I reassure her everything is fine. I tell her about Hettie's emergency outfit and she splutters with laughter.

'I'm just about to download all of the photos I took in Italy. If you're passing, drop in sometime for a coffee and you can take a peek,' I offer.

'I'd love that. And you are sure you're okay?'

'Everything is back to normal. As far as I'm aware there's only the here and the now. I still have a little glow going on, though.'

'Sickening. Anyway, must go. See you soon.'

When I slide the SD card into the slot in the PC it takes a few seconds for the screen to spark into life. There are two folders on the card, but one contains the stuff you can't touch and the other one, entitled DCMI, is the digital camera interface. I open the folder, highlight and copy all of the tiny icons and paste them onto my desktop. A box pops up and confirms it will take eight hours and thirteen minutes to copy the files. In real time it will probably only take fifteen to twenty minutes, but I head off to the kitchen to pour a glass of wine and leave it to chunter away.

As I'm in the kitchen uncorking the wine, my phone pings. It's a text from an unknown number. I click on it without thinking and up pops a photo of a wrought-iron table decoration.

Hi Ellie, Max asked me to send you this photo. It isn't on the website yet, but it's a special piece that Eduardo Camillucci's son, Piero, made. He thought you should have first refusal, as it's rather special. Anyway, hope everything is good with you. Bella

Max is right. It's definitely something Livvie wouldn't want me to turn down. Piero's a very talented young man.

Very interested, can you get me a price? How's the sunshine? E

A moment later my phone pings again.

Hot. I'll find out and send you an email with a couple more shots. I'm now doing the cooperative's admin, sort of working as Max's assistant. If you need anything at all please let me know. Have a great weekend. Bella

As I take a sip of wine, I realise that Italy isn't behind me at all. This is the beginning of what could be a growing association. Did I really think I could shake it off as if it never happened? I feel both crushed and elated at the same time. And grateful that Max has clearly also realised it's better if we don't stay in close contact. Bella is the perfect person to be our point of contact.

I head back upstairs, glass in hand, to monitor the upload. As the natural light in the room begins to fade, I sit watching the progress bar edge along, while my mind sifts through a tirade of thoughts. I wonder what Bella feels about what happened and how Max has been treated by Aletta and her family, not to mention the rest of the community? She touched upon it briefly; I mean they all obviously still live under the shadow of it. And Max is on the edge, of what, I don't know. A nervous breakdown? Or like a volcano about to explode when some silly little thing tips him over the edge? What concerned me was that he didn't appear to have anyone to talk to. I don't mean in English, but someone he could trust. A confidante. I wondered about the guy from the restaurant, Luca. There seemed to be a strong bond between the two of them, but that doesn't necessarily mean that Max won't have to tread carefully. I wondered whether the police were watching him still, hoping a clue would—

'Mum!' Rosie's voice hits my ears at double the normal volume and I turn to look at her, surprised.

'What's wrong?'

'Nothing's wrong, but that's the third time I had to say your name. Were you back there in Italy, you know, enjoying the sunshine?'

Rosie tips her head and I spin back around to glance at the computer screen. To my horror the download has stopped and the last photo is open on the screen. It was taken on the terrace on my last afternoon at the villa. I wanted to get a shot of the front facade to show Livvie. I was so caught up in making sure I caught the beautiful oleanders and the herb pots, as well as a getting a glimpse of the mountain range behind the building, that I didn't notice Max standing watching me. I spin around, wondering about Rosie's reaction to the photo.

'Nice flowers, Mum. I need a sugar rush, is there any chocolate?'

Glancing back I see that, of course, the first thing anyone is going to notice is that vast expanse of colour. The second thing is the beauty of the villa.

'Left-hand drawer, next to the cutlery tray. There might be a bar or two in the fridge, Dad likes his ice-cold.'

She laughs, 'Good job he doesn't have veneers. No one eats chocolate from the fridge.'

Veneers? What has she been reading?

Once more I spin around in my seat and my eyes go straight to Max. He seemed to know I was totally unaware he was there and he has a slightly amused look on his face. I close my eyes, but the picture's imprinted on my mind's eye. I step forward into the scene, imagining the heat on my face and that bubble gum smell from the red oleander blossom.

'I was watching you,' Max's voice seems to echo around the room.

'I didn't know. I wasn't expecting to see you.'

He smiles and I step back, opening my eyes. In some cultures they believe that a photograph can steal a person's soul and some religions forbid it. That thought has always fascinated me. I know mediums often ask for an article, or a photograph, during a sitting and from that they can glean a lot of information. Can something as simple as a photographic image transmit energy and information? I dismiss my thoughts with a scathing laugh. I think I'd better check all of the photos before I show them to anyone. But now is not the time. It's too soon and if one glance can tangle me up in a myriad of thoughts, I need to come back to this when I feel more detached.

~

When Hettie returned home from the party she was buzzing. I hoped the outfit was a winner.

'Did you have a good time?'

'Oh, Mum! Everyone wants a top like this. I didn't say it was homemade, of course, I just said I bought it online and now it's out of stock. That's okay, isn't it? I mean, it's only a small lie.'

I look at Josh, who shrugs his shoulders with an air of I-don't-know about it.

'Well, maybe in this case it's okay, but don't make a habit of it. I'm just glad you were happy you looked good – and we will go shopping. I keep forgetting how fast you're growing.'

I touch her shoulder, giving it a light squeeze. When did my baby become so grown up? And now, according to Rosie, a boy called Alex and Hettie are always together at school. They sit apart from their large group of friends every lunchtime so they can talk. That's a big deal at their age. I have no idea how Josh is going to cope with this.

A week ago life seemed rather ordinary, in fact comfortingly ordinary. Suddenly my head is full of new worries, and it isn't just about my blossoming daughter.

Chapter 18

Josh's problems at work continued to grow. Over the next couple of weeks we spent most of our quality time together talking it through. People leave, as they tend to do, but they aren't being replaced. At first the impact isn't that damaging. Josh said the targets were still being met and no one was complaining. But now Josh is very worried. A lot of the team spirit evaporated after a recent staff meeting where management confirmed they were going to streamline operations. It's a large IT department, but with more and more satellite offices coming online and increased numbers of staff working from home, Josh freely admits it's too much to manage. He's hoping that the streamlining will split the section into two and he'll be left to manage the core operations. He's been asked to write a report outlining the various options and potential savings. So, as usual, the bottom line is all about reducing costs. But things just became a whole lot more serious.

'If I get it wrong it isn't just my job that is on the line, Ellie. To be frank with you, I'm worried sick about it.'

'What does Nathan have to say?' I think I already know the answer. Nathan's mid-life crisis is an accident in the making and all of his friends know that.

'Nathan's off sick with stress as of a week ago.'

'What?' Josh never said anything to me about that and now I understand the pressure he's been under. Nathan's role is to attend board meetings and give the directors an overview of IT's performance. He's the buffer that allows Josh to concentrate on the real job of running the department. The only person Nathan manages is Josh. Josh has more than fifty staff to manage and he's the trouble-shooter, and the fire fighter, when things go wrong. And they do, all of the time, because that's the nature of the job.

What I don't understand is why Josh didn't tell me this before.

'Is there anything at all I can do to help? I'm disgusted with Nathan. It isn't stress, it's over-indulgence. Too many parties and too many alcoholic binges. At first, I didn't believe the gossip I'd heard. Even though I knew Nathan was capable of being that stupid. Liz deserved a medal for making their marriage last as long as it did. But now he's a player and there's no one to rein him in'.

Josh shakes his head. 'To be honest, Ellie, the next few weeks are going to be little short of hell. We have hackers causing major problems and staff morale is the lowest it's ever been. Somehow I have to turn things around, while coming up with a master plan for the future. I have no idea when, or if, Nathan will return, so it's down to me. But if they don't agree with what I say, then I fear they will outsource the whole thing and everyone will lose their job.'

I sit back against the cushion, the impact of Josh's words almost beyond my comprehension. I grab his hand and he gives mine a gentle squeeze, lifting it to his lips. As he very tenderly kisses the back of my hand he looks into my eyes.

'I don't want you to worry about it. This is one problem where all I can do is my best. But I need you to understand that it's going to affect us all. I will be staying late and heading out earlier than usual for a little while, until this is all sorted out. That means I'm not going to be around much to help out. We need to let the girls know that it won't be forever, but I want them to pull their weight so it's not so hard on you.'

Josh, you are my protector, my lover, my best friend and my salvation. I'm here for you no matter what. The pressure he's under scares me, but I can't let him see that and add to his worries.

'Do what you have to do and let me handle the domestics. The girls will be fine, well, as fine as two warring teenagers can possibly be. Just promise me one thing.'

'What's that?'

Josh turns towards me, wrapping my hand in both of his.

'If it all becomes too much, just walk away. No job is worth driving yourself into the ground, or shouldering so much responsibility it becomes stifling. You have a good CV and, if necessary, Livvie would let me work full time if we needed a little extra income. Don't try to carry this burden alone, Josh, let's work together as the team we've always been.'

'I hope it doesn't come to that, Ellie. But you need to know what's going on and I hear what you're saying, it means a lot. You've always had my back, that's why we're so good together. I love you.'

He leans in to wrap his arms around me and we hug out the worry and the stress.

'Life, eh?' He mutters, taking the words out of my mouth.

~

'Sorry it's been a while. We've had a lot of people off sick at work and I've had to do extra shifts. Even nurses succumb to the lurgies that are going around.'

Aunt Clare leans forward for a hug and pushes the front door closed with a deft kick of her foot. 'I bring gifts. Low-calorie yoghurt instead of cake. I'm on a health drive.'

Yoghurt?

'I think I might actually be allergic to anything low-cal at the moment. Stress levels are through the roof here and if it isn't highly fattening or full of sugar it will remain uneaten.'

'Things are that bad?' She grimaces, then follows me through into the kitchen. 'Where is everybody? I mean, it's Saturday afternoon and I thought it would be buzzing here.'

'Nope, it's just me. Josh is at work. He has almost taken up residence there at the moment. He's fighting not just for his own job, but for those of the entire department. The dirty word is 'outsourcing'. The girls are on a trip to the cinema to celebrate a friend's birthday. Thankfully it's a mutual friend, so I don't have one moping teenager feeling left out. I don't envy Alice's parents, though. It's a party of ten and you know how boisterous they can be when they get together. I'll pop the kettle on. Tea, or coffee?'

'Tea, please. Do you have anything herbal?'

I wince. 'Ooh, that would be a *yes*. Can't say how long it's been in the cupboard, though.' I open one of the unit doors, move a few boxes around and shout 'Eureka!'

Begrudging, I join Aunt Clare, knowing I've already drunk way too much coffee and now she's made me feel guilty.

'Tea for two, then.'

'Has it been like this ever since you returned from Italy?'

'Pretty much. To be honest, we are preparing for the worst. Josh won't give up until every last option has been exhausted, but I'm trying to get him to start unofficially looking elsewhere. I've spoken to Livvie and if we end up having to rely on just my income for a while, she's happy to increase my hours. We're luckier than some. That's why Josh is hanging in there.'

Aunt Clare frowns. 'When will you know for sure?'

'Well, that's just it. Josh has put forward a report but there's been no action, so things continue to deteriorate. It's coming up to the end of the company's financial year, so he thinks that's why everything is on hold.'

'Is there's anything I can do? You know, help out with the girls, or something? How is life in Livvie's growing empire?'

I laugh. 'Expanding too fast! I'm rushed off my feet. At the moment I'm managing to get by working part-time and doing a few hours in the evenings. The girls eat and then tend to go up to their rooms, anyway. In this house the iPad rules. Rosie wants to be around Hettie, of course, but Hettie wants her privacy. There's a boyfriend involved now, but it's not strictly official. As in we aren't supposed to know and can't acknowledge it. Furtive phones calls and all that.'

Aunt Clare's eyebrows shoot up. 'Ah, the joys of seeing them grow up. Always something to worry you, isn't there? Poor Rosie, though, I can imagine the frustration.'

'I'm organising regular sleepovers for Rosie's friends most Friday nights, to keep her occupied. She loves it, although Hettie keeps complaining about the late nights and the constant giggling. We have inflatable mattresses we lay out in the sitting room. Hettie says she can hear them through the floor. How that works, I don't know, as she's always either on the phone talking, texting under her duvet, or listening to her iPod. Of course, she thinks sleepovers are beneath her now.'

That raises a laugh.

'Your mum would have loved all of this and I'm sure it would have reminded her of you growing up. You were quite a precocious teen, you know. Thought you knew best.'

Was that me? I can't remember anything that stands out as a vivid memory.

'I popped in to see those photos you promised to show me and hear more about your fancy Italian trip. Are there any more jaunts planned for the future?'

'I haven't even bothered to show the photos to the girls, or Josh. Everything has been so hectic recently. You might find them rather boring, actually, as most of them are photos of coffee tables, tiles and items of pottery. Livvie glanced through them, but by then I'd already placed the order. The first container will arrive next month and the next order has already been placed. I don't know if Livvie will fly over at some point in the future. It sounds like they have further plans for expansion as things are going so well.'

'Gosh, you really are a buyer now, in the true sense of the word. I'm impressed. Livvie and you go way back, and of course she trusts your judgement, who wouldn't? So that next trip might see you heading back out there. Anyway, come on, get out the holiday snaps.'

'It wasn't a holiday, as I keep telling you!'

I pretend I'm cross, but I know she's only joking around. As Aunt Clare follows me upstairs to the study she's muttering away to herself. Something about how it's alright for some, being whisked away to exotic destinations.

'And it wasn't exotic. Just beautiful,' I correct her, but as soon as I open up the photos she exclaims.

'It's paradise, Ellie. No wonder you were at home. Who wouldn't be relaxed in that setting?'

The first photos are the ones I took the day I arrived. I was standing on the terrace and snapping away to try to capture the panoramic view.

'The photos don't do it justice. You can't get a real grasp of the scale, but see those little dots here and here? Those are fully mature trees. This swathe in front of the villa is mostly olive groves, almost as far as the eye can see.'

I can tell she's captivated. I click onto slideshow mode and the photos automatically roll forward every ten seconds.

'This is Villa Rosso. Most of this part of the building is guest accommodation. The owner, Trista, has a suite in the adjoining part that nestles between the two wings.'

'It's much grander than I imagined.'

The slide moves on to a shot of the reception and the beautiful cascading metalwork chandelier. I pull up a chair alongside Aunt Clare, each new photo taking me back to a precise moment in time.

'This was the day I toured the villa with Bella, taking photos of some of the furniture and decorative items produced by the cooperative. Isn't that coffee table amazing? If you stay in a Parkhouse Hurst hotel once the refurbishments are finished early next year, that's the coffee table you'll find in the executive suites.'

'Who's that?' Aunt Clare points to one of the workshop photos I took.

'It's Eduardo Camillucci. This piece in the front of the photo is a garden sculpture. That's his son, Piero, who works alongside him. You can just make out Eduardo's wife, Cristina, standing in the doorway to the kitchen. They made us so welcome that day, insisting we stay for lunch.'

I didn't think the memories would feel this fresh, but looking at the photos, nothing has diminished.

'Us?' Aunt Clare's question makes me stop mid-thought.

'Myself and Mr Jackson, who escorted me on the tour of the various facilities.'

Aunt Clare studies my face. 'You didn't mention an escort. Mr Jackson, you say.'

Awkward moment. 'Max, his name is Max.'

'Do you have a photo of him?'

What is this, twenty questions? 'I don't have photos of everyone.' Not an outright lie, just a misdirection. 'He's the general manager, I suppose you would call him, who runs the Ormanni family's businesses. The cooperative venture was his idea.'

As the photos flit across the screen we're almost at the end and I move the mouse to click stop, just in time. The last photo is the one of the front of the villa, with Max standing in the open doorway, watching me. I acknowledge, with more than a little unease, that I won't be able to control the expression that appears on my face when I find myself reliving that moment in time. If only I'd dropped his name into the conversation before, then I wouldn't be feeling so defensive now. I don't want Aunt Claire to make a big deal of this, because even though I've done nothing wrong, something doesn't feel quite right about it either.

'What a wonderful experience, Ellie. You're more of a business woman than you give yourself credit for. I'm really impressed. No wonder you were a bit stressed. That was a lot of pressure to be put under at such short notice. I mean, it's not like you've ever flown on your own before and, judging by the look on some of those people's faces, your visit was important to them. How did you avoid getting pulled into their life stories? I know what you're like.'

I keep forgetting that Aunt Clare knows me almost as well as Josh. But not quite.

'I was sending a stream of photos I took on my phone to Livvie from the moment I arrived. After that first day I was able to pass on the good news that it was a *go* for the first order. Once that had circulated, things were a lot more relaxed. If Livvie hadn't liked what she saw, I would have had to face the disappointment of those hard-working people. They accept their lot without question, but it is a hard life for them. Those with land are dependent upon a good harvest, but even then it only gives them a basic living. Branching out and using their artisan skills gives them a second line of income. I learnt a lot about the area in a short space of time and it was humbling how welcome I was made.'

'Pity you didn't get a photo of Max. He obviously has their interests at heart. I suspect he's a man with an interesting life story of his own to tell.'

A part of me wants to tell Aunt Clare everything, but it was told to me in confidence and I can't betray that. It's also none of my business.

'Josh was rather lost without you, Ellie. My phone didn't stop ringing. He was worried you'd get lost, or mugged, or lose your passport. I think he felt life was on hold until you got back. It's wonderful to see that level of devotion, but he was definitely moping around.'

I had no idea. I assumed it was just the one call to let

her know what was happening. Then I realise that with things going so badly wrong at work, I wasn't here when he needed me the most. I wonder if he rang her, desperate for someone in whom he could confide. But I know it would have been an impossible conversation to begin because, by then, he felt he was letting a lot of people down, even though it wasn't his fault. Aunt Clare would be upset to think he couldn't open up to her.

'He didn't say, but that's Josh. Of course, if I'd known about his problems at work I wouldn't have been so quick to step in for Livvie. Maybe suggested she postpone the visit instead, so I could be here for him to at least give what support I could. It's so typical of Josh putting me first, though. I'm really lucky and I know it.'

She nods.

'You couldn't find one like him for me, could you? I can't remember the last time I went out on a date with a guy who was worth talking to.' She eases herself up from the chair. 'Maybe I'll try one of those online dating agencies. Can't do worse than your ex-uncle, can I?' She laughs, but there's a hint of sadness wrapped up in it. 'You're a sensible woman, Ellie. You found the one and you've both worked together as a team. It's wonderful to see and your mum would be very proud.'

She touches my arm lightly and we make our way downstairs.

'Don't forget, if the worst happens and you need a bit of extra help, I'm just a phone call away.'

As I close the front door the strangest thing pops into my head. If my adult daughter went missing with absolutely no clues about what might have happened to her, would I want her fiancé to remain in the family home? Family means something; it's a bond that exists even if there are arguments and petty jealousies. But in Italy that family tie is even stronger. Isn't it more than a little strange that Trista never doubted Max for even a moment? My conscience niggles away, but I try not to think of Max and the pain I saw in his eyes that night in the restaurant.

Time to distract myself with a stack of ironing that needs my attention before the girls run out of things to wear.

Chapter 19

By the time I realise that Josh probably isn't coming home again tonight, I'm cross with myself for not having checked my phone. Sure enough, there's a text sent at six minutes past eight this evening to say don't wait up. A few of them use a local bed and breakfast if they are working very late and starting early. He's been sleeping away from home at least two, or three, nights per week for the last three weeks.

The girls are both sound asleep and I've been struggling to keep my eyes open for the past hour, but I was reluctant to give in. I don't like Josh coming home to a house in darkness. Usually he's so exhausted he just wants to drop into bed, but I try to make him eat something first. Sometimes he wants to talk and at other times he doesn't. I take my lead from him.

As soon as my head hits the pillow I relax. The cool cotton of the recently ironed pillowcase gives off a pleasant spring-fresh odour, proving that advertising does work.

Fresh as spring flowers, the ad for the fabric conditioner boasts. Whether it's the floral smell that reminds me of the oleander blossoms, I don't know. But as I begin to drift into sleep mode I'm transported back to the villa. In much the same way as you would take a virtual tour, I find myself walking across the patio and pushing open the door to the reception. No one is around and I climb the stairs, heading towards Trista's suite.

I tap on the door, but there's no answer. I have no idea what time of day it is, but it's very quiet. Turning the handle to swing the door open, I walk across to the ornate wooden table and the silver-framed photographs. I trail a finger along the top of a frame and my hand slides down to pick up the photo of Aletta. The eyes staring back at me are fiery. Her dark hair hangs like a silky frame for that perfect face. No wonder Max was besotted. Up close she's even more beautiful.

Suddenly Trista's voice makes me turn my head.

'*Non sai nulla.*' She crosses the room and snatches the frame out of my hands.

'Why did you believe Max was innocent of any wrong-doing? Don't you miss your daughter? Don't you want to know what really happened?'

The words are in my head and I realise that even if I had voiced them, her English isn't good enough to understand what I'm asking her. I turn and begin to walk away, but each step seems laboured, as if I'm walking in slow motion.

Bella appears in the doorway. 'I've asked her the same questions, Ellie. But she wouldn't answer me. Max didn't have anything to do with it, I'm sure of that. But we need some actual proof, or he'll always have it hanging over his head.'

Bella begins to cry and when I turn back to look at Trista she has disappeared. Bella shakes my shoulder and I try to brush her hand away. I need to find out where Trista went.

'Ellie, Ellie, it's me. Are you having a bad dream? You were talking in your sleep.'

Josh's face looms over me in the darkness, concern etched onto his drawn face. I drag myself back into consciousness.

'You came home. You must feel shattered, way beyond tired.'

He nods. 'I am, but the drive was worth it just to see your sleepy face. Go back to sleep. This time have a nice dream.' He plants a kiss on my forehead and that's the last thing I can remember.

~

I creep out of the bedroom, gently closing the door behind me so that I can warn the girls to be quiet. Josh is still sleeping soundly and I don't want them disturbing him as they get ready for a Sunday-morning swimming session. The fact that Josh hasn't set the alarm means he wants to wake up naturally and it's hard to keep the noise level down as the girls bustle around. Thankfully, two of the other mums will be supervising today, so I'm only the taxi service.

'Is Dad okay?' Rosie asks across the breakfast table. 'He's never here. It can't be much fun driving home so late at night.'

She's worried, bless her. 'We all have responsibilities, Rosie. Sometimes things go smoothly and sometimes there are problems. A bit like your homework, when you find something difficult and you have to keep working at it. It won't be like this forever and we have to get through this bit as best we can.'

Non sai nulla. Non sai nulla. I shake my head to chase away Trista's words.

As I begin to clear the table and start getting things ready for the school run, the words seem to echo around me. Is it possible to dream in a foreign language? And what does it mean?

'Mum, we're waiting.' Hettie and Rosie are standing side by side, staring at me.

'Sorry girls, I'll fetch the keys. Last one out of the door make sure you close it quietly, so we don't wake Dad.'

~

When I arrive home Josh is up. The smell of coffee perco-
lating is the first thing that hits me as I walk into the
kitchen. He isn't dressed for work and that means he can
at least enjoy a relatively normal Sunday at home.

'Hey you. Sorry I missed the girls, but I needed to catch
up on a little sleep. Yesterday was a long day.' I slip off my
coat and watch as Josh makes coffee for two. 'Come and
sit up at the breakfast bar, we need to talk.'

I swallow hard. This isn't going to be good news and
yet, looking at his face, it reflects acceptance. I notice the
dark smudges beneath his eyes, which are slightly bloodshot
from all the late nights.

'They've pulled the plug. A contract to outsource the
entire IT services has already been signed and a team will
be brought in to begin organising the changeover tomorrow.
This was the plan all along and how did they tell us? By
email. Alistair Peterson himself sent it out to every member
of the team at half past nine last night. What a nice little
surprise for everyone to open up first thing Monday
morning. Except that he didn't know a dozen of us were
working all weekend to sort out another of the little problems caused by the cutbacks. Five of us immediately
resigned by email. The others chose to stay. It wasn't
awkward, everyone's position is different. I know I should

have stayed, but the anger was mounting. To withhold this information and lead everyone to believe there was still a chance to come up with a solution was wrong on so many levels. Nothing they've done is illegal, but it's immoral.'

Josh suddenly stops talking and the colour drains from his face.

'What have I done?' He stands there with a coffee mug in each hand, as still as a statue. I quickly step forward, take them from him and put them on the counter top. Then I throw my arms around him.

'It will be alright, Josh. It will be alright, I promise. In a way I'm glad it's over.'

He buries his face into my neck, dry sobs shake his torso and I hold him even tighter in my arms until he's calm.

'What have I done?' he asks, once more.

'You stood up for yourself and I'm proud of you. Look Josh, you have to listen to me. You are exhausted and you couldn't have continued like this for much longer. We have savings and we are better off than most, so we have to count our blessings. I have a good job and Livvie will be delighted if I can offer her more hours. We will survive and by the time you've found yourself a new job you'll be back to your usual self. At the moment you are running on empty. You are stressed and exhausted from lack of sleep. All we've been doing as a family the last few weeks is to exist and that isn't what we want for the future, is it? I'm glad this has happened and it's going to be a new start for you. The company don't care about individuals and you've sacrificed far too much already. I don't want you jumping to their every order right up until the minute they flick the switch, or whatever stops those damned computers and servers running. So no regrets, you understand?'

He nods, drawing back a little to look at me.

'Repeat the words.'

'No regrets, Ellie. No regrets.'

'Right. Let's have a day with the girls. How about we head off to the arboretum for an hour or two? The fresh air will do us all good.'

'Can't think of a better way to spend my first Sunday as an unemployed man.'

Chapter 20

Monday mornings the girls are always slow to wake up. After coffee and cereal I persuade Josh to go back to bed. He has a cracking headache and after taking some painkillers he doesn't need any convincing.

I'm not due into work until ten-thirty this morning, so I head upstairs to the study. I'm on a mission. Josh will need somewhere to work and there's only one desk. I suspect he will have handed back his top-of-the-range laptop and I look at my three-year-old PC that is more than adequate for me, but will drive Josh mad. He's always saying I need to upgrade, but it suits me fine. I guess we'll be sharing it for a while until he sorts himself out some new kit.

I log in, but the first thing I do is to Google those words that keep going around and around in my head.

The translation for non sai nulla, is literally *you know nothing*. Why would Trista say something like that to me? And then I remember that it was only a dream. It seemed so very real, though, especially to remember a phrase that is very foreign to me in both meanings of the word. My imagination took all of the thoughts whizzing around in my brain and turned it into a story, I suppose. Then I remember what Bella said about how Max would always be under a cloud of suspicion until the truth was known. Okay, so my head was trying to make some sense of the little I know about it. But Bella was there during the whole thing and she must have drawn her own conclusions. My gut instinct tells me she's on Max's side, as she never said anything even remotely negative about him to me. However, I'm not sure she knew Max was opening up to me about it. Anyway, enough. I came up to sort things out so my clutter doesn't get in Josh's way.

I go back to the desktop and move my photo file into a folder I have for work stuff. My conscience niggles away in the background. Am I hiding it, just in case Josh opens it by accident? I shrug off that thought as being totally ridiculous and open my mailbox to have a quick check before I leave for work.

Ironically the first thing I spot is a message from Bella.

From: sales@villaormanni.it
To: elliemaddison@bradleys.com
Subject: Delivery date

Morning Ellie
Max is working on your second order and says things

are looking good to get that out to you in about eight weeks' time. The only item likely to cause a problem is the batch of bedside table lights, due to the number you've ordered, but he's arranging for additional labour to be brought in. Once the container is loaded I'll send you confirmation of the due delivery date. As with the first container, it will take about ten days from the time it leaves our storage facility.

Hope all is well with you. Things are quite busy here, which is great. Max has been very quiet since you left, spending a lot of time in his office. Trista is worried about him, so all the good news is sort of offset by the tension here at the villa.

Oh, and I'm hoping to plan a trip home very soon, so watch this space!

Bella
Bella Williams
Sales Administrator
Artigianato
Part of the Ormanni Group

I click on reply and my fingers hover above the keys. It's so tempting to ignore the business part and start talking about Max, but I'm mindful that Bella's email account might be accessed by someone else when she's not there. Even Max himself.

From: elliemaddison@bradleys.com
To: sales@villaormanni.it
Subject: Delivery date

Hi Bella
Thank you for the update. I'll phone you when I arrive in work as I have an item I need added, but I don't have the details here.
Enjoy your morning and we'll speak later.
Ellie
Assistant Buyer & Lead Designer
Bradley's Design Creative

I press send, knowing that I'm making an excuse to phone her. As Hettie would put it, I'm telling a little lie. After my dream last night it's too coincidental to sit here and read those words and not want to follow them up. I think I'd have to be a hard person indeed to know that Max is probably slipping into depression because of the isolation he feels and ignore the situation. You can't keep running away from your emotions and everyone has to vent their feelings to stop the pressure building up. But he has no one to support him, or see things from his viewpoint. How can I pretend I'm not aware of that, or the fact that he chose to turn to me? Wrong place, right time. Or maybe not, if I manage to do at least some little thing that helps.

I clear down a few other items I'd left on the desktop but no longer need and put the PC into sleep mode. Then I tidy the desk, jamming most of the clutter into the bottom drawer. Josh is going to need space as he'll be updating his CV and, fingers crossed, drafting lots of cover letters. I don't want him to feel he's invading what has been regarded as my space, as this is going to be his new office now. It will be strange, though, knowing he's here when I'm at work.

I glance at my watch and see that it's time I left. Popping my head around the bedroom door, Josh is on his side facing away from me, snoring. One arm extends up over his pillow and that's his comfort position. I want to walk over and touch him, but I'm scared even the slightest noise might wake him. That's not fair when I'm literally going to be out the door in the next thirty seconds. Sleep well, my love. We will get through this.

~

'You look rather worried. Problems?'

The moment I walk through the door Livvie can tell something is wrong. The open office isn't the place to talk and I nod in the direction of the tiny kitchen. She immediately pushes back on her chair to follow me.

As I slip off my coat and hang it on the hook, Livvie flicks the switch on the kettle.

'Is it to do with Josh?'

I nod. 'As we feared. A handful of them walked out on the job late Saturday night. Josh was one of them. He told me that the handover begins today, would you believe. It sounds like the contract was set up quite a while ago. Things like that don't happen overnight.'

Livvie looks shocked. 'Ellie, I'm so sorry to hear that. How will you manage? I mean, are you alright for money? You only have to say if you need a loan to tide you over. Please don't go borrowing money at an extortionate rate of interest. Poor Josh. Searching for a new job is tough, even when you are in employment, but looking for something when you are in this situation adds a lot of pressure. I can't even begin to imagine how worried you are about him.'

Livvie steps forward to give me a hug.

'Thank goodness we're strong. It's at times like this that the cracks show up, isn't it? I keep telling him we'll get through it and we'll be fine, but I won't pretend I'm not scared. We're okay for money at the moment and our savings should last a few months if we are careful. I'll sit the girls down and explain what's happening, so they know we have to start counting the pennies. If you need me here to work extra hours then I'd appreciate that, although at the moment it's going to be all about giving Josh whatever support he needs. But he's probably going to appreciate it if the house is quiet during the day and it might be a good idea if I'm not there to disturb him. Just until he's established some sort of routine.'

'I understand. You know that I've wanted you here full time for ages now. We are getting to the stage where we need to consider growing our admin team. In the meantime I'll take any extra hours you can fit it. But if Josh needs you around, I'm more than happy for you to do some of the work from home.'

I feel my eyes well up and once more Livvie throws her arms around me. I let the tears slide down my face, thinking that it's better to let it all out in front of my best friend, rather than Josh. He's going to be feeling so insecure at the moment and I know he will think that he has failed his family. That thought grates on me more than anything, because when he hurts, I hurt.

'Thank you, Livvie. I needed that.' I wipe my eyes and blow my nose. 'Right, it's back to work for me. Bella has been in touch about the second order. It looks like eight weeks, tops. That fits in rather nicely with the work schedules and everything should be here at least a couple of weeks before we need the goods.'

'That's great news. They've really stepped up to the mark, haven't they? I'll be honest and admit that I did have my doubts. Not having met Max in person, it was a bit of a leap of faith to assume he could deliver on his promises when they are running things on a very small scale.' Livvie pauses for a second. 'Actually, that's not strictly true. I gave the go-ahead based on your first impressions and you weren't wrong. You never are. I don't know what I'd do without you, Ellie, because you really are my right-hand woman.'

I smile, but it's a watery one. My life seems so full of problems at the moment. It's as if the universe is sending everything my way, in the belief that I can actually make a difference. Well, at least I can tell Josh the good news tonight, as the extra money will really help. I'll ring Bella next and see where that conversation leads. I might be fooling myself that I can help Max from a distance, but my conscience is saying I have to at least try.

~

'Hi Bella, thanks for your email.' I ignore the flood of Italian when Bella first picks up the phone, even though it does sound rather charming in her wonderful sing-songy voice.

'I have one item to add to the second order.' Damn it, I meant to think of something before I made the call. I quickly run my finger down the printed copy of the order sitting in front of me. 'I need two of the garden sculptures, not just one. That won't hold the order up, will it?'

'No, that should be fine. And I have news I think you'll be interested to hear.'

My heart skips a beat. Has Aletta returned home?

'On the strength of the second order, Max has arránged a loan for Eduardo Camillucci to expand his workshop. He worked his magic and managed to get a small parcel of land to the rear of Eduardo's property at a bargain price. And there's more. Not only are they going to extend the workshop and create a storage area, but they are building a bungalow for Piero.'

It's not what I was hoping to hear, but my heart lifts as this isn't just good news, it's great news for the Camillucci family. It means Piero is more likely to remain working in the family business and, when the time comes, he will be able to raise his own family there.

'Bella, that's wonderful news. Max has such a good heart and I know it isn't just about the business side of things.'

I hold my breath. Will she grab this as the opportunity I meant it to be?

'They have always supported Max and won't tolerate those who spread gossip. I'm sure you can imagine the stories that went around the local area like wildfire when the police were questioning Max. It was heart-breaking.'

I hesitate, wondering how much I can say without making Bella feel my curiosity is out of place.

'Actually, Max and I had a talk that last night I was there.'

'I guessed as much when I came out to hand Max the keys that night. I believed you had been sent to us for a reason. Not just in your capacity as an important buyer, but because Max is so alone. He would never talk openly to me about personal things, as he's such a professional. With Trista he's all about supporting her and she never seems to think about how he's coping as time drags on. I mean, I find that strange and I'm sorry if I'm talking out of turn here.'

I can feel her dilemma. She's sitting on the sideline in much the same way that I am, really. Unable to do anything practical, but annoyed by the unfairness of the situation.

'Well, if you need to chat then give me a call. Is your email account secure? I mean does anyone else use it?'

'I'll text you my personal email account. When I head back to the UK to visit my family someone else will have to take over my role for a couple of weeks. I'm not sure what Max will do, as there isn't anyone else here who has really good English or is computer-literate. He might even take on the task himself and get one of the cousins to support Gianni, so he can delegate some of his work. I feel bad about the timing, but I can't avoid going back home for much longer and I do need a break.'

'Yes, all that sunshine must be wearing and you must so miss the rain!'

She laughs. 'Hey, we did have some rain the other day, but it didn't last for an hour. Anyway, if you get a chance to email Max, his address is the same as mine, but substitute Bella for Max. He might be grateful to hear from you personally as he has sunk into some sort of low. At work he seems almost his normal self, but outside of that he's unusually withdrawn. I know it's a lot to ask, but he was very comfortable around you.'

Bella thinks she's asking for me to do her a favour and I feel a little guilty when it's exactly what I was hoping she would say.

'It's no problem. Having met everyone I don't feel like a distant stranger, although that's really what I am. But if I can help in any way at all, I will. I can't bear to see a good person suffering. And don't forget that you promised to visit me next time you are in the UK. We'll be able to catch up properly and you can meet my girls.'

'Ah, thanks and that will be great. I'll add that item onto your order now. Have a lovely day, Ellie, and thank you for being so ... compassionate.'

As the line disconnects I'm left feeling grateful. Bella, too, needs someone to confide in and rather me than someone who might share her confidences far and wide. I feel relieved that at least Max has someone there watching out for him, even though Bella has to be very discreet and can't voice her concerns to him. But it's better than nothing and if things start to escalate, I'm sure she'd feel she has at least one person she can turn to.

With that problem simmering away in the background, there's a pile of work awaiting my attention before I can go home to sort out the girls and give my lovely husband the support he deserves.

Chapter 21

Arriving back home, everything looks quite normal at first glance. Josh has made a start on dinner and is standing at the cooker, as he often does at weekends. Except that this is Monday, of course. Hettie is in her room, hopefully doing her homework in between texts. Rosie is sitting at the kitchen table doing her maths homework and chewing the end of her pencil.

As I lean in to give her a hug she screws up her face.

'Does anyone ever make sense out of this x and y thing? I mean, who cares if $2x + 3y$ is 146? It's not something anyone uses, Mum, so why do they make us learn it?'

Josh and I both stifle laughs and the eye contact with him is warm. At least he's not feeling down; I'm delighted to see him dressed and looking a lot more like his old self.

'You look good,' I comment, walking over to give him a lingering kiss.

'Yuck, Mum. I'm going upstairs. Call me when dinner

is ready.' Rosie scoops everything up in her arms and flounces out of the kitchen.

'Are we going to tell the girls after dinner?'

Josh nods his head, moving an inch or two closer.

'You smell good,' he breathes into my hair.

'You do, too. Bolognaise sauce, I think, and I'm starving.'

'The way to a working woman's heart is through her stomach.'

I frown and search his face, and when I see the cheeky smile sliding over it, I realise he's joking.

'Any news today? Have any of the guys been in touch?'

Josh gives the pot a good stir, places the lid back on the simmering sauce and indicates for me to take a seat at the table.

'My phone hasn't stopped and I've received at least a dozen emails. I also spoke to Nathan and I think I've managed to piece it all together now. The bottom line is that it really is all over. A couple more of the team resigned this morning and everyone is just walking out and saying screw you to the money. The union will sort out what we're due from an employment law standpoint. But we have ammunition, now.'

Josh walks over to the dresser to pick up a bottle of wine and two glasses.

'Here, you're going to need this.' He hands me a glass and we both immediately take a gulp. There's nothing to celebrate other than the end to the weeks of misery.

'Nathan really did get a doctor to diagnose stress but, as we both know, it's mostly self-imposed, given how he's running himself into the ground. But it was also a tactic and guess what? The next day he was offered a large pay-off to take voluntary redundancy.'

My mouth drops open.

'He said that he already knew we were being set up to fail. We'd lost eight good people with no replacements. Extra work was also being put our way to further destabilise the situation and money to replace servers that needed to be urgently upgraded was refused. If only I'd taken a moment to step back and see the bigger picture. Nathan took the money and has already found himself another job.'

'What a rat. Why on earth didn't he call you? He's supposed to be a friend. But it's good news in a way. If Nathan can get another job that quickly, that bodes well for you.'

Josh's eyes narrow and his brow crinkles in a particularly unattractive way.

'The position he's accepted is up in Scotland. He's heading up the IT department for a huge call centre and they have several managerial vacancies. He's trying to talk me into applying and he says it would be a formality; they'd pay a premium to get me.'

Scotland? My heart sinks.

'How do you feel about that?' I ask quietly.

'It can't be solely my decision, Ellie. This would throw all of our lives up in the air. I could probably get a job tomorrow in any number of similar set-ups, but a lot of them will be a long way away from here. I either go where the jobs are, or accept that it might mean less money and a smaller operation. Even then, there are no guarantees it will be on our doorstep, so there's commuting time to take into consideration. And the cost of diesel is rising, which doesn't help.'

'I hadn't considered how lucky we were that your drive to work was only half an hour. It's a lot to take in. It will mean uprooting the girls and, as for Livvie, I don't even want to think about what her reaction would be.'

'I'm not going to jump into anything and it has to work for all of us. All I'm saying is that it might not be as easy as Nathan's situation. He's free to go wherever he chooses, because he only has himself to consider. There is another way. I want you to consider it and give me an answer before we sit down and explain the options to the girls. I could go for the money and rent accommodation nearby, just coming home at weekends. It's not ideal, but mull it over and let me know if you think it's worth considering.'

I've never been prone to despondency, always looking at a problem and immediately exploring the possible solutions to overcome it. But this floors me and my spirits take a sudden nosedive.

When Josh and I sit the girls down to explain that daddy

has lost his job, they receive the news in silence. It's hard telling them that we aren't sure what will happen in the longer-term. In the short-term Josh will be based at home, because I'll be working more hours. Josh tells them that he doesn't think it will be long before he gets another job but explains that it might be in another part of the country. Hettie mutters something about it not being fair and Rosie bursts into tears, saying she doesn't want to move anywhere. At that point Hettie walks out of the room, as the enormity of the situation began to sink in. Josh looks across at me as I put my arm around Rosie, pulling her close. His face looks ashen and I know this is tearing him apart.

'That's enough for now.' Josh addresses Rosie and myself, unable to take any more. If simply talking about it is this hard, then what follows is going to be really, really tough on everyone.

'I'm sorry, Dad.' Rosie stands up and walks over to Josh, learning onto his shoulder and giving him a reassuring pat on the back as one might with a child. It's touching to watch.

'Hey, pumpkin, it happens. There's nothing to worry about. It will all be sorted, but in the meantime we have to establish a new routine. Mum is going to need some help around the house. I'll be here to do as much as I can, but I need to focus on finding the right job. You understand that, don't you?'

'Yes and I'll help, I promise. I just don't want to leave my friends, or my school, Dad. I really don't.'

'I understand, Rosie, and that is going to be the absolute last resort. So let's not dwell on that and hopefully I'll find something local and we'll be able to get back to normal.'

'It's nice to have you back again, Dad. I didn't like the last few weeks. It isn't the same when you aren't around.'

As Rosie heads up to her bedroom to watch a DVD, Josh and I reflect upon her words. We've all struggled to maintain a semblance of normal family life and I know we are both thinking the same thing. If Josh is only home at weekends it will save disrupting the girls, but at what cost to us as a family?

Chapter 22

This last month we've all been through so much and yet the girls have been marvellous. They've turned off lights when leaving the room and insisted they don't need all the products we normally pile into the shopping trolley, so they can emerge from the bathroom shiny and clean. Hettie even suggested she get a Saturday job so she could pay for her own makeup and clothes. Rosie thought up a few money-saving ideas for the lunch boxes. It left Josh and me feeling proud of our caring, empathetic daughters. We were even more determined to find the right solution and not a quick fix that turns into a nightmare.

The problem is that it's hard to turn down the offer of a really good job, particularly when you are headhunted. And that's what happened, which was a real boost to Josh's self-esteem. He asked for time to consider the offers, but all of them involved a major upheaval of one sort or another. He stalled into week two and then into week three. A week ago we sat up late into the night to make the final decision.

It came down to which was likely to cause the least impact to the family as a whole. Eventually we settled on a job based in Milton Keynes and Josh went back to them to negotiate terms.

He has a permanent contract with a six-month opt-out option at one month's notice, if it doesn't work out. After that they will require him to work four months' notice, but he told me that isn't unusual. He leaves home at six o'clock every Monday morning and stays locally throughout the week. At three o'clock on Friday afternoon he drives back home for the weekend.

The girls were stunned when we broke the news. We didn't gloss over the sacrifice Josh was making, so that they wouldn't have to be uprooted. We decided that they were old enough to understand that life isn't always easy and that this solution was still going to mean a huge adjustment for us all. The big plan is that if Josh settles in and things continued to run smoothly here, then we will review the situation in two years' time. Having a potential end date in our minds somehow made us feel a little better about our nightmare situation.

I had to break the news to Livvie that I couldn't continue to work full time, but had to work around the daily school run again and any after-school clubs. Then our neighbour, Dawn, offered to act as a taxi and do the afternoon run. It means that she has a little income and I can work from nine-fifteen in the morning, through until four-thirty. Livvie was simply relieved that I wasn't handing in my resignation. The new lady, Eve, is going to take over some of my less-demanding tasks, so I can focus on buying, and supporting Livvie.

Suddenly there was a glimmer of hope on the horizon. The mortgage would continue to be paid, the girls were relatively happy and, courtesy of FaceTime, they can see their dad each evening. When they were done, Josh and I could have some one-to-one time. At first I dreaded the thought; it seemed a strange way to have quality time. But over the past few days I've come to see that it's more personal than just hearing someone's voice and often we chat while I'm in the kitchen making dinner for the girls. Josh feels he's still a part of what's going on and soon it will all begin to feel normal. Just a different sort of normal, that's all.

As for the physical side, well, it's lonely – for both of us. This is Josh's second week and it's true what they say, absence does make the heart grow fonder. Last weekend flew by, but we probably packed in a lot more family, and couple, time than we had for ages. When we reflected upon it last night, Josh said he thought it was because we no longer have the fear of uncertainty hanging over us.

In my head I have all of these little compartments, like boxes. In one is Josh, in another Hettie, then Rosie, then Aunt Clare. Livvie has one, too, and now Max. Why?

Because he has no one and because fate sent me falling headlong into his little world for a reason. Perhaps it's my turn to repay that fateful day when Livvie introduced me to Josh. It changed my life forever and I'm hoping that if I help Max, then it will change his life forever, too.

Josh and the girls are now reasonably settled into our new living arrangements, so that's three boxes I don't have to dive into for a while.

Livvie's mum is doing well and she has admitted to me there are times she forgets that her mother is living under her roof. Having settled into the guest annex with the live-in nurse/companion, life seems to be continuing as normal. As for Aunt Clare, she's about to go on a second date with a man she met online and seems quietly optimistic for a change. Well, he didn't run screaming from their first date and he thinks her sense of humour is a bonus. Yes, really.

That leaves one last box. With all the others firmly shut, because that's the only way I can cope with it, Max and Castrovillari still invade my dreams most nights. I've tried everything I can think of to blot it out, but nothing works. So now I have to accept the fact that I can't control how my brain functions when I'm asleep. Whatever happens is driven by fate and fate alone.

Bella's latest email from her personal account is open in front of me.

It's all booked and I arrive at Heathrow Airport on Saturday evening. I promised Mum I would stay for three days before I head off to see a few friends. Are you sure it's okay if I get to yours Wednesday afternoon/ early evening? I can only stay the one night, as there's been a change of plan. I'll tell you all about it when I see you, as it's rather complicated.

I've been doing some digging and I've found something. Something I don't think Max has seen and probably doesn't even know exists. If you speak to him and can steer the conversation around to talking about Trista, ask him whether she ever talks about Aletta. Or if he can remember when she last talked about her.

Max seems a little more relaxed and I think your emails brighten his day. I hope Josh's new job is working out and the girls aren't driving you mad.

See you next week; I can't wait to catch up.

Bella x

Max never talks about Trista. He writes about the cooperative, what's happening at the refinery and life at the villa. Considering my stay was so short, the connections I made feel so very strong, as if their lives touch mine. I can't stop myself caring about their day-to-day concerns. I love to hear how the cooperative is growing and Max is, I think, grateful to have someone to share his news with, who understands how important it is to him. I cursor down the screen looking for his name and, sure enough, about a dozen items below Bella's latest email, he's there.

Buongiorno, Ellie

I promised you a photo of Piero's newest sculpture. He says it's not for sale, unless his favourite English lady finds the perfect setting for it. He now regards you as little short of a patron saint for his family. The building work has already begun on the extension and Piero will have a little bungalow that will be quite separate from the family home.

The villa is busy and we are down to our last two rooms. Everyone is helping out, even one of the cousins I'd never met before. There is a feeling of optimism here at the moment that changes the whole ambience. People are busy and happy to be busy. And the harvest is looking good.

I will miss Bella, though. She deserves a holiday and I know that it's long overdue. But she says she came here to escape her family, which I find rather curious, as she seems to fit right in and has become close to us all. Here, of course, the fact that her mother is still remembered with great fondness means she is only one step removed from a family association, anyway.

Today is a good day. Catch me up on your news if

and when you can. I wish you could drop by for a coffee
on the terrace. Maybe next time.
   Fino a quando ci incontriamo di nuovo,
   Max

I know that tonight I will dream about coffee on the terrace and my heart soars at the positivity in Max's words. Bella is right and each day his emails seem to get a little brighter. Maybe it's because all of his efforts in the business are beginning to make a difference, or perhaps it's easier to chat via email. It's almost like talking to yourself, as you allow your fingers to fly around the keyboard. Then you press send and it's forgotten. No one stops to think about the reaction of the person at the other end until they get a response. And then you realise you aren't just talking to yourself. In the past I've re-read my original emails, wishing I'd re-phrased something. Transferring the thoughts inside my head into text isn't always clear, or it's coloured by my emotions at the time. Because he's feeling happier, he's able to share that with me. Max always signs off with 'until we meet again' and that makes my heart skip a beat. We'll never meet again, well, not in the flesh.

I can't explain our relationship, if it could even be called a relationship. We met because of business, but now we are like any online friendship, whether it's social media, or a group chat room. But if Bella has a lead that could help unravel the puzzle Aletta left behind, then I need to talk to Max about Trista. I can't do that via email, it would be too awkward. So I press reply.

Buongiorno Max

Or good evening now, by the time you read this.

I'm so happy to hear that everyone is busy. It's raining here at the moment and a typical June for us in the UK. Please remind Bella to come prepared, as she might have forgotten how wet our summers can be.

Piero owes me nothing. His work is amazing and he's a very talented sculptor in his chosen medium. Bradley's Design Creative can find a home for any of his one-off pieces, but he shouldn't look to sell anything that has meaning to him. Unless the money will help his future, of course. I'm just relieved Eduardo and his wife realise he needs his own space if he's going to stay and continue with the family tradition.

We are into the second week of Josh's new job and surviving. The girls have a lot going on at school and I'm busy at work. A neighbour collects them from their after-school activities and they usually get home just before me. They FaceTime with Josh while I'm cooking dinner and it helps a lot. Seeing someone, rather than just hearing their voice, makes a big difference. Once they're in bed, though, it's very peaceful. Something that is still a bit alien at the moment.

I'm around this evening if you wanted to chat. After eight is best for me.

I suppose it's time I wandered into the kitchen. Maybe tonight I'll take my inspiration from the wonderful pasta dishes I had while I was in Italy. I will never forget the pink spaghetti.

Until we speak again, take care,
Ellie

There, it's done. The offer to talk has been made and now it's in Max's hands. The lid slides gently back onto the box and now they are all lined up neatly in a row. It's time for me to unwind.

Chapter 23

'Mum's making pink spaghetti. It has wine in it, Dad.' Rosie's voice sounds almost scandalised, as she chatters away to Josh in the background. I concentrate on chopping onions, smiling to myself.

'Only a little red wine, Rosie,' I throw over my shoulder.

Hettie walks into the kitchen, obviously hungry. 'When's dinner going to be ready, Mum? Oh, hi, Dad. I forgot it was that time of the day. How's work?'

'Good. But when I'm at the hotel it's very ... quiet, let's say. I miss the noise you guys make. I don't miss the fight over the bathrooms in the morning, though. The ensuite here is just for me.'

I laugh. 'Don't get too used to it. You'll be back to sharing at the weekend.'

It's so lovely to be able to come together still as a family and each talk about what we've been doing. We all miss the hugs, of course, but it's the next best thing.

Josh comments on my perfect pink pasta, as I scoop up

the long strands and coil them onto the dinner plates.

'Can you make that for me at the weekend?' He asks.

'Anything you want. Ristorante Maddison will be open and very accommodating to its regular clientele. I can't wait to see you tomorrow, although this week hasn't dragged as much.'

I leave the girls to sit and eat, taking the iPad off into the sitting room.

'Are you really okay? You're not just being upbeat for the benefit of the girls?'

We're looking directly as each other and I reach out to touch his face, forgetting it's a touch screen. I quickly clear the icons that pop up.

'Sorry, I forgot.'

'It's weird, isn't it? Still, it won't be forever. Although the way this job is working out it's a real shame it's so far away. I'd forgotten what it was like to be appreciated and to be given a decent budget to work with. Being here on my own I can really focus on work and most evenings I grab a quick meal and then I'm back in front of the PC. I've tried watching TV, but the screen is too small and it just makes me long for my home comforts. I have a few books down-loaded, though, and I try to read for at least an hour before I go to sleep. It usually helps to stop me obsessing over the fact that I'm not with you.'

Guilt hits me like a punch in the gut. I haven't told Josh

very much about Italy and I didn't tell him anything at all about the Ormanni family. Or Max's problems. We usually share our innermost thoughts and worries, unless we're trying to protect each other. Josh held back for a while about his work pressures because he didn't want to worry me unnecessarily. He thought he could fix it. So why don't I tell him about Max? Am I hiding it from him, or am I simply choosing not to involve him as it's work-related, really?

'You've gone very quiet.'

'I'm having very complicated dreams at the moment. You know, when your thoughts get all mixed up and you wake up having to sort out what's real from what isn't.'

'I've put you through a lot recently, Ellie. Things will settle down for all of us. But if any problems arise, please don't feel you have to cope on your own. Let's address them together. Promise?'

'Promise.' Josh is talking about our own family and so I feel I can reply with honesty. 'And if you need me for anything, or just to talk, I'm available 24/7.'

'See you later, alligator. Well, tomorrow, actually.' His voice lifts.

'In a while, crocodile. And drive carefully.'

I suddenly feel angry that fate is meddling in my life at a time when things aren't settled. I'm happy to help anyone at any time, but why now? If things were normal here, of course I would be talking to Josh about the Ormanni's. I mean, it's a mystery and having been there and met the people, I'm sure he'd understand how I feel.

In the kitchen, I see that Hettie has already disappeared back upstairs and, much to Rosie's annoyance, has taken the entire bag of pretzels with her.

'It's not fair, Mum. She never listens to me. I bet she's texting her boyfriend again.'

It's now an open secret, it seems. But we wouldn't dare raise the topic if Hettie was still in the room.

'It's an age thing, pumpkin. In two years' time you'll be hiding yourself away and doing the same thing. Do you want to sit and watch a film together?'

Rosie's eyes narrow. 'Do you want us to watch a film together?'

Is there an echo in here? It wasn't a trick question. And then I realise that she thinks I need her company because I'm lonely.

'Only if you want to. If not, I'll go up to the study and sort through my photos. I need to move them all into one folder, have a bit of a cull and then do a back-up. But I can do that any time, so if you want to do something together, I'm free.'

'Well, I did have plans.' She looks at me in a matter-of-fact way, as if weighing up the pros and cons of the situation.

'Oh, plans, eh?'

'I want to enter a short-story competition. It's only a thousand words and there are three age groups. There will be a winner in each category and the prize is a gift voucher and a medal. My teacher says entries have to be in by tomorrow, so they can get sent off in time.'

Her little face is so serious. I'm thrilled she's doing something that will stretch her mind and doesn't involve playing computer games or watching the TV.

'Sounds like fun. Will I get to read it before it's sent off?'

'Maybe yes, or maybe no.'

I pull two apples out of the fruit bowl and a small bar of chocolate from the drawer.

'Here, you'll probably need a little sugar boost to help the thought processes. Shout if you need anything.'

'Thanks, Mum. Let me know if you are lonely, though.'

Josh and I are so lucky. I know Hettie is a bit distant and moody at the moment, but it could be a lot worse and Rosie, bless her, is still at the stage where she's fairly easy to please.

It's time to look at those photos. Josh only shared my desk for a couple of weeks and now all of my clutter is back out of the bottom drawer. Mostly it's cuttings from home interior magazines, especially new trends. My involvement with design is certainly a big help now I'm in buying. Livvie relies upon me to keep putting fresh ideas in front of her that will excite the client. But everything revolves around being able to find a reliable source, at the right price.

Josh said my computer is creaking along and he hoped I was backing everything up, because one crash and I could lose everything. Now he's working again I suspect he'll talk me into an upgrade, so I'm going to back up the important stuff to a new external hard drive he bought for me, in readiness.

I plug in the iPad and connect the lead, ready to download the photos onto my desktop, when the FaceTime icon pops up. I smile, thinking Josh has forgotten something, then see that it's Max's name on the screen. I press the green accept button.

Nothing prepares me for the sensation that hits my stomach as Max's face appears in front of me. He's here and he's real. This isn't a dream. As my life goes on as normal, so Max's life in Italy is being lived out as if we are in parallel realities.

'Ellie, it's good to see your face. Is this a bad time? You said after eight.'

I shake my head and raise a smile, willing my heartbeat to slow down.

'No, it's fine. The girls have settled down in their rooms and I probably won't see them until morning now. Teenagers like their own space.'

He nods and I realise he expects me to continue. All I can think about is how good it is to see him and how tired he looks.

'Emails are so cumbersome, aren't they? I mean, the emotion is lost and it's just a jumble of words. I always feel they should be short and to the point, when often it's not easy to stop the flow. I've never been the sort of person to fit what they want to say into a 140-character Tweet.'

He laughs.

'You Tweet?'

'For the company, yes. We all take a turn. But not a lot gets said.'

He laughs again and it's good to see, as he begins to feel more comfortable in this surreal setting.

'So, where are you in the house?' he asks.

'This is the study. But it's actually my study, because no one else really uses it. I keep all of my design stuff in here, as I often play around with mood boards and then take my ideas into the office.'

'Am I stopping you from working?'

'No, tonight I was going to begin sorting out my photos. One of those jobs that I keep meaning to get around to, but can't quite find the motivation to tackle. So you are saving me from hours of weeding out, and deleting, those out-of-focus snaps I won't even remember having taken. Where are you?'

He looks as if he's sitting outside, so I'm surprised there aren't people milling around.

'I'm at the refinery, still. Most people have gone home but I've been catching up on paperwork. I like sitting here at the end of the day when it's quiet. I'm in a little corner, tucked away and with a stunning view of the mountains in front of me.'

He raises his wine glass to me.

'Give me one moment.'

I head out of the room and downstairs to the kitchen, returning with a glass of red wine.

Settling myself back in my seat I raise the glass to the screen and say, 'Cheers.'

'It's like you've never been away.' Max's words have a sad ring to them.

'Except for the rain. It's awful here at the moment. A few low-lying areas have had flash floods.'

He grimaces. 'Sorry to hear that. I'll send some sunshine your way.'

'So what's been happening? You sound a little more optimistic and that's nice to hear.'

Bella's questions are whirling around inside my head. I just don't know how to broach them.

'I will admit I've had an awful time of it lately. As you so intuitively picked up when you were here. It's hard sometimes. Something sparks a memory and it all comes flooding back. I can't live in the past, I have too much to do in the present to keep everything going.'

'How's Trista?'

'Taking the hotel from strength to strength. Her managerial skills reflect her character; she's a strong woman who doesn't give in easily. Nothing can dent her motivation, no matter what goes wrong. She's unstoppable and she has one goal, which is to provide for the wider family around her. But she wears a mask and behind that is a lot of sadness and pain. Without Stefano she feels alone and isolated, but she should still have her daughter to help her through that.'

Max sounds angry and I can see that etched onto his face. Anger isn't an emotion he's ever displayed in front of me before and this is a real step forward. But I have to tread carefully.

'Does Trista ever talk about Aletta?'

He's staring into space and I have no doubt he's replaying some incident in his head. The sound of my voice brings him back into the moment and he turns square on to the screen.

'Not since the day of Stefano's funeral and the family have taken their lead from her.' His tone implies it's only to be expected.

'That can't be good for her, Max, bottling up those feelings. Maybe she's waiting for someone to let her know that no one expects her to keep holding back. Trista probably needs to step aside from her role as the head of the family and allow herself to simply be a mother whose daughter is missing. She's a victim, too. When it first happened I assume everyone talked about it openly?'

Max has relaxed a little and his body language indicates I haven't said anything he considers to be out of order.

'Aletta left for London planning a five-day stay. It included a trip to some sort of trade show, she'd said, that was showcasing luxury and boutique hotels. But when the police investigated they could only find details of one exhibition fitting that description. Aletta was travelling a full month before it was due to begin.

'When the police interviewed me they kept going over and over that point, seemingly convinced I was covering up the truth. She was my fiancée, and it was supposed to be a business trip. Obviously, they thought it was bizarre that I didn't know the details of her itinerary. I had to agree it was odd, but for Aletta it was the norm. No one told her what to do, or when.'

'But surely Trista would have said pretty much the same thing. It wasn't as if you were the only one explaining her rather strange behaviour?'

'Trista was watching her husband grow weaker by the day and the stress became almost unbearable. Her state of mind would have made her very difficult to question. You have to understand that it was also the year of the bad harvest and emotions were running high throughout the region. Locally, tough decisions were being made, as sons and daughters headed for the city hoping to get jobs and earn money to send back home. But everyone knew that if they succeeded they were unlikely to come back here to work, ever again. So it was a bitter-sweet solution that ended up tearing families apart. Trista was beside herself as the tension built up and up. That's why she begged me to stay, because she couldn't face what lay ahead. Everything she had ever known as a constant was being taken away from her, piece by piece.'

I sip my wine, hearing the despondency in Max's words.

Then he adds, 'Hey, I didn't mean to suck the joy out of your evening. Bad things happen and yet people survive. The success of the cooperative is like a blood transfusion, putting life back into the community. And you are a real part of that!'

He smiles and those mysteriously deep, hazel eyes twinkle back at me. I feel myself blushing, but in the semi-darkness of the room, and with only the light from the screen, I don't think Max can see that.

'I'm glad some good came of my visit. As soon as I arrived I could feel the passion and the will to succeed running alongside a real fear of failure. Livvie's business is in a strong position and going from strength to strength, so your order book should continue to grow. It means so much more to me, I suppose, because I've met some of the people and seen for myself the impact this will have on their lives. And their skills are matched by their determination to guarantee a future to hand down to their children. I know exactly why you couldn't walk away, but that doesn't mean you can't have a life of your own.'

Max stirs in his seat, readjusting his position. 'You've seen the way things are here, Ellie, but what you didn't witness was the doubters, or the damage that a scandal like this can do. Trust is quickly eroded away and slow to re-build. I'm in limbo and until the situation is resolved there are no options open to me. I have to sit and wait, but there's more than enough to do to fill every hour of my day.'

With each sentence Max is filling in the gaps and as the picture begins to reveal itself I, too, can see it's a hopeless situation to be in.

'But if you could find someone to share your life with, then you could move out of the villa. That doesn't stop you managing the Ormannis' affairs, it would simply allow you to escape the constant pressure. You aren't giving yourself a chance, Max.'

'Maybe I feel the situation is partly my fault. I was so besotted with Aletta that I didn't try to curb her unacceptable behaviour. If only I had challenged her; walked out, or something, then maybe she would have come to see reason. Trista and I had to work hard to keep everything from Stefano and look how it all ended. Imagine any woman walking into this situation now. Wouldn't they always wonder if I'd had a hand in Aletta's disappearance? Wonder if she pushed me once too often and I did the unthinkable? After all, what kind of a man doesn't know exactly where his fiancée is going, because they hardly talk to each other any more? I guess the moral of this story is that sometimes what you want isn't necessarily what's good for you.'

'It's easy to be wise with hindsight, Max. Does it help to talk about it?'

He nods at the screen, raising his hand to sweep them over his eyes.

'It does, actually. Anything that gives me a reprieve from this constant swirl of questions and scenarios that I can't get out of my head whenever I'm alone. I imagine her being involved in a car accident, but realise even if she lost her memory her personal effects would confirm her identity. Or what if she was kidnapped and before they were able to ask for a ransom something awful and unexpected happened?

'I feel she is no longer with us, but how, or why, remains a mystery. That's something I would never admit to anyone else but you, Ellie. Aletta is gone; there, I've said it. You never once looked at me with that question in your eyes, even though you were a stranger and must have been shocked at what you were hearing.

'And now it's time I left you in peace. Please don't go to bed with all of this running around inside your head. If you have to dream of Italy, then let it be about the view from the terrace. That earthy smell as the cool evening air brings with it the scent of the forests high above Castrovillari, or the rich perfume of the oleanders.'

He yawns and I think that maybe tonight, after finally unburdening himself, he will sink into a deep, untroubled sleep.

'Nothing would please me more. Sleep well, Max.'

'Thank you once again, Ellie, for your trust and for your friendship. *Fino a quando ci incontriamo di nuovo.*'

As I press the end call button I'm left with mixed feelings. Anger at Trista for what she did, and didn't, do. Anger at the people who doubt Max's innocence without a shred of evidence to support their hastily drawn conclusions. Anger at Max for accepting the situation he's been forced into, but that's accompanied by an overwhelming sense of respect.

I have no idea what Bella has discovered, but it must be something significant. Max seems unaware of it, of that I'm very sure. But what if some sort of evidence does exist, something that could shed light on the mystery that is trapping him there? What would Max do with his freedom, I wonder?

Checking on the girls, I find them both tucked up and sound asleep. I turn off Rosie's TV and gently kiss her cheek. I have to ease out Hettie's earphones, untangling her iPod, placing it under her pillow.

After a quick shower I sink, very gratefully, into bed. Italy is waiting for me in my dreams.

Chapter 24

We begin the day counting down the hours until Josh is home again. Tonight we are going to the cinema, so I'm taking the girls out for pizza first and we'll pop back to collect Josh at around seven o'clock. We never used to plan our weekends with such precision, but it's something we talk about each evening now, when we are all gathered around the iPad. It's funny how habits are formed and we often wasted Friday evenings just lolling around and doing nothing in particular. That included constantly flicking around channels on the TV in an effort to find something everyone could agree on, which rarely happened.

Josh has arranged for the two of us to go and look at some cars tomorrow. So Hettie is going to Charlotte's house and her mum will take them to their ice-skating lesson. Rosie will be spending the day with her friend, Alice, and in the afternoon they are going to a friend's birthday party.

The plan is that Josh and I will grab some lunch out, in between test drives. He's worried that my old car will break down when he's not around and leave us stranded. I told him I was sure it would last a while longer, but he was adamant. The girls love his new company car because it has all of the latest gadgets and, parked alongside, my old, well-loved Mini just looks well-worn. He has a point, I know that, but I begrudge what I see as the waste of a day.

But, first things first. I drop the girls off and head into work. Livvie is bursting to tell me some good news.

'I had dinner last night with Richard Dale. The rumours about his latest acquisition are true. It's costing him four and a half million, so you can imagine the size of the budget for the refurbishment contract.'

'You mean THE Richard Dale? As in TV's most celebrated chef to the stars?'

'The same one. A signed contract will be in our hands by the middle of next week. He's a man who likes every-thing done yesterday, Ellie, so we need to start pulling things together very quickly. You'd better put your friend Max on high alert. Richard will want unique pieces and it's a very big house. We are probably talking air freight for this one.'

I flinch. 'Your friend Max', she said. What if Livvie calls round to the house and says something like that in front of Josh?

'He's only a business contact, Livvie. He also happens to

be a very nice man, a gentleman. We aren't friends, merely business acquaintances.'

Livvie looks surprised. 'Oh, sorry. Slip of the tongue. Anyway, isn't Bella your main contact now?'

I almost blurt out that she's on holiday and is flying to the UK next week, but as the first word is about to leave my mouth I manage to cut myself short and cover it with a fake cough.

'Sorry about that. Yes, Bella is the new contact since she was promoted.'

Livvie doesn't seem to have noticed my moment of hesitation, but it's a wake-up call. Now, though, I feel awkward not having at least mentioned Max and what he's been going through. How on earth I'm going to casually begin talking about it to Josh, I have absolutely no idea. The only person whose advice I can seek is Aunt Clare's. If I sit down and explain the whole thing to her, then maybe she will be able to think of the right way to tackle it. Max's face flashes through my mind and pieces of last night's dream start to come back to me.

We were sitting on the terrace and it makes me smile as that's exactly what Max said last night. 'If you have to dream of Italy, then let it be about the view from the terrace. That earthy smell as the cool evening air brings with it the scent of the forests high above Castrovillari.'

In my dream I was sitting at the little bistro table by the

fountain and suddenly I noticed him in the reception doorway, watching me. Just like in the photograph. He smiled when I looked across at him and began walking towards me. Then Trista appeared and called his name. Max stood still, turning his head to look back at her and suddenly I was afraid. The darkness around me became oppressive and I wanted to go home. I tried to move, but I couldn't and Max turned back to look at me, extending his hand to reach out.

'Don't go, Ellie, please don't go.' There was panic in his voice and a wild look in his eyes.

'Ellie, are you okay?'

Livvie is staring intently at me and I realise she's been talking to me throughout my little daydream.

'Oh, I, um ... just remembered an order I need to amend. You were saying?'

'I said, let me know if your desk starts piling up. Things are about to get really busy and if we need to draft in more help, then I'd rather do that sooner rather than at the last minute.'

Livvie hasn't taken her eyes off me.

'Everything is okay at the moment, really. I have time in the evenings and can easily do a bit extra from home,' I reassure her.

'If you say so, but don't overdo it. I don't want to overload you when there's so much going on.'

I plaster on a smile. Livvie's usually too caught up in her own thoughts to notice the little things in life and if she's scrutinising me, then she's noticed something. That means I need to be more careful or I'm going to start worrying the people who love me.

'I can't wait to see Josh tonight. We're taking the girls to the cinema.'

I make my voice sound bright and breezy. In my head the vision of Max's hand reaching out for me tugs at my heartstrings.

~

'Aunt Clare? Is there any chance we could meet up for a quick coffee? I can get away from work in about an hour, so any time after eleven-thirty.'

'Hi, Ellie, it's lovely to hear your voice. I've only just woken up. I've recently finished four late shifts in a row. Let me see what time it is, oh, right. Guess I needed a lie-in this morning. Give me an hour and a half and I'll meet you in the coffee shop around the corner from your office. Is everything okay?'

'Fine. I need a listening ear.'

'I'm yours. I'll jump in the shower, grab some breakfast and head over. See you in a bit.'

I'm hoping Livvie won't notice my absence, as I think

she has a couple of meetings today. But just in case she does, I mention to the new lady, Eve, that I'm meeting my aunt for lunch. Livvie is bound to be curious if she spots my empty desk, as I don't usually take a lunch break as such. But I really need some advice and I need it now.

~

'Hi, Ellie. How's Josh's new job going?'

We exchange hugs and Aunt Clare pulls out the seat opposite me. The café is full and I was lucky to get a table, but it's not the most private of places to talk. I bring her up to date on Josh and the girls, happy to report that things are ticking over rather well, all things considered.

Aunt Clare gives me an encouraging smile. 'That's good to hear, Ellie. I was worried the strain would be too much. Even for you.'

She reaches across, patting my arm affectionately. I know we are both thinking of Mum and how different life would be if she was still here. She would have loved picking up the girls from school, taking them to their after-school activities and generally sharing quality time with them.

'You look well. And happy,' I remark, thinking she sounds a lot more upbeat than usual. 'Oh, it's a man, isn't it?' I begin laughing and she actually blushes.

'There is a little company in my life at the moment, I

will admit. Don't go reading anything into it, well, not just yet, anyway. But we're having fun and we'll just have to see where it goes.'

'Is it the same guy? The one who thinks you have an amazing sense of humour?'

She bursts out laughing, but I can see from her reaction that I'm right.

'Maybe. Now let's change the subject. What's important enough to pull you away from work?'

I let out a sigh and Aunt Clare frowns. 'Trouble?'

'No, I don't think so, more of a dilemma.'

'Okay, you have my undivided attention.'

I toy with my coffee cup, trying to decide where to begin.

'Is this about the déjà vu thing we discussed after your return from Italy?'

I look up at her, surprised she's connected the dots.

'Yes, and I wish it wasn't. I know it sounds a little ridiculous, but I'm even dreaming about it. I know that's understandable in one way, as having met the people I appreciate the impact of the business Bradley's is putting their way. I mean, it's personal now and the more contact I have, the harder it is to distance myself from it, even if I wanted to.'

Aunt Clare puts down her coffee cup and leans forward, concern written all over her face.

'I think you'd better be a little more specific here. What aren't you telling me?'

I close my eyes for a moment, suddenly fearful of what she will think.

'Max Johnson and I are emailing and last night we made contact on FaceTime. Most of the work orders I place are through his assistant, Bella. Bella is coming to the UK next week to visit her family. I've invited her to stay overnight.'

'Stop there. That doesn't make sense. You deal with Bella, so why are you talking to Max?'

'I told you, we had this ... connection.' I sit looking at her, hoping she'll understand without me having to explain – because I don't really understand it myself.

'No, Ellie. You told me you felt some sort of a connection to Italy and the villa, remember? Are you saying now you felt a connection to Max specifically? Because that isn't quite the same thing.'

She looks appalled. Panic begins to rise in my chest as I realise I can't back down now, even though this isn't going quite the way I'd hoped. The least I can do is make it seem matter-of-fact.

'He's isolated, Aunt Clare, and his situation is impossible. All he needs is a friend, someone he can talk to. You know me, I'm a good listener and it's no coincidence I was whisked away to get a glimpse of the pain in his life. Now I understand that, how can I simply ignore it? I didn't mention it to Josh when I came back because we were all preoccupied with Josh's situation at work. I mean, there's nothing else going on between us on a personal level. I just listen to Max. That's not wrong, is it?'

Aunt Clare sits back, her eyes searching my face as if she's mulling over my words and not sure what conclusion to draw. A few seconds of silence hang between us before she replies.

She leans forward, speaking softly. 'You haven't fallen out of love with Josh, have you? I mean, this guy hasn't come between you two?'

My reply is instant and heartfelt. 'Of course not. Josh is my soul mate and I love him more than life itself. That will never, ever change.' My eyes fill with tears and I look away for a moment, not wanting her to see how torn I feel. 'But I admit I do feel a certain connection with Max because he has no one else.'

'Okay, perhaps I over-reacted there for a moment. It came as a bit of a shock, I mean, you and Josh are such a solid couple. This isn't like you, at all. You have so much to lose if you make a silly mistake for the wrong reason. If this isn't some transient feeling of attraction, I need to understand why you can't walk away from him. I know you are a sensitive soul and you care about people, but Italy is a long way away. There's a limit to what you can do to help, anyway. You might want to consider it as damage limitation, as good intentions can often go more than a little awry. You said Bella is your new contact over there, so what am I missing? Does Livvie know about this?'

I realise I'm going to have to trust in her discretion and reveal what Max has confided in me. I pull my chair closer to the table, not wanting to raise my voice, but it's getting increasingly difficult to hear her over the background buzz.

'Max's fiancée, Aletta, disappeared a little over two years ago. He initially went there for a holiday and ended up staying to help the family, who were struggling to cope. Aletta's father was recovering from his first stroke, at the time. As the only child, there was no one else able to manage the operations and help Aletta, and her mother. Many of their wider family members are employed in either the production of the olive oil, or the hotel side of the business. Max's arrival must have made him look like a saviour, as he had the right skills to take over the reins. As his relationship with Aletta deteriorated, his sense of responsibility was growing. He soon realised they were in a serious way, financially. After a disastrous year for the olive harvest, he encouraged them to diversify. Unwittingly, he was getting pulled in beyond the point of no return.'

I can see by the expression on her face that this wasn't at all what she expected to hear. I indicate to the waitress to bring two more cups of coffee, as one thing is for sure, this story isn't a short one.

'We are talking about the livelihood of so many families.

Max was interviewed by the police, but released when they were able to confirm that Aletta had flown to London, as planned. It turned out that the trade show she was supposed to be attending was merely an excuse. It was more than a month away and she'd told Max she would be back five days later. At the time her father was going downhill, rapidly, and he died a little over two months later. Max won't walk away, even though there are still people who think he might have been involved with Aletta's disappearance. But it's only his efforts that have kept that community going and the Ormanni family's business interests continuing to thrive.'

Aunt Clare breathes out heavily, her eyes reflecting the fact that she, too, can see it's an impossible situation.

'It's a harrowing story, Ellie, but you have to remember that this isn't your life we are talking about.'

It's a difficult conversation to have in such an open place and Aunt Clare can see I don't know whether or not to continue.

'Come on, finish your coffee and let's take a walk.'

She doesn't wait for me, but heads off to the till to pay the bill. I gather together my things and make my way outside. My head is buzzing, but at least I don't feel so closed in.

'Thank you. I couldn't have stayed in there for much longer. I really value your opinion. But first, I need you to understand why I feel so involved and explaining that isn't easy. I love Josh and the girls with all my heart, but it's almost like I now have two lives running in parallel. The reason I can't let go of Max is too difficult to put into words. Please believe me when I say I have done nothing wrong, nothing to feel ashamed of. I would never betray Josh and the girls. It's not possible to have two soul mates, is it? Or maybe Max is my soul mate from another lifetime and what has stirred inside of me are feelings I'm not even supposed to remember? It's the only way I can explain a connection I can't ignore. In the same way that I knew as soon as I saw Josh that our life together was destined, I feel something very similar with Max. That sort of thing is so rare, Aunt Clare, some people don't even experience it once, so twice takes that way beyond a coincidence. Why did Italy have to happen?'

As the full impact of my words hit me, I realise I was fooling myself to think I was in control. Now I'm caught up in something that is beginning to rip my life into two. In exactly the same way that Max is unable to walk away from the situation he's in, through no real fault of his own. It seems fate has decided that I, too, am a pawn.

Aunt Clare's face looks pained. 'Two lives. Two connections. Is this some sick joke fate is playing?' She isn't talking to me, but to herself and she shakes her head.

'What do you mean? I don't understand.'

She comes to a standstill, leaning against a large brick wall for support. I walk around to stand in front of her, trying to read her face.

'You can't live two lives at once, can you? Of course it's ridiculous, but I wonder – isn't that technically what identical twins do? But then, there was nothing to say you were identical.'

'What do you mean? I don't understand you. Please, talk to me.' I grab Aunt Clare's arm, making her look into my eyes.

'Obviously she never told you. You were one of twins, but the other embryo didn't survive and your mum miscarried it at twelve weeks. She feared she'd lose you, too, but fate was kind. Of course, you might not have had an *identical* twin, but two lives ... is that a weird sort of coincidence? Maybe this isn't just about you, Ellie, and you are right, there is a connection you don't understand. There are too many unknowns in this world and I, for one, prefer not to over-think things because it's easier to keep it simple.'

She hugs me and we stand, totally oblivious to the people passing by.

'You don't think I'm going mad, or that I've done anything wrong?'

'I think you are confused and you've been pulled into a situation by a set of circumstances that were outside of your control. Clearly this wasn't of your making, Ellie and you don't deserve to have your life disrupted in this way. All you can do is to cut all ties to Max and keep telling yourself that you are doing it for Josh, Hettie and Rosie. But I feel for you, as it means walking away from someone who is obviously desperate to reach out to you. I don't know Max, but his situation sounds like an impossible one. You are taking a big risk getting involved in this any further, and you have no idea what information might come to light in the future. And yet you seem to believe he's innocent, without any hesitation whatsoever.'

My stomach churns and nausea rises up within me, leaving a bitter taste in my mouth. I will myself not to throw up.

'If I don't get involved something really bad will happen, Aunt Clare. I know it, deep down inside of me. Do I want that on my conscience? I fear that I'm already past the point of no return. Bella says she has uncovered some new information about Aletta. What if the end is in sight and if I step away now my part in this will be the missing link that means it's never resolved? What if, when Bella arrives, I tell her everything I know and hope that's enough? Maybe then I will be able to accept there is nothing more I can do and let him go.'

'My poor, dear, girl. This is the worst possible thing that could happen to you, because I know how deeply you feel things and you have such a big heart. It's hard to be different, isn't it? But you must beware of giving too much of yourself, Ellie. That's about the only advice I can give you. Josh won't understand this, of that I'm sure. It doesn't matter that you aren't having an affair with Max in the usual sense. He'll be hurt because you have developed a connection with another man; someone who should be a stranger to you, but whose life has touched you in a very personal way. Some things should never be said and this is one of those things. How you are going to cope and not let this come between you and Josh, I don't know. But if Josh finds out it could rip your marriage apart.'

'I can't let that happen, Aunt Clare. I won't let that happen. Josh and the girls have to come first. After Bella's visit I will make it clear that there really isn't anything I can do for Max. I'm sorry to have dragged you into this, but I needed to hear your take on it.'

'Be strong, dear girl. Ring me at any time, night or day.'

Chapter 25

What should have been a wonderfully relaxing weekend ends up being a nightmare, as I struggle to maintain my composure. A part of me wants to sit down with Josh and let it all out, but another part of me knows that Aunt Clare is right. I can't risk anything that might rip my family apart, even though Max's face now haunts me at every turn.

As each hour passes I feel this impending sense of loss, similar to when Mum died. In those final days I found myself willing the end to come to spare her the pain, but a part of me also didn't want to let her go. Saying that final goodbye was beyond painful; it leaves a scar on the heart that never heals. I fear the same when I tell Max I can't be there for him.

I am full of anger for the way fate has chosen to inflict this on us all, because nothing will be quite the same after it's over. I'm counting down the hours until Bella arrives on Wednesday and I can tell her what I know.

After that, the pain will come from not knowing what is happening, but the line will have been drawn. I can only hope it doesn't affect me to the extent that Josh decides to broach the subject and ask me outright what's been going on.

I feel awful wishing today away, precious hours during which we should all be relaxing together, because this is our quality time. We spend the morning having a late brunch and then head out for a family walk. It's a glorious day and being out in the fresh air helps to clear my head. When we get back the girls are tired and want to laze around. After a few board games Hettie disappears up to her bedroom to text Alex and Rosie follows shortly afterwards, enticed by the thought of Minecraft.

I head into the kitchen to make a cup of coffee and by the time I walk back into the sitting room, Josh has a film all ready to go.

'In the mood for a little romantic comedy?'

He looks up at me and my eyes go straight to his birthmark. That little kiss from an angel was the first thing I noticed about him, quickly followed by that tousled hair that won't be tamed. Even kept very short, it has a will of its own.

'Sounds good.'

We cosy up together and for the first time all weekend I finally begin to relax. Maybe I'm getting things out of perspective, and lending too much weight to my involvement with Max's situation. Every now and again Josh laughs at some silly line, or scene, but I keep switching off as the humour is lost on me. Two guys are sitting at a bar, chatting. And then it happens.

'She thinks I've been unfaithful,' one of them bemoans to the other. In the context of the film it's hilarious, as his other passion is a part-share in a thoroughbred horse. He promised he would quit gambling, but his prize investment is winning race after race, so everything has to be done in secret. She knows there's something up, but thinks it's another woman.

Josh bursts out laughing. It's supposed to be a comedic moment, as the horse standing behind the actor begins to nuzzle his ear.

'If you ever get tempted, you would tell me, wouldn't you?' Josh says, half-laughing.

I don't know if my own laugh is convincing enough. Josh is only joining in the general fun of the situation and doesn't appear to be monitoring my reaction. I sit there wondering if I told him what had happened he would think I had betrayed what we have. I can't deny the strong physical and mental attraction I feel towards Max. It's not in my makeup to be unfaithful and I could never do that to Josh, but in my head—

Can I be held responsible for where my dreams take me,

or when my thoughts run away from me in wild daydreams? What have I done? What am I doing?

I hardly sleep a wink all night and when the alarm goes off at five in the morning my hand instantly slides the switch across. Even so, it disturbs Josh, who has slept like a log.

'Good morning. I can't believe it's that time already.' He stretches, then rolls into me. 'Wouldn't it be nice if we could have another hour?'

Lying there cuddling, I don't want to think about the week ahead. It's going to be a tough one and I pray that by the time Josh is here again next weekend, it will all be over.

'Thank you for humouring me about the car. I know you were annoyed because our weekends are precious, so I won't push for a decision. But if I'm going to get through this separation I need to know my girls are all safe. Your car is holding up at the moment, but I'd feel a lot happier if you had something a bit newer.'

He's about to face a long drive and I can't leave him thinking he's made me feel cross.

'No, you're right. I was simply uncomfortable about spending the money, but it's probably a false economy. They were all reasonable, so I'll leave it up to you.'

He wraps his arm around me and squeezes.

'The sporty Suzuki, then?'

'The Suzuki, it is.'

'Great, I'll give them a call as soon as I'm in work. Thanks, Ellie. You have no idea how relieved that makes me feel. Another tick on my "to do" list.'

'You have a list for us?'

'I want to make my wife and my girls as happy as I can. I'm not quite there, yet, but I'm working on it.'

It is with great reluctance that I kiss Josh goodbye. Nothing has changed between us. I know that sounds almost unbelievable, given the circumstances. But what I feel for Max is nothing at all to do with my life. It isn't real, at all, it just feels real at times.

I shut the front door with a quiet click and walk into the kitchen to make coffee. Another hour and the girls will be filling the house with their noise and bustling. It's another Monday morning.

~

'Livvie, can I have a word?'

She looks up from her desk, glasses perched on her nose.

'No problem. I hate reading the small print in a contract.' She sits back and indicates for me to sit down opposite her. I'm conscious that I'm going to have to handle this delicately and even going over and over it in my head, there is a chance I will mess up.

'I think I underestimated how demanding this new regime at home was going to be. The weekend was lovely, but I was so tired and I knew I was letting the family down. They all want to do active stuff and I seemed to be lagging behind. I know I said I could do a little work from home, but I'm beginning to see that isn't as practical as I'd hoped. With dinner to make and homework to supervise, the evening flies by and I don't think late nights are an option.'

'At last! You haven't been yourself for a while there, lady, and something has to give. I want the old you back. I bet you have a solution.'

'Eve is very capable and seems keen to really establish her role here. I thought I could prepare the orders and she could take over responsibility from there. Placing the orders, progress-checking and making sure deliveries arrive on time. That includes unpacking and checking off the items against the invoices. It would free up a lot of my time for other things.'

Livvie chews on the end of the arm of her glasses, nodding appreciatively.

'What an excellent idea. That works out rather well, as it's something she can own from start to finish. I readily admit that I have so much work piling up here and there are things I know you would very quickly knock into shape. At the moment I'm being pulled in all directions. I also need to sit back and look at our manpower situation again, too. With work flooding in I'm not sure we have enough people to deliver on time and that's an overriding concern at the moment.'

'I have a few ideas for working smarter and not harder, Livvie. Throw whatever you want my way and leave it to me. If it gets too much, I'll shout.'

Busy is good. Once this week is over I'm going to need the distraction.

Chapter 26

It seemed like a normal Tuesday. Josh texted to say he'd arranged for us to pick up my new car on Saturday. The girls were delighted, feeling the old car was an embarrassment. My attitude is that it has four wheels and it gets us where we need to go, but Hettie was always scandalised that there is no USB port for her iPod. And it doesn't have a satnav, or DAB radio, or a good sound system.

I told them both about Bella, saying she was a friend visiting the UK and that she was going to be staying over on Wednesday night. I wasn't expecting her to arrive until late afternoon, or early evening, which was perfect. They were mildly curious and I chose not to mention that I was planning to be home on Thursday, so that Bella and I could talk without fear of being overheard.

When I'd mentioned it to Josh he was very relaxed about it, probably thinking it was some company for me. I didn't labour the point, but threw it into the conversation and then I changed the subject as quickly as I could.

Mornings are always a rush, but today we were already halfway to school when Rosie remembered she'd left a homework book in her bedroom. She suddenly had a little meltdown and I had no choice but to return to the house. Hettie wasn't impressed and kept muttering under her breath. We parted company under a cloud, neither of the girls in the mood to say a proper goodbye and I arrived at work late, hot and flustered.

Two cups of coffee later and I'm feeling much better. I do wonder how on earth teachers put up with a class full of teenagers. It must be hell at times. Shaking off the remnants of a bad start, the next couple of hours is very productive.

When the phone rings, I pick it up and say my usual introduction. But it's not a client on the other end of the line.

'Mrs Maddison, it's Sarah Grant, Hettie's head teacher. There's been a little incident at school, I'm afraid, and I need you to come in for a chat.'

Alarm bells start ringing.

'Of course. When?'

'Now. Ask at reception and someone will escort you to my room.'

The line clicks and it really does feel as if I've been summoned. What on earth has happened?

I let Livvie know about the call and say I'll ring her as soon as I know what's going on, and then I head off.

There's no point ringing Josh until I've spoken to Sarah

Grant. From her tone, whatever Hettie has done hasn't impressed her.

When I arrive at the school one of the admin staff walks me around to Miss Grant's office. After knocking on the door, we wait until a voice calls out, 'Come in.' She opens the door, but doesn't venture inside, indicating for me to enter. My heart begins to race a little.

I shake hands with Sarah.

'Please take a seat.' Sarah picks up the phone. 'Hettie's mother has arrived. Can you bring her down to my office please, Sylvia?'

My heart is now pounding in my chest and I really wish Josh was sitting next to me. We've never been summoned to see the head teacher before and, clearly, whatever this is it's serious.

After a couple of minutes' awkward silence, there's a knock on the door and Hettie walks in looking sheepish. Sarah doesn't tell her to take a seat, although there are two other unoccupied chairs. She then turns her attention to me.

'I'm afraid you've been called in because Hettie was involved in a fight, which took place in the school corridor about an hour ago. Three girls were involved in the incident and I've spoken to each of them to establish their side of the story. While it appears Hettie wasn't the one who started the fight, she was an active participant in it and has admitted as much. I have decided that in this instance all three girls will be suspended from school for two days. If I thought any bullying had taken place, then that would have been an even more serious matter. However, I'm satisfied that wasn't the case and will leave you to talk it through with Hettie.'

I gulp. Hettie won't look me in the eye. She just looks very pale, except for a horrible red mark on her cheek.

'We'll see you on Friday, Hettie. I trust that will be sufficient time for you to consider your part in the incident and realise that this sort of behaviour is not acceptable. Thank you for coming in, Mrs Maddison.'

Talk about being dismissed. Hettie has already opened the door and I'm only a second or two behind her. In tandem, we both let out a big sigh of relief as we hurry along the corridor in search of freedom.

'What on earth happened?' I ask in a semi-hushed tone. She turns her head to look at me and I see that her cheek is beginning to swell.

'This stupid girl hit me and I hit her back. It really wasn't my fault, Mum.'

'Well, that's a relief. Tell me all about it when we get home. Are you feeling alright? Not dizzy or anything?'

'No. I'm fine. One of the PE teachers is a first-aider and we were marched off to see her individually.'

Marched off?

~

'Josh, sorry to ring you at work, but there's been an incident with Hettie. She's fine, but by the time you FaceTime tonight she's going to be sporting a rather large and angry bruise on her cheek. I think it's best not to mention it, as I'll let her know I've spoken to you about it. But maybe at the weekend you need to sit down with her for a little father/daughter chat.'

'Are you saying it happened while she was at school?'

'Yes. She's been suspended for two days. I'll tell you all about it later. It's to do with Alex, but he wasn't involved in the incident.'

'She's not being bullied, is she? I mean, sometimes kids cover things up rather than confronting their issues head on.'

'Hettie wasn't just on the receiving end, Josh, she was actually fighting.'

'What on earth? That's the last thing I ever expected. I mean, Hettie. She's a moody teenager but she will grow out of that. But our Hettie, fighting. I can hardly believe it.'

'She's not denying it, Josh. But you need to let her tell you the story in her own words. I'm not saying I condone what happened, but when girls wind each other up over a boy it can get pretty heated. She realises now that she should have walked away and it's taught her a valuable lesson.'

'And she's okay, you say? Would it be better if I came home now?'

'She's fine. FaceTime later and unless she starts talking about it, wait until the weekend. She knows I'm doubly annoyed, because I'm losing an extra day's holiday. I'm off on Thursday, of course, because Bella is here, but it's such a waste of a whole day tomorrow, which could have been a family day. So I'm making her clean her bedroom and sort out her wardrobe as a punishment.'

Josh laughs and I picture his face, those little lines around his eyes all crinkled up.

'If you're sure there's nothing at all I can do to help, I'll leave you to it, then. I imagine it's not going to be the easiest couple of days. And I'm sorry you won't have some peace and quiet when Bella is there. Some lessons have to be learnt the hard way, I'm afraid, and hopefully Hettie will realise she isn't the only one affected by her behaviour. Good luck, Ellie, and stay strong. See you later, alligator.'

'In a while, crocodile.'

When the line disconnects I whisper, *I love you* into the phone, as if it's a portal between us and the echo of my words will still reach him. Like a comforting hug. It's guilt, Ellie, and Josh is right. Some lessons have to be learnt the hard way and I'm not thinking about Hettie, but the lessons I need to learn. I go to check on her progress, feeling dejected.

'How is it going? Do you need more black sacks?'

The reply is muted, 'No, Mum, I'm good for now.'

I have about an hour before Dawn drops Rosie back home. I didn't want to upset the usual routine and I also don't intend having the detail of this sorry incident discussed in front of Rosie. I pop up to the study, disconnecting from today's unsettling episode and open up my inbox. This is the hardest email I've ever had to write. I would rather talk to Max over the phone, but I know if I do I will weaken.

Good afternoon, Max

I wanted to let you know that there's been a reorganisation in the office. I'm not sure if you've spoken to Eve before, but she's taking over part of my workload. I've been drafted in to help out Livvie, as things are really hectic at the moment.

Eve will be your point of contact from now on and she'll be in touch on a regular basis to place orders and check on progress of deliveries etc.

If we can't work harder, we have to work smarter and I suppose that's the nature of the business we are in. I've always found it difficult to delegate, but I know you will be in safe hands.

I also wanted to share the news that we have another large, one-off project just about to go into design. I'll be

*helping out on that, so there will be a big order coming
your way in the next couple of weeks.*

*Anyway, take care of yourself and send everyone my
best regards,*

Ellie

Max will understand what I have chosen not to say. Things
that simply cannot be said in an email and I couldn't bear
to see staring back at me in stark black and white. I always
sign off with 'until we speak again', but this time I'm really
saying goodbye. I wish my heart didn't feel so heavy, or that
I'm abandoning him. Bella will be shocked, I know that, and
I'm going to have to be strong. I have to do the right thing
for Josh and the girls, even if it's the wrong thing for Max.

As soon as the girls retire for the night I jump online.
Livvie rang earlier to say there was no way she would count
this as holiday leave, as it's a domestic emergency. She was
very supportive about the whole thing and rather surprised
when I told her what had happened. I fully intend to make
up for as much of the lost time as I can. How I'm going
to manage with Hettie here on Thursday, when I'd planned
to have the whole day alone with Bella, I don't know.

Opening my work inbox I clear as many things as I can
and make a few notes. I'll ring Eve tomorrow to check the
schedules and then I'll be able to respond to a few
outstanding queries.

I begin sifting through some of the cuttings in my ideas file in preparation for the mood boards, for what Livvie is calling the twenty-first-century Manor House. Celebrity chef, Richard Dale, has a vibrant personality and he isn't going to be easy to impress. Livvie will want to throw a lot of very different ideas at him during the first meeting. It should help us to quickly identify what he does, and doesn't, want so we can plough forward.

Suddenly, the iPad sitting next to my PC lights up and the tinkle of broken glass confirms that someone is FaceTiming me. I glance across and see it's Max. I ignore it. Sitting there I squeeze my eyes shut as my heart thuds in my chest. Please don't do this to me, Max. Please. It's hard enough to stop dead like this, but it will be impossible if you won't let go.

He tries three times. Then the message box opens.

I'm sorry and I want you to know I understand.

I stare at the words with sorrow in my heart, then cradle my head in my hands. When I look up there's another message.

I know you're there, Ellie. I can feel it. I'm sorry that I dragged you into my problems. You were kind enough to listen and I took advantage of that because I have no one else to turn to; suddenly you were there, like an answer to a prayer. But I did listen. And I will try, because I never want to hurt you in any way.

This time a few minutes elapse before my determination evaporates into thin air. I swing the keyboard across in front of me and begin typing.

The email did what I needed it to do, but it didn't reflect what I really wanted to say. I knew that you would be able to read between the lines. I can't do this because it's ripping me apart. Something that happened to my daughter today made me realise that if my attention wanders for even a moment, the ones I love will suffer. That doesn't mean I don't care, because I do. You will always be in my thoughts.

My finger hovers over the return key for a moment and then click, it's gone. In mere seconds it will appear on Max's screen. He will be sitting alone somewhere, probably on the terrace with the gloom gathering around him. Feeling isolated and helpless. For such a vibrant and strong-willed man, that's a devastating situation to handle.

I reluctantly slip the iPad into the top drawer. Tomorrow Bella will be here and I'll share whatever I can in the hope that she can help Max in some way.

Why? Why me? Why Max? I know that tonight a part of me will, once more, visit the terrace in my dreams. I'll hear the incessant chirping of the tree crickets and breathe in the warm air that carries the sweet scent of the oleanders. Max will be sitting opposite me and I will make my peace with him.

Chapter 27

Dawn offers to take Rosie to school and as soon as they leave I set Hettie to work again. I tell her I want the mountain of clothes she has sorted out for the charity shop neatly folded and put into recycling bags ready to go. Today she's going to clean her own bedroom window for the very first time and I can see her visibly sag at the prospect.

'I expect this room to sparkle,' I add, as I close her bedroom door behind me.

Walking into the study I know it's going to be a long day. I'll stop to make lunch for us both and at the same time I'll put a casserole in the slow cooker, so at least dinner tonight will be easy. I know Hettie will no doubt tire after an hour or two and probably watch a DVD. But she didn't start the fight and, from what I gather, it wasn't until she was punched in the face that she threw a punch back. We've had the talk and she'll have it again at the weekend with her dad, so I think from here on in I can ease up a little and let her do battle with her conscience.

I have a mountain of work to get through before Bella arrives. And then I need to sit down and think about what I'm going to tell her. When she tells me what she's found, unless it's really significant, or some sort of proof of his innocence, then what Max has told me has to be treated in confidence. I can only breach that for the right reason and it has to be something that will help Max in the long run. It's a judgement call, but one that comes with nothing but good intentions out of my respect for him. However, Aunt Clare's words of warning still ring in my ears.

And last night, in my dreams? Italy did not disappoint. The stars seemed to wrap themselves around the night like a blanket and Max was there, smiling. Telling myself it's a big mistake, I pull the iPad from the drawer and open it up.

There is a new message from Max, sent several hours ago.

You were in my dreams and we were on the terrace. There were a million stars above us and I realised how insignificant this life probably is in terms of our existence. One thing of which I am sure is that you will always be in my dreams.

I reel with shock. Is it possible for two people, so far apart, to share the same dream? I Google it, wondering if it's a question many people ask. Of course it is; an endless number of pages come up. One of the short descriptions seems to leap off the page.

It has been known for twins, for example, to share common dreams. Often occurring at the same time.

My eyes eagerly move down the entries, looking for anything linked to research, real evidence to support the theory. One such paper talks about people who have learnt to control their dreams by maintaining a degree of awareness throughout. It says it is possible for people to share the same dream, where two parties have a link and goes on to talk about psychic awareness and telepathy. Is that the link I feel with Max that threatens to overwhelm me? Or is this to do with the twin I never knew existed? The only thing I know for sure is that, whatever the reason, I'm the one who has to deal with it.

I long to talk to Max about it, but the line has already been drawn. What happens in my sleep isn't something I feel I can consciously control, or maybe Italy has become my guilty pleasure.

I close the iPad and place it back in the drawer.

~

'Your girls are amazing, Ellie. And Josh is such a sweetheart. It was lovely to meet him, even if it was virtually. I hope some day I'll have a family around me who don't drive me crazy,' Bella says.

'They always drive me crazy, but they were on their best behaviour this evening. Hettie is still very quiet and feeling guilty about being suspended. Rosie is always bubbly; at thirteen they are fun to have around as they want to share everything with you. They simply have a million questions, for which you are expected to have instant answers. On the other hand, getting anything out of Hettie is particularly hard work these days. But our pre-dinner family chats via FaceTime actually bring us all together, which is really special.'

Bella chuckles.

'You should meet my mother. She's either criticising or complaining. The moment I walked through the door the hot topic was why I haven't found a man yet. To which the answer was, of course, that I'm not ready. It wasn't what she wanted to hear.'

I look at her, noticing a hint of something in her face.

'Come on, you can tell me.'

'Well ... Piero and I have grown very close. Eduardo and his wife, Cristina, are thrilled. My mother would be appalled for all of the wrong reasons.'

'Oh, Bella, that's wonderful news. Is that why Max pushed to get the land, so they could extend the workshop and build Piero a bungalow?'

Her face breaks out into a beaming smile.

'Yes. When he found out, quite by accident, he didn't say anything at all, but within a couple of days he had everything sorted.'

'What will you do about your mother?'

Bella nestles back into the cushions, stretching her legs out along the sofa.

'We'll get married first and then I'll break the news over the phone. At some point Piero and I will fly over for a visit so my family can meet him. I'm teaching him English as he wants to impress my father. I've tried to warn him about my mother, but I'm not sure he understands. At least he'll get one tick, as he's Italian. Piero is a hard worker and between us we'll be able to manage once the bungalow is finished. Max insists we have the ceremony on the terrace at the villa and the Ormannis have offered to lay on a wedding banquet. We can't believe it, it's like a dream. I wish you could be there.'

I sigh, because a part of me wishes that, too.

'I'm stuck behind a desk now and it's where I'm at my best. Livvie is an experienced traveller and takes it all in her stride. For me, family always has to come first.'

Hettie traipses through in her PJs to grab a bottle of water from the fridge. I glance at the clock and see that it's gone nine.

'Are you settling down now? I think Rosie is asleep.'

'Yes, I'm tired. Goodnight Bella, 'night Mum.' She leans over me to give me a kiss on the cheek. I don't always get one nowadays; sometimes it's a passing hug that lasts for mere seconds, other times I get a high five.

As she disappears upstairs I turn to look at Bella. 'Don't be fooled. It isn't usually as quiet as this. Rosie has been on a field trip and all that fresh air seems to have zapped her energy. And Hettie, therefore, has no one to argue with.'

I'm impatient to find out what Bella has discovered and am tempted to start talking about Max. But one look at her face tells me she's ready to drop into bed.

'Come on, let's get you settled for the night. I'll grab a bottle of water and then I'll show you to your room. It's tiny, I'm afraid, but the bed is comfortable,' I laugh. 'Welcome to hotel Maddison. Actually, that sounds rather posh.'

'And it's wonderful of you to invite me here, Ellie. In the morning, when I'm refreshed, I have quite a lot to tell you. I think you'll be shocked.'

As I give Bella a goodnight hug, my head begins to buzz. What could Bella possibly have found that made her sound so upbeat and excited? It's going to be a long night and, for once, I hope it's a dreamless sleep, because I feel tomorrow's conversation might shake everything up.

Chapter 28

I awake refreshed, no memory whatsoever of having had a dream. Maybe, by cutting myself off from Max, the disconnect has already begun. With no moments of flashback to contend with, we breeze through breakfast and I head out to drop Rosie off at school. I leave Hettie and Bella at the breakfast table, chattering away about funny things they've seen on YouTube.

When I return, Bella is in the bathroom and Hettie is already dressed.

'What do you want me to do today, Mum?' She asks, waiting to hear what mundane task I have in store for her.

'As you did such a good job with your bedroom, I thought today you could tackle the black hole.'

She looks at me as if I'm joking.

'But that's not my mess. It's everyone's mess. I mean, all those games in there and probably a few spiders too.'

I give her a look that makes her hang her head. 'Okay, Mum.'

'You know which games we play regularly and which ones we haven't touched for years. Some of them you girls have now outgrown. The cupboard needs to be emptied out in neat piles in the hallway and vacuumed. If you sort out a pile of things you think can go to the charity shop, we'll go through it together, later today. Bella and I are going to be up in the study for a bit, talking about work.'

'But what about all the other stuff?'

'Hettie, I have no idea what's in that cupboard and I haven't seen the back of it for years. Try using your common sense. If it's something useful, it stays. Wellington boots definitely stay, but if there are a ton of recycle bags we don't use, those should be … recycled. You'll figure it out.'

There are a few snorting noises as I leave her to it and climb the stairs to the study. Bella is standing on the landing, trying not to laugh. I put up a finger to my mouth and point in the direction of the study. Once inside I close the door and we both burst out laughing.

'The black hole?'

I nod. 'It gobbles everything. Seriously, I can't remember the last time it was emptied out. Goodness knows what she's going to find, but it will keep her busy.'

. 'It's not easy having kids, is it?' Bella muses, a frown settling on her forehead.

'No. It changes everything and your life is never, ever the same again. But in the best way.'

I move a second chair across in front of the desk and we sit down.

'Did you manage to talk to Max about Trista?' Bella enquires.

This is the point of no return. I wasn't going to say anything to begin with, but Bella's face tells me this is big and we have to begin somewhere.

'Yes. We spoke on the phone and it turned into a rather lengthy chat. There wasn't anything out of the ordinary, only that Trista had begged him to stay and continued to hold out hope that Aletta would return some day. I thought that was rather odd as time went on, but he did it out of respect for her. Maybe hope is all she has left.'

I'm not sure if Bella is expecting more, but I want to hear what she has to say before I share anything further.

'That's something, then. I wanted you to focus on Trista, as when you hear what I have to say your opinion will help determine what I do next. I've always been very protective of Trista in the past. You know, the sadly dignified, grieving widow who lost her daughter. Everyone wondered if Stefano would have rallied and even recovered if it wasn't for Aletta's disappearance. The double tragedy seemed too much to bear for anyone and she's always had this air of fragility. But do you know something? I'm beginning to think she's more of an ice queen. So far removed from her emotions that to her, few of us represent a relationship. We are merely here to serve a purpose. If that purpose changes and we are no longer useful to her, she casts people off.'

I do a double-take, rather shocked at Bella's attitude.

'What on earth makes you say that? I mean, I admit my initial opinion of her has changed. But I know Max is still fiercely protective of her. None of this can be construed as her fault and now she's the head of the family. It's a lot for one woman to bear.'

'Ha! See? No one ever really questioned Trista about it because it was all "poor lady, how sad her husband is so unwell. It's all so unfair". People treat her as this fragile, lonely woman, but what if she's just aloof and uncaring by nature?'

'I think maybe you are being a little harsh, there, Bella. Unless there's any real evidence to confirm your suspicions, then it's nothing more than a theory. You could be very, very wrong about her.'

'Just hear me out. After you left, Max became very withdrawn. Oh, he continues to run everything as efficiently as usual, but in quiet moments the despair he's feeling is tangible. It was Trista's reaction that astounded me. I assumed she'd rally round him but, on the contrary, it seemed to unsettle her. I noticed it because I'd begun to watch her and monitor her reaction to things. She goes on and on about family, but to her they are little more than servants. And, what's more, they seem to know that and accept the situation without question. She's never kind to anyone; she simply tells them what she wants them to do. Did you ever notice that?'

Something stirs in the pit of my stomach and I'm pretty sure it's unease.

'Yes. The only person she seemed to fuss over was Max.' Bella nods in agreement.

'At first, I wondered if there was something going on between them.' She looks me firmly in the eye and my brow lifts, my eyes showing the surprise I feel.

'What do you mean, at first?'

Her face begins to colour. 'Having grown close to the Camilluccis, I'm aware there is a lot of support for Max. What wasn't so apparent is that there are still a handful of people who feel justice hasn't been served and they're pushing to have the case reopened. People who feel Max must be responsible for Aletta's disappearance and as the Ormannis' business interests grow, it serves only to strengthen his motive.'

'But he stands to gain nothing, other than the income he earns. Max told me that Gianni will inherit everything when Trista dies. And it's funny you should begin by looking at Trista, because I was uneasy around her. There was something not quite right about her reaction to what had happened. I mean, Aletta is her only daughter and yet, with the mystery still unsolved, she treats Max better than if he's her son. Wouldn't a mother harbour a tiny seed of doubt about him, until the truth is known?'

Bella gives a satisfying grin.

'Exactly my point. But it wasn't obvious until I watched her reaction to Max's recent descent into what I think is a form of depression. It's clear to me now that there is no romantic association between them, even though for a while I feared that might be the case. He's so overly protective of her and the age difference isn't that great. He's what, early forties and she's not yet fifty, having has Aletta in her early twenties.

'Anyway, as Max's emotional well-being plummeted, everyone was worried about him, except Trista, who seemed to be increasingly irritated by it. To the extent that she moved her desk out of the office they share in the villa and into her private sitting room. She said the reason was that it was more convenient, and no one questions Trista's actions.'

This seems to mirror my appraisal of Trista, but there isn't anything Bella has said that changes anything.

'Eduardo and his family weren't able to add anything to the story?' I wondered if there was hope from that direction.

'No, not really. But Eduardo and a group of the cooperative members rallied together and pressed upon me that there must be something that was overlooked at the time.'

'You're investigating it for them?'

She looks smug.

'I'm the insider. But you said that Max had no motive because he has nothing to gain from Aletta's disappearance. Shortly after Stefano died, Trista had her will drawn up. The Testamento Pubblico is drafted by an Italian notary and in the case of a formal will, which is then lodged with the notary, the process requires it to be read out in front of the witnesses.'

Bella looks at me and nods. 'Yes, the notary brought someone with him and Trista called me into her room to act as the second witness. After the reading, Trista then had to confirm her agreement to the content, and we witnessed her signature. At the time most of it went over my head, because all I could think about was the loss of Stefano and wondering when Aletta would return.

'Having done a little research, I now realise that Trista could simply have hand-written her will. But there is always the chance it could get lost, or be disregarded in favour of the Italian intestacy laws, which follow the blood lines. Obviously the fact that she sorted this so quickly, bearing in mind this was very shortly after the funeral, was a clear indication of how important it was to her. What was particularly shocking was that the police were still talking to Max about Aletta. Max will get everything and if he dies leaving surviving children, then they will inherit the estate.

If not, then it all goes to Trista's parents, or her siblings, should they not have survived. Not only was Aletta cut out of the will, but so were the Ormanni family.'

I inhale deeply, realising that at the time it was much too soon for Trista to give up on the chance of Aletta returning. Particularly as she herself had asked Max to promise he wouldn't do the exact same thing. How would the wider Ormanni family react if they knew about the will? And why would Trista have done this and not informed Max of her decision?

'You didn't tell anyone about this, did you?'

'Gracious, no. Trista took me aside and told me that what I had heard was in strictest confidence. To be honest, I thought she was simply panicking and ensuring that whatever happened, Max would be there to keep things running. I mean, there's no one else capable of managing the business and that situation hasn't changed. But if Gianni knew – I mean, the Ormanni family have become the workforce with no line of inheritance. It's shocking in more ways than one.'

We stare at each other, trying to make some sense out of it.

'And Max really has no idea?' I double-check.

'As far as I know, no he doesn't, but if this was to become common knowledge it looks bad for him, doesn't it?'

Bella reaches down and zips open the handbag lying at

her feet. She extracts a folded piece of paper, handing it to me.

As I open it I can see it's a photocopy of an actual photograph of a woman holding a newborn baby and shows both the front and rear of the hard copy.

'This is Aletta, although she looks very different from the photo I saw of her in Trista's bedroom. Whose baby is it?'

Bella frowns and our eye contact lingers for a couple of moments.

'I don't know, but look at the date stamp on the back. It was taken seven months after her disappearance.'

Chapter 29

It's a lot to take in and Bella and I go down to the kitchen for a break from the tension, as suddenly I'm in need of a really strong cup of coffee.

'It's a lot to process, isn't it?' Bella leans back against the worktop counter, watching me as I grab two mugs and spoon in the granules.

'How did you come across the photo and why haven't you taken it to the police? Or, even, talked to Max about this? If this isn't a hoax, then surely this proves that Aletta is still alive.'

Bella breathes out, her chest slumping as she expels the last of a long breath. I can see that this is something she's been over and over in her own head many times already.

'The only person I've confided in, aside from you, is Piero. And he will tell no one. When Trista made a fuss about moving her desk into her sitting room, it was left to Gianni and me to organise it. A couple of guys brought the desk up to the room. She wanted it by the window and,

268

if you remember, there was an ornate wooden table standing there with a collection of framed photos. I cleared them off, they took the table away and put the desk in situ. I was left on my own to polish the desk top and arrange the photos.

'Eduardo's increasing concern about the situation and what he had told me about some people still suspecting Max was very much in the forefront of my mind. I knew it was probably my only chance to have a good look around. Trista was out, Max was at the refinery and I was unlikely to be disturbed. I went through the drawers and there didn't seem to be anything related to Aletta. So I began polishing the silver frames and setting the pictures back up. When I picked up Aletta's photo I stared at it for a while, as if her face would give me some sort of clue. I mean, I was there with Max and Trista to wave her off as the taxi pulled away the day she left for London. It was like all of her other trips and there was nothing to indicate otherwise. But I was still in detective mode and I asked myself where I would hide something I didn't want to be seen. It was a long shot, but I unclipped the back of the frame. And that's where the photo was hidden. Trista has had this for quite a long time and she chose to keep it a secret from everyone, including the police. I'm not sure that's a crime, exactly, but morally it's definitely wrong.'

I put my finger up to my lips, remembering that Hettie

is working only a few feet away. I grab a carton of apple juice, a small chocolate bar and a banana from the fruit basket.

'I'll be back.'

Hettie is on her knees, surrounded on one side by a pile of boxes and on the other side by a mountain of shoes.

'Is it possible to have only one Wellington boot?' She moans. Her eyes light up when she notices the snacks.

'You are doing a good job there, Hettie. Take a break, but don't forget you have a job to finish.'

'Aww, thanks Mum. You are a star.'

Going back into the kitchen I shut the door firmly behind me.

'Bella, before you go any further, I need to tell you something. None of my family knows anything about this situation or Max. Yesterday I sent him an email letting him know that in future our new lady, Eve, will be his contact. I feel I've become too close to this and I'm not completely sure Josh would understand or approve. My family have to be my first priority, even though my heart aches for what Max is going through.'

She looks disappointed, clearly sad to hear this.

'Max feels something for you, Ellie. I know that's wrong and meeting Josh and the girls makes that even more apparent. If you didn't have anyone, I mean, if—'

'But I do, Bella. I already have my soul mate and nothing

can change that. I want to help you, and I'm here to listen, or do whatever I can. But you can't tell Max about my involvement, as I've made it very clear there can be no more contact between us.'

I immediately wonder if she'll read something into what I've just said, thinking it implies something other than what it really is. I listened to Max, yes, and sympathised with him, but that's as far as it went. Other than a sense of connection that was only in my head and is still in my dreams, but isn't real. There's no point in going into detail and I can only hope she understands.

'This is my parting gift to Max, as a friend. So if you haven't taken the photo to the police, what's your next step?' I'm leaving her in no doubt whatsoever about where my first loyalty will always lie.

She wriggles around in her chair, outstretched hand cupping the hot mug of coffee.

'Piero and I agreed that I should run this past you first. I don't really want anyone to know I found the photo. I love my job and any further scandal could jeopardise everything. I fully understand your concerns, Ellie, but I desperately need your help. This isn't solely about Max and Trista, but the whole family, and everyone connected to it.'

'So what's the alternative?'

'I want to find Aletta. I'm convinced she's living in the UK. We know from the photo that she's changed her hair colour and style. What we don't know for sure is whose baby she's holding. I've managed to get the address of the hotel Aletta stayed at in London, from the invoice files in the office, and I thought I'd start there. I know it's been almost two and a half years, but I have the photo to jog people's memories. Do you think I'm doing the right thing?'

I sit back and mull it over, considering the options. Renewed police interest is something I don't think Max could handle at the moment. What further damage might ensue as a result, I can't even begin to imagine. Trista, well, whatever sympathy I had for her is rapidly being replaced by anger and disbelief at her lack of action.

'I think you are doing exactly what I would do in your situation. However, I'm not sure about the likelihood of being able to find anyone who will remember her after all this time. Staff turnover in the hotel trade is notoriously high. It might mean you'll struggle to find someone whose employment with the hotel stretches back that far. But it's a start. What can I do?'

Bella looks relieved. I hadn't appreciated what those on the edge of this have to lose just from the association of a new scandal breaking out if the case is reopened. Or if Max was suddenly arrested, what would happen then? I know in my heart he has nothing at all to do with this, but everything revolves around proof.

'This is just me thinking outside the box. Although you

didn't meet Aletta, I think you heard enough to gauge what type of person she was and the lifestyle she wanted. I'm assuming Max probably told you a little bit about her too. She was a party animal, very into fashion and very out there on social media. If she wanted to disappear and start over again without the obligations of family duty, I seriously doubt she'd be happy with an ordinary lifestyle. Oh, and I have this. I talked to one of her best friends and made a few notes. It's a list of people Aletta knew and places they'd visited when they all went on shopping sprees together, in London and Paris. She's high maintenance and always will be. Someone will have to have funded her new life.'

'Thanks, Bella. I'll trawl through this and see if there's anything I can add. Then I'll start looking online. It must be hard for anyone to completely disappear, even if they change their name. And you are right. Aletta doesn't sound like the type of person who would settle for a simple exist-ence. I have the entire rest of the day, but tomorrow I'm back in work. This might take a while, though. How long before you fly back?'

'I have a full week and I can only hope it gives me enough time. Let's see if we can do what the police couldn't.'

Bella high-fives me.

I tell myself that this is a little harmless research to help Bella in her quest. It's no longer about Max, as such, so what's the harm?

'Right, I'll pack up my things and head off to London. It might be a day or two before you hear back from me, Ellie. If you find anything you think might help, text me and I'll call you as soon as I can.'

~

I make a start, only stopping briefly to make some lunch and heading back to the study with a plate of sandwiches. Hettie feigns exhaustion and I let her watch a film on the condition that she finishes sorting the cupboard by dinner time.

I've added a few items to the list of bullet points Bella gave me. As it appears that Aletta was very into the selfie culture, I wonder if she would have been able to curb that, or maybe set up an account under an alias? With a totally new look, and country, was it enough to keep her true identity safe? Might she be on Facebook now under her new name? Would she attend fashion shows? Would she have a job? Even if she was being very careful and not in character, it's hard to avoid being photographed when you are out in public places. With people constantly taking photos, posting on YouTube and blogs, it's a long-shot but worth thinking about. It's a case of knowing where to look, but my main problem is that I don't really know where to start.

As I read and re-read the list Bella gave me, I decide to Google her name as a starting point. As with most people who have a social media platform, there's page after page, after page. None of it is recent, obviously. I click on the links to the usual accounts, Twitter, Facebook, Instagram, but nothing has been posted to any of the accounts since the day she flew to London. I trawl through for a while, adding another couple of items to the list.

Sitting back in my chair I look out of the window, noticing that it's actually a beautiful day. I wonder how Max is doing. Then an idea pops into my head. Let's assume the baby is Aletta's. Crazy, I know. She could be a nanny, although it's hard to see her slotting into that sort of role, but when you want to disappear I suppose anything is possible.

I draw a straight line on a piece of A4. I don't know the exact date Aletta disappeared, but I remember Max mentioning two years and three months. And maybe a few days or a week, or something. Okay, that was about two months ago. So that's around the end of April of that year. I write April at the start of the line and then divide the line into twelve equal sections, filling in the rest of the months. I can't remember the time stamp on that photo Bella had, but she said seven months after the disappearance. I put an asterisk against November. No one knew Aletta was pregnant, but if it was true, this could all be making a lot of sense. She wasn't happy with Max and she'd already made it clear to him, in confidence, that she thought her future lay elsewhere. Paris and London had the cosmopolitan vibe she was after and she might have been seeing another man for months before she plucked up the courage to leave.

I also mark the date of Stefano's death, which was about two months after Aletta's disappearance, so that would be May/June. Looking at the info Bella gleaned from Aletta's friend, I know from her birth date that she is now twenty-nine. So what does this give me? She isn't the sort of person who would sink into the background and be satisfied with life in a quiet suburb. I'm sure of that. So we are talking London, or a big city. What I need is someone who can trawl through records and I know just the person.

'Hi Michelle, it's been a while. How is everyone?'

My cousin Michelle lives in Southampton and we usually catch up a couple of times a year. As with a lot of families these days, we tend to only meet up with the more distant relatives when there is a christening, a wedding or a funeral. Michelle is one for detail and twenty minutes later I think I'm up to date on what everyone has been doing.

'I'm actually ringing to ask you a favour. Are you still into genealogy and all of that stuff?'

'Yes. I've done research now for quite a few friends. It's only a hobby, but it's fascinating. You won't believe what it throws up. Illegitimate babies, marriages and secret divorces – and we think we have big scandals today. Nothing is new, Ellie, they just swept it under the carpet and didn't talk about it.'

I feel a twinge of excitement.

'How would you feel about doing a little research work to help out a third party? I instantly thought of you as it's beyond my capabilities. We need to trace someone's daughter. It's all very confidential and rather sensitive. It's a client, actually, so this is literally for their eyes only. I'm happy to pay for your time.'

'Ooh, a real-life mystery, count me in. Of course I don't need paying. I already have a subscription to some of the larger databases and other sources I use are free. I love a challenge. Now you're going to tell me you don't have much to go on, right?'

I smile to myself. 'Right. I have a few dates and things, and a general location. I'll email you everything I have: full description of Aletta Ormanni, age, approximate dates I think she might have given birth to a baby, although the sex is unknown. She's Italian by birth, but may have changed her name shortly after she arrived in the UK. She wanted to disappear, but she's a lady who wouldn't simply fade into the background. I'm convinced she'd still have quite a high-profile life. And I can't stress enough that this has to be treated as very confidential. Not only would I lose my job, but the case of her disappearance has never been solved. The police still have her listed as a missing person.'

'I feel like Sherlock Holmes. Of course I'll handle this sensitively. Thank you for thinking of me. Send it over and I'll start work. I will warn you that it's a case of trawling through a lot of records and finding something, only to discover it's a false lead. Then back-tracking and going off in another direction, or widening the area of the search. But that's what I love doing and I'll do my best.'

I pull the email together and press send, feeling it was the right decision to make. I wouldn't know where to start and Michelle is virtually an expert. I'll continue to pursue other avenues, but it will be sheer luck if I stumble across anything. Before I quit for the day, I watch several YouTube videos of recent London fashion shows. Trawling the footage for a glimpse of the audience in the background, I hold onto a mental picture of the new Aletta. I wonder if, as time has gone on, she's settled into a false sense of security. I'm sure that at first she must have been in an almost constant state of paranoia. The fear of discovery in those early days must have been hard to ignore. But you can't live your life looking over your shoulder every minute of the day.

Finding nothing at all, and conscious that it really is time to stop, I reluctantly close down the PC. Dawn will be dropping Rosie off after her gymnastics class very soon.

The iPad is still in the drawer and although it's calling to me, I turn and walk out of the room. I'm helping you in the only way I can, now, Max. I pray we can free you of this burden.

Chapter 30

With Josh due home early evening and both Hettie and Rosie at school, it's back to work for me.

Livvie and I are now working more as a team, as Eve takes away a lot of the repetitive admin side of my job. Some of the design ideas I put together while I was at home pique Livvie's interest and we spend the day developing them.

'You seem a bit more like your old self, today. If the job ever gets you down, you only have to say, Ellie. If it stops being fun then we know we're heading for a disaster.'

'This never is going to be just a job to me, Livvie. You listen to my ideas and put your faith in me, which is good for the morale. It has added a little something extra to my life, a sense of rising to a challenge, I suppose.'

My words are received with a short, sharp laugh.

'I think having kids is the real challenge. I admire the way you manage to juggle everything. There can't be much time left for you, Ellie. Now that would drive me mad as I need my space to relax and get away from people.'

I suppose she's right in one way. What would I do with lots of time on my hands and how would I fill it?

'I have all the time I need, really.' If I want to get away I always have my dreams.

'Have you let Max know a big order is coming his way very shortly?'

'Yes, but I've also told him that Eve is the contact from here on in. It makes a lot of sense and you really do need a lot more support, Livvie.'

She agrees, surveying the large, if incredibly neatly stacked, project folders.

'Ellie, it didn't cause you any problems going to Italy, did it? I mean between you and Josh?'

I freeze. Livvie doesn't usually notice anything if it's not business-related. I swallow hard.

'No, not at all. He just gets lonely when I'm not around. Men, eh?'

She smiles and her mind moves off onto something else. I think I drew that line at precisely the right time. As far as anyone is concerned now, all ties are cut. Bella won't tell anyone what we're doing and, hopefully, we'll know before too long whether all of this research is going to lead anywhere.

~

The weekend flies by. On Saturday we pick up my new car and I wave a tearful goodbye to the old one. There are a lot of memories attached to it. The girls can't understand my sentimentality, too excited to have something much newer in which to be driven around.

Aside from Friday night, when we did laze around, we didn't stop the entire time. We took the girls swimming, had two meals out and visited a car boot sale. Oh, and on Saturday night Rosie's best friend came for a sleepover.

Josh was very relaxed the whole time, except for when he went up to Hettie's room for the talk. I made her tell him the whole thing, because he needed to hear it first-hand and in her own words. Alex, Rosie's boyfriend, had nothing to do with it. It was simply two girls winding Hettie up by suggesting Alex was going out with someone else. One of the two girls admitted that in front of the headteacher, Hettie had confirmed. When Hettie had told the girls she didn't believe it, that's when the punch came her way. I think they were hoping to put doubt in her mind, and that Hettie would storm off and have a row with Alex. But she stuck with what she believed to be the truth and I was quite proud of her for that. There are times in life when you have to go with your gut instinct. Unfortunately, though, she retaliated in the same manner and then all hell broke loose.

It's Sunday night and Josh and I lie side by side in bed, aimlessly chatting about nothing in particular.

'It's working, this new arrangement, isn't it?'

He sounds positive and accepting. It can't be easy for him and he must get lonely and miss the general hubbub of family life.

'It is and it's another mountain we've successfully climbed. The thing with Hettie served to confirm that you never really know what's around the corner, do you? Life is full of surprises.'

He snuggles closer as his hands start exploring my body in a familiar yet still exciting way.

'That's why we have to live in the moment, Ellie,' he whispers into my ear, before moving his mouth softly across my cheek. As we kiss passionately, all of my worries melt away.

~

Eduardo and his wife, Cristina, are showing Max around Piero's little bungalow and I'm trailing around behind them. The pride in their eyes makes me well up. Next they escort us back to the compound to look at the new extension to the workshop.

'This is incredible. What a superb job you've done here and now you have room for Piero's masterpieces.'

Max translates and Educardo and his wife bow their heads, smiling.

As Max escorts me back to the car I look down at my feet. Am I really here?

'Is this real, Max?' I ask, the lightness of my body making me feel that something isn't quite right.

He nods, closing the door, but the next moment we seem to be walking through one of the olive groves. Max stops every few paces to inspect the ripening fruit.

'Lean forward and smell this, the fruit is almost ready.'

Taking a slow breath in, the slightly bitter, pungent smell that has a fruity quality to it, is very real. I reach out to Max and he takes my hand, holding it in his. The feel of his skin, the warmth of his body and the smell of his cologne fill my senses. He pulls me close and I let myself relax into him. This isn't an alien feeling; my body knows his in an intimate way.

Then as solid as the picture around me is, it suddenly begins to dissipate. Two hands touching begin to fade away until once more the image inside my head is simply one of darkness, and a deep sleep.

~

I open my eyes and an amazing feeling of complete and utter well-being washes over me. The aftermath of a peaceful night's sleep sends a warm rush of energy around my body, the endorphins acting as a happy drug. It gently and pleasantly kicks my senses into touch. Even though I'm still sleepy, the enticing warmth of the sunlight filtering in through the open window promises a bright new day ahead and I feel energised.

Without warning, my lazy thoughts are suddenly replaced by an unwelcome, and rather frightening, wave of rising panic. I'm not sure where I am. My heart begins to pound and my chest tightens; my breathing becomes rapid and shallow as I fight to take in air. I try to ignore the stifling wave of fear that threatens to overwhelm me and focus on regaining control. Stay calm, Ellie, stay calm.

Then reality comes flooding back in a rush. My first thought is what time is it? The second is where is Josh? I look at his pillow and there's a note pinned to it.

My darling, the alarm didn't wake you and I didn't have the heart to disturb your peaceful sleep. I kissed your cheek and you didn't even stir, so I hope when you wake up you will forgive me.

I'll text you when I arrive at work and speak to you this evening. Thank you for a wonderful weekend and some lovely memories.

See you later, alligator. xxx

Ah, my darling husband has reset the alarm for seven and it's almost a quarter to now. I snuggle up close to his pillow, where a trace of the smell of him still lingers. All thoughts of my dream have disappeared and I'm back in the present again, grateful for the blessings life has bestowed upon me.

Chapter 31

Driving to work my phone starts to ring and almost before I have a chance to think about it, the radio switches from a rock song to a ring tone. I press the button on the dash as Josh had shown me, and Bella's voice fills the car.

'Morning, Ellie. Are you good to talk?'

'Morning. I'm driving, but I now have the technology to talk on the phone too. It's all hands-free. I still miss the old car, though.'

'Nothing lasts forever. I didn't call over the weekend as I thought it might be awkward and it's your quality time with Josh. I might have a lead on Aletta. You were right about the hotel staff; most of the people in reception had been there less than a year. However, I passed this little old lady pushing a laundry trolley. Turns out she's the house-keeper and has been there as long as anyone can remember. She says it's nearly thirty years.

'She looked at the photo and it didn't seem to mean

anything at first, so I described Aletta. I said that at the time she might have been a little upset, or nervous; not behaving like the usual tourist, or visiting business woman. Mostly, I imagine, guests get up and have breakfast, then don't return to their rooms until late afternoon.

'Aletta may have spent most of her stay actually in the room and maybe, even, put up a *do not disturb* sign. I followed the housekeeper around the hotel, talking to her as she dropped off towels and toiletries ready for the maids who were working on each floor. Something I said did the trick, because eventually she took me to the actual room. She remembered Aletta, of that I was sure. It was, as you would expect, one of the most expensive rooms. I didn't give any background, just implied it was someone with whom I had lost touch. One thing that I immediately noticed when I entered was that there was an adjoining door to another room. I asked her if she could remember whether the door remained locked when Aletta was there. She shook her head without even having to think about it; it had never been locked, although the man in the adjoining room had had a different surname.'

'Wow. That's almost unbelievable. How could she remember his name?'

'It was David Lancing. He's an internationally known artist, who lives in London. And I was right, Aletta spent the entire time in her room. The man gave the housekeeper a big tip when he left, which might have accounted for her temporary amnesia. I checked with reception and they both signed out on the same day. The day Aletta was due to fly home. I thanked her, gave her a twenty-pound note, saying it would mean a lot to reconnect with my friend. If anyone asks about me, hopefully she'll remember the friend bit. Then I made my way out of there as quickly as I could. Not quite as big a tip as the one David Lancing gave her, I suspect, but she seemed pleased. I'm texting you a link to this guy's website. I haven't even had time to take a look myself.'

'This is big, Bella. I mean, I'm not sure what you are going to do next, but it's a real lead. Just to let you know that I haven't found anything online. All of her old social media haunts drew a blank; she stopped posting the day she arrived in London. But I have a cousin who is brilliant at investigating family trees. I gave her a little information and a timeline, stressing how sensitive this is and she's going to look at the birth and marriage records in and around London. What if the baby is Aletta's and this artist guy is the father?'

'Well, that would make sense with the connecting door. Maybe she'd been having an affair with this man for a long time, hence any excuse to fly off somewhere and use one of her vague *business trip* excuses. Getting pregnant changed everything for her.'

'Look, I'm about to arrive at work and I can't do anything

at all while I'm there. Can you ring me tonight, after eight o'clock?'

'Will do. Wouldn't it be wonderful if we could find her, Ellie? Max's nightmare would finally be over.'

'I know. Well done, Bella. I'm proud of you!'

Parking and walking into the offices I feel it's like a jigsaw puzzle. Without that photo this is an option that would never have cropped up. Why did Trista hide it? The only conclusion I can come to is that it was to make sure Max remained at the villa. If he'd known Aletta was cheating on him, then he might have simply walked away; the memories alone would have been hard to bear. Being able to think about her being alive for the first time since I heard the sorry tale, makes me feel lighter and brighter. If I feel this way, then how would Max react? This isn't good news, it's great news and if Michelle can find proof that a child exists linked to Aletta, under whatever name she's now using, this could all be resolved very quickly.

Although my working day is busy, I keep Max in my thoughts. I want him to know help is coming and to hang on a little longer. If life has a way of sharing one's thoughts and positive karma, then it's worth the effort. I can't be there for him in person, so this is all I can do.

~

As soon as the girls are in bed I jump online. Bella hasn't phoned and I try ringing her, but the phone is switched off. Clicking on the link she sent, my heart sinks a little. I was expecting to see a young artist whose work was perhaps a little too avant garde for my taste. Instead there's a head shot of a much older man, with greying hair around the temples. I'd say David Lancing is in his very late forties. He's clearly extremely successful, the website boasting that his paintings hang on the walls of some of the richest celebrities around the world. It's not my taste, but then art appreciation is very subjective.

For me, it's like comparing jazz to my preference for soul music. His style is referred to as hyper-realism. As I click through the pages, I would describe the paintings as having an unreal quality to them. A very talented artist, without a doubt, and I'm sure he could paint a portrait as well as any old master. But his style, while executed faultlessly, is to turn whatever he's painting into a sort of surreal version of the real. That's the only way I can describe it. It grates on my eye and I find myself slightly irritated by the simple changes that turn it from a mirror image of reality into a slightly dream-enhanced, or worse, computer-generated look.

But this man has enough money, and resources, to help someone disappear. He can control his online and media exposure quite easily and avoid Aletta being photographed with him. Aletta obviously prefers older men and there is a slight resemblance between the artist and Max. Tall, sophisticated air, slightly greying hair, although less noticeable in Max's case, being a good few years' younger than David. For Aletta I could see this working as it would also give her total freedom. And David acquires a trophy wife with no strings. Just one who prefers to stay out of the limelight, but would shine like a star in small social gatherings.

My phone pings. It's a text from Bella.

Sorry, battery ran out. Have to be quick. I tracked down David Lancing's home, which is in Knightsbridge. He and his wife are away. They have a second home in Plan de la Tour, a 12th-century village near St. Tropez and aren't due back until the end of August, by the sound of it. I couldn't find out much, just that his wife is quite a bit younger than him. But the guy was a contract gardener, so I wasn't surprised he didn't know much. We'll speak tomorrow. B x

I immediately email Michelle and say that Aletta might be using the name Lancing and could be living in Knightsbridge.

It was beginning to look promising that this might come together quite quickly, but August means we will have to be patient. Even if Michelle comes up with something, we still have to establish that it really is Aletta. If Bella takes this to the police, it might not turn out to be any quicker. I presume the Italian police would have to liaise with the English police force, which is bound to require a lot of administration.

Hold on, Max. Just keep going.

Chapter 32

We're halfway through July before the pace at work begins to even out. Poor Eve is stressed as the orders keep piling up on her desk, faster than she can clear them.

The pressure is on as our celebrity chef rang again yesterday to say that the prestigious *Celebrity Style* magazine want to do an in-depth interview. It's going to be an *at home with the star* feature and the deadline is only five weeks away.

Livvie took the call, replaced the receiver very calmly and then let out one almighty groan.

I ran into her office, wondering what was going on.

'The man is insane. I seriously doubt there is another interior design team out there who could have pulled everything together as quickly as we have. There are containers being air-freighted in from Italy and Germany, and I've called in a lot of favours for some of our orders to jump the queue. But this is beyond ridiculous!'

I calmed her down, made a strong black coffee with two

sugars and we set to work. Eve gave us an update on the containers and went away to ring the textile people to press for a delivery date.

'The painters still have at least another week and if they over-run, it's going to eat into an already tight timetable. And there's another problem. He's called for an emergency meeting at the house to deal with the latest issue. He's still not happy with that huge wall in the entrance hall and we need to come up with a solution. My patience is running thin and I might need you, not just for any ideas you might have, but to restrain me if I lose the plot and start attacking him.'

I grimace. 'Oh dear. Surely there can't be many more changes he can make at this late stage? When are you thinking of going?'

'I have to be there tomorrow at eleven. Chobham in Sussex is about a two-hour drive at least; you can add another hour onto that if the traffic is bad. I know that means you won't be able to take the girls to school, but I'd really appreciate you coming along on this one. You always manage to find a solution that pleases the client and you'll get to see how the other half lives.'

To be honest, I could do with a few hours away from everything and no doubt we'll stop for a nice lunch on the way back.

'I'll ring Dawn and ask her to do both school runs

tomorrow. I'm sure it will be fine. In the meantime, I'll kick-start the thought processes. I'm sure I can come up with a few options, but whether or not he'll like them is another matter. The problem he has is that the house is an old Victorian building, with various extensions from differing time periods and he's throwing into the mix contemporary and country. That's a big ask.

'It could be a recipe for disaster. Sorry, couldn't resist that one. But when you are dealing with bricks and mortar it's too much going on. I know you jokingly refer to it as a twenty-first-century manor house, but there is a limit to how far you can go, unless you are starting from scratch. That's why the entrance hall doesn't work, but once you walk into the heart of the house I think we've given him everything he asked for, and more. Well, once all of the furniture and fittings arrive and they can be installed.'

'We'll talk about it on the way there tomorrow so we can go in ready to pre-empt his every mood. He's a wonderful man when he's in the kitchen, but his divorce is getting messier by the day. No wonder he wants the new house finished quickly, as I can imagine their rows must be spectacular.'

A small smile creeps over my face as I, too, have leafed through the celebrity gossip magazines while I've been queuing in the supermarket.

'How are all my girls this evening?' Josh's face appears on the screen and Hettie repositions the iPad on the corner of the table, so we can all see him.

'We're good. How was the drive up this morning?'

The picture pixelates for a few seconds and it reminds me of Star Trek when they teleport people. I wonder if Josh will suddenly rematerialise here, in front of our eyes. It's a pity technology can't keep up with the imagination of writers.

'Fairly good. A stretch of motorway is down to fifty miles per hour because of roadworks, but it only added about fifteen minutes to the journey. What's happening there?'

'Nothing with me,' Rosie throws into the conversation. 'Oh, I did get an A minus on a geography test.'

'Well done, that girl, I'm proud of you, Rosie.'

Hettie doesn't look impressed. 'Don't all look at me. It's Monday, for goodness' sake. Nothing ever happens on a Monday.'

'Ah, no, you're right,' Josh says, rather diplomatically.

'Well, I have news. I'm off on a jolly tomorrow,' I say.

All eyes are on me.

'You aren't going to Italy again, are you?' Josh asks, his face dropping.

'No, nothing like that. Just a day trip, so Dawn will be

chauffeuring you tomorrow, girls. I'm off to Sussex to meet the dashing Richard Dale.'

Hettie is impressed. Oh well, two out of three isn't bad.

'Livvie and I are going to his new house to finalise a couple of design details. The house is going to feature in *Celebrity Style* magazine when we've finished fitting it out.'

'Sounds like fun. Will he cook you lunch?' Josh asks.

I laugh and even the girls giggle.

'It's a nice thought, but no. The transformation is a work in progress at the moment and he can't live there. In fact, there's a huge container on its way from Italy packed full of items for this very property. And another one coming from Germany.'

'That reminds me, isn't it about time we thought about having that extension built on the house? Give the girls their own sitting room,' Josh remarks.

The girls both spin around to look at me because I'm clearly going to be the bad cop here. I give Josh what I hope he realises is a stare of utter disappointment.

'We've just replaced my car and the cost isn't warranted. It's a nice-to-have, not a must-have.'

Rosie grabs an apple from the fruit bowl, turns on her heels and starts walking out of the kitchen.

'Depends on who you are and how big your bedroom happens to be. Some of us live in a shoe box, remember. Night Dad, off to watch a DVD.'

Josh and I start laughing, the tension suddenly broken. 'She does have a point, love. It's okay for Hettie as she can get an extra single in there when a friend stays over. It was only a thought as you raised the subject of renovation.'

Hettie grins, 'Night, Dad, I'm off to do my homework.'

'Night honey. Say hi to Alex from me.'

'Oh, Dad! Of course I won't.' With that daughter number one exits the room, too.

'And then there were two. Seriously Josh, I know you plan to be up there for another what, one year and nine months is it now? But after that things will be up in the air again. We could maybe knock the guest room and Rosie's room into one instead. It would be much cheaper to do and it would save Rosie having to have her sleepovers in the sitting room on the inflatable beds.'

'Clever you, what a great idea. I'll leave it in your capable hands.'

I can't believe Josh has talked me into this off the back of such a flimsy excuse.

'If you're going to make trouble every time you ring us, I'll start pretending no one is home. And now you've committed us to spending a couple of thousand pounds by the time we put in fitted wardrobes.'

'Who said anything about fitted wardrobes?'

'You know it's what I do, Josh. You sowed the seed and

now I'll make sure it's done properly. Let this be a lesson to you!'

~

When I check my emails there's one from Michelle and nothing at all from Bella. That's not unusual, because I've only been getting short updates until she decides how to handle the next step. And everything is on hold until the artist and his wife return at the end of August. I assume Michelle's email is a progress update, as she tends to talk me through every single step and every frustrating dead end. It's interesting, but rather depressing at times.

Hello Ellie

I have some news. After those false starts I think I've solved the mystery! It seems that Aletta Ormanni changed her Christian name to Vittoria by deed poll. I can't be sure of the actual date of that, as there is no central database for name changes, still. That's why genealogists often hit a brick wall; unless you know the new name, the trail suddenly stops dead.

However, it was before she married David Morgan Lancing, a month after the date you say she arrived in the UK. The marriage certificate clearly shows her as Vittoria Ormanni, so I'm ninety-nine per cent certain it's the right woman. Once I'd established that, it was pretty easy to trace the birth certificate of her daughter, Elouise Morgan Lancing. She was born on the third of November at The Portland Hospital in London and the father is shown as David Morgan Lancing. So very unusual that father and daughter share the same middle name, but it works so well.

If you require copies of any of the documents, let me know. A lot of people think genealogy is dull, but believe me, I've yet to look at anyone's family history without unveiling a few secrets. Sometimes it's sad, like dead siblings, or step brothers and sisters who are still alive but whom they have never met. It's one surprise, after another.

We must make the effort to meet up very soon. Maybe you and the family can come down here for the weekend and we can do a little sightseeing.

All the best, Michelle

Chapter 33

In the early hours of the morning my mind is still whirling, as a chill starts to pool in the pit of my stomach. Because I've hardly slept, my dreams have evaded me and I wish I hadn't checked my emails before getting into bed. I haven't relayed the news to Bella, yet. When Max finds out this is going to devastate him. Even if he can cope with the thought of losing Aletta for good, what about his reaction when he hears she is married? How hurt will his pride be when he finds out about the affair with David Lancing? And then there's the baby; that's going to come as a massive shock and such an unexpected one. She's named Elouise, too. I mean, what a strange coincidence – I can't remember the last time I came across a namesake. It feels like yet another little strand linking me to Max in some curiously inexplicable way, as if I was always meant to bring about this discovery.

By six a.m. I've probably had about three hours' sleep in total and I decide to get up and send Bella an email. It's unfair of me to withhold information. Dawn will be here at seven-thirty to sort the girls' breakfasts and Livvie is picking me up at eight, because she thinks the traffic will be heavy.

As the PC kicks into life and my inbox opens, the first one is from Bella's personal email account.

Hi Ellie

I'll be brief. I'm really worried about Max. He's taken on an assistant and the new guy, Luca, starts next week. Trista isn't at all happy about it and things are very tense here. I think she fears he's preparing to leave and is training Luca to take over.

I guess I'm not surprised about Max wanting some help, though, as he was rushed off his feet even before he set up the cooperative. But I'm not sure Trista really understands how fast the new side of the business is growing.

Aside from that everything is fine and you should see Piero's bungalow. It's wonderful and I know we are going to be very happy there. Let's just hope things keep going as they are.

Enjoy your day! B x

I slump forward, my aching head now having to weigh up the pros and the cons. Do I tell Bella, or don't I? Will this information tip Max over the edge he's been sitting on for so long? How long can I hold off and what good will it do? It won't change anything – apart from clear his name, of course. It's a double-edged sword.

Hello Bella

I was sorry to hear that Max is still struggling, but maybe having someone else there will be good for him. Not just to share his workload, but in general. It might help normalise things a bit, because of the situation. I really hope Trista doesn't make a fuss and doesn't fight with him over this. It will benefit everyone in the long run.

I have news and I'll forward you an email from my cousin, Michelle, next. I'll leave you to read it first and maybe we can talk about it tonight. I'm away most of today and will be travelling with my boss, so I won't be able to talk.

It's something I think you need to read and think about before you do anything. What we hadn't thought through was Max's reaction when the truth is finally exposed. You'll understand what I'm talking about once you've read it.

Anyway, I should be here from about eight o'clock onwards.

Speak soon, E x

By the time Livvie arrives I'm happy to shut the door on the chaos I'm leaving behind. Bestowing kisses, I then grab some headache tablets and a bottle of water on my way out.

'You look tired,' Livvie utters, turning her head to check her wing mirror before pulling away from the kerb.

'Awful night.' I take a big gulp of water to swill down the tablets. Twenty minutes and the pain will begin to lessen.

'Problems?' She sounds concerned, taking her eyes off the road to look at me for a moment.

'Eyes ahead, Livvie. It's not my problem, it's someone I know. But it's a tough one.'

She lets out a deep sigh, tinged with annoyance. 'You really are your own worst enemy at times, Ellie. If it's not your problem, do what you can and then let it go. Are they worried about your problems?'

Why did I even start this? Livvie looks at everything in a detached way. There's black and there's white and there's nothing in between. Her business head isn't something she can switch off. Problem. Solution. Done. Plus, she'd be mortified if she knew this harked back to my trip to Italy.

'Let's not fall out, Livvie. Anyway, can you run through this little meeting? What's the plan of action?'

Another sigh, this time followed by something that sounds like *harrumph*.

'You and I both knew that wall was going to be a problem when we originally saw the plans. With the staircase sweeping up behind it and the fact that it's a support wall, the only solution was to put up a small extension on the front in reclaimed brick to match the facade. At the moment he's right, you open the front door and it's a corridor.'

'But you discussed this with him at the start – warned him about it. I remember it coming up in our team meeting.'

'We did, but now the other building work has been done he's regretting that little wave in the air he gave, totally dismissing the idea. I've brought the original 3D interior design model so we'll revisit that. I can't remember what we had on the wall. Was it a large ornamental mirror?'

'I checked it yesterday before I left, and yes, it was. It brightens the area and makes it feel bigger because it reflects the light from the front door.'

'Well, Richard is now saying it lacks impact. And he is right. You turn the corner and there's this vast open-plan space, so of course it now puts an emphasis on the narrower space leading into it. He needs to remember that prior to the internal walls being taken down it was all in proportion. The architect is saying that the only other option is to move the entrance around to the side of the house. Of course, Richard doesn't like that idea because at the moment it looks out across the lawns and the lake.'

As Livvie pulls up at a set of traffic lights, she turns to look at me and we start laughing.

'Oh, the problems that having money brings with it. What are we going to do?' Her exaggerated tone sends me into a fit of the giggles. I've seen Richard on TV and he does love a bit of drama.

Already my headache is subsiding and I don't allow myself to think about anything other than the two ideas I have to present to Livvie and Richard.

I check the file on my lap and everything is there. I pull out the iPad to assess the battery level and instantly a message flashes onto the screen.

I listened. I'm still trying.

It's from Max and it was sent yesterday. I quickly close it down, trying not to appear flustered.

'Are you all prepared?'

'Yes. Richard Dale likes bespoke and something different. I can't wait to unveil the two options I think will take the focus off the problem.'

'I appreciate your company today, not just as the ideas lady. We don't seem to get time to sit and chat any more. It's good that business is booming, but it's non-stop, isn't it? All or nothing.'

'Well, I'm glad it's a busy period because Josh has talked

me into knocking our guest bedroom and Rosie's room into one. At least sleepovers will be easier, as at the moment we turn the sitting room into a mattress factory. But that's a couple of months' salary tied up. His reining back on expenditure phase didn't last long.'

'Use our guys. They'll give you a healthy discount and whatever furnishings you buy, do it through the company account. Just write out a cheque when you know the costs and I'll pass it to the accountant. It's in my interests to keep your family happy and that way I don't feel so guilty dragging you away from them.'

'Really? That's a kind offer, Livvie, and I wasn't dropping a hint or anything.'

'I know, it's not your style.'

As we lapse into silence my head begins to droop. I see Max's face. He looks up from reading my email and he looks ashen. In my mixed-up thoughts it appears as if the email I forwarded to Bella went to Max by mistake. I jolt forward suddenly and realise I've been asleep and dreaming again. For how long exactly, I have no idea.

'I was about to wake you. You'll feel much better for that little rest. Welcome to Chobham.'

I've seen the file and the photos of the house and grounds; ten thousand, six hundred square feet, with ten bedrooms and six bathrooms. It now comprises a massive open-plan, living/dining/kitchen area, three large reception rooms, one of which is a thirty-five-feet-long billiard room, complete with a fully fitted bar. Newer extensions to the property house a second kitchen/breakfast room, a butler's pantry and a staff annexe.

Pulling up at the electric gates, Livvie presses the intercom and it takes seconds for the gates to swing open. Ahead of us is a driveway with a large turning circle at the end.

The house sits sideways on to the parking area and as we walk around to the front I can see exactly why Richard won't move the front door, or build out from the front elevation of the house. The facade still retains all of the glory and proportions of a solidly built Victorian house. Two gabled roofs, with two very domineering chimney stacks either side, add to the grandeur. Turning around, Livvie and I look out over the beautiful lawns that sweep down to a lake. There are about a dozen aged trees, of different varieties, that look so perfect in the setting that it almost looks unreal. Too perfect.

'Not bad, eh?' Livvie says, turning to me. 'And now for the corridor.'

Spinning back around, the entrance to the house is in the centre of the building with nicely proportioned bay windows either side of it. The door is quite wide and as it swings open I don't think either of us is looking at Richard, because instead our eyes go straight to the vast expanse of wall behind him.

'Ah, you've noticed our little problem.'

We step inside and shake hands.

'I don't think we've met before,' Richard says, as he takes my hand. 'I would have remembered. Shall we head into the work room?'

As we turn an immediate right and follow him along the twelve-foot-long, four-foot-wide corridor, we all pause at the end to look back. It's crazy. To the left is, as Richard pointed out, a corridor and now, from this vantage point, to the right the open-plan area looks cavernous by comparison. With no furniture yet to define the various areas, the space seems to go on forever.

'I know what you are going to say, that it's my fault because you did warn me, Livvie, that once those walls came down that entrance wasn't going to look right. What can you do in five weeks, as the clock is ticking? A magazine spread is good publicity, but the pressure is enormous. I'm guilty of the same thing myself, flicking through and finding fault. You know they always do that opening shot, with the front door open and the celebrity there with the big, welcoming smile. It's their signature for this feature and whatever is on the wall behind me has to be spectacular, because it's all about first impressions.'

We follow Richard through into a side room, our hollow footsteps ringing in our ears.

'This is the cosy room.' He throws open the door as a

wry smile creeps over his face. There are a few picnic tables and some plastic chairs in here at the moment. It's the painter's tea room.

Livvie sets up the laptop and opens the software programme.

'Remember that this is the vision, Richard, and once the painters have finished it will all start to transform very quickly.' As the screen takes us on a virtual 3D tour and we move from room to room, he seems to relax a little. It reminds him how the space will look when it's furnished. At the moment it feels almost clinical. It's a new interior inside of a classic, old building that wraps around it lovingly. Having taken the full tour, Livvie runs the intro again and pauses on the shots of the entrance hallway.

'This mirror is coming from Italy and will arrive next week. Because it's over-sized it will reflect the light from the front door and make the space appear much larger than it really is. You will notice a huge difference, Richard, I can promise you. At the moment I can see why you are having second thoughts.'

'Yes, the mirror is very nice, but it's not spectacular. It's not a conversation piece. It's modern and elegant, but predictable. And I know I signed off on it, but it would look equally as good practically anywhere in the house.'

Time for me to jump in, I think.

'If it's impact you are after then I have two ideas, one is

very much in keeping with our theme, the other is a little out of the box.'

I open up the iPad and tap the photo icon.

'This chandelier is hanging in a villa in Italy. It's a one-off piece made by a very talented young designer. It's twelve feet long and the staircase, as you can see, wraps around it. The modern elegance of the metalwork leaves, enamelling and a cascade of tiny lights make it a statement piece. What I propose is that we commission him to make two wall-mounted chandeliers. So instead of having something rounded, like this one, imagine it cut in half and the depth reduced a little so it doesn't project too far into the space. But the cascade of tiny lights would begin about six inches above the skirting board and extend up as high as you like. It would be a waterfall of lights, or rather, two waterfalls of lights. Behind both, simple frameless mirrors will give the look a 3D effect.'

I can see that I've impressed Livvie, but Richard is harder to read.

I pull two hard copies of the photograph from my file and hand them out.

'The second idea involves thinking outside the box. It's an investment opportunity and a statement piece rolled into one.' I slide my finger across the screen and a collage of David Lancing's paintings comes into view.

'I don't know if you are a collector of art, Richard, but

David Lancing is a world-wide renowned artist. His style is hyper-realism and I can guarantee you that every single one of his paintings is a conversation piece. Now, the only potential problem is the timescale. I can call in favours and have the chandeliers here in time for the photo shoot. One of David's paintings might be harder to acquire, but I'm not ruling it out as an option for you to consider.'

As I flick through the photos, which are screen shots from David's website, Richard's face kicks into life.

'I like it. In fact, I like both options. Order the lights and let's go big. If we can't get a painting in time, then we have a fallback. As for the paintings, find out what is available and I'll make a decision. As an investment, price is not really a problem. Hyper-realism, you say. I want big, bold and talking-point. I wonder if he has anything food-related? It's rather clever, perfectly executed but almost too perfect. Genius.'

Livvie looks relieved. 'So that's settled, then? You're happy?'

Richard gives me a wink. 'What can I say, other than I'm excited. The next few weeks are going to blow all thoughts of divorce out of my head.'

I ignore the comment and jump in to fill the awkward silence.

'I'll get straight onto it today. You might like to keep these to look through. But I'll talk to the artist and let you know how I get on.' I hand Richard a folder with about a dozen A4 screenshots of David's paintings.

'You must come to my house-warming party, ladies. I'll send you both invites. If you absolutely have to bring menfolk with you, then the offer extends to partners. There will, however, be quite a few eligible bachelors here.'

I look at Livvie, 'I'm taken, but Livvie is free.' She shoots me a black look, turning to face Richard with an awkward smile.

'That's very kind of you, Richard,' she mutters as he escorts us back through to the front door.

Once we are safely in the car Livvie turns to face me.

'That was inspired. I mean, I hate the paintings. Dreadful. But it's just what Richard is looking for; do you know the artist personally?'

My stomach flutters.

'No, but I'll be talking to him very shortly.'

Chapter 34

'Mum, can I go to the cinema with Alex?'

I haven't even had time to take off my coat before Hettie looms up in front of me wearing her serious face.

'Thank you, Dawn. Much appreciated.'

'But can I, Mum?'

I give Dawn a hug and we exchange glances.

'I'll leave you to it. I popped the casserole in the oven; give it another ten minutes and you can dish up. See you tomorrow afternoon.' Dawn flashes me a sympathetic look and heads for the door as quickly as she can.

'Mum, I have to design a maze and then make a model of one. I need your help.' Rosie sidles up next to Hettie. Both are looking at me, expectantly.

I slip off my shoes and coat, and they follow me like sheep into the kitchen.

'Welcome home, Mum. How was your day?' I mutter to myself, but there is no reaction from the girls, only hopeful looks.

'We could go into town by bus on Saturday, have a pizza and watch the afternoon viewing.' Hettie is trying to play down her excitement.

'Bus, pizza, film and then home? Saturday?' I pretend to give it some serious consideration. 'Okay, but I want you to phone me after the film and either Dad, or I, will come and pick you both up.'

I don't want to spoil her fun, or her first real date, but I also want her to know that there are rules.

'But, Muuuum. What will Alex think? It will spoil everything.' She looks at me with doleful eyes.

'Alex will think that you have parents who care about you, but trust you enough to allow you out on a date. Take it or leave it, but those are the terms.'

I turn to Rosie.

'We'll jump on the internet after dinner and look at some examples, Rosie. You can draw up a plan and then we'll look at what materials we can find, ready for you to build it. What's the deadline?'

'Next Monday.'

'Good. Maybe we can get Dad's ideas, as well, and you can work on it over the weekend.'

'Ah, thanks, Mum.'

Hettie adds a semi-grateful 'thanks' of her own, but it's an afterthought.

'And I had a very busy, but productive day, thank you,

girls. Now if one of you can lay the table I'll sort the iPad, as it's about time for Dad to FaceTime.'

~

Once Hettie accepts my decision she brightens up and I don't mention it to Josh. Our little girl is turning into a young woman and this is only the start of her testing the water and extending her freedom. We both knew it was coming, but it still feels much too soon. Is any parent ever really ready to begin letting go?

After saying goodnight to Josh, we spend an hour around the table playing board games before the girls go up to their bedrooms. As I go in to kiss Rosie, she jumps straight into bed. Hettie is sitting up in bed and has a school book in front of her, but I can see her phone peeking out from beneath it. I give her a peck on the cheek and a quick hug.

'I know you think we shouldn't worry, but we do. That's what being a parent is all about. Alex will understand. He's a nice young man and his parents will be saying much the same things to him.'

I pull away and she looks up at me. 'You can trust me, I am sensible.'

I smile, 'I was fifteen once and I thought I knew everything. We don't want to stop you having fun, Hettie, but this is a journey you need to take one step à time.'

I think we both know what I'm talking about. We've had the talk and they do sex education at school. I simply want her to take her time and not try to rush the process.

Making my way into the study, I reflect upon how lucky Josh and I are to have the girls. Children add pressure, dominate your lives and cost you a fortune, but life without them wouldn't be nearly as exciting or wonderful. Every day my girls remind me about what is important. As adults we attached significance to things that really don't matter. As long as we have a roof over our heads, food on the table and everyone is well, then no obstacle is insurmountable.

My heart tells me that Max would love to have a child and that makes his situation even worse. What I can't understand is why Aletta had to run away, rather than admit to having an affair? It's not a crime to fall out of love with someone and then fall into love with another man. She wasn't married to Max, although I can understand it would have been hard to face both him and her family, to break the news. It wasn't the easiest situation, given that Max is now a key figure in the Ormanni family's future.

I pull out the iPad and see that I have a missed call from Bella. I immediately call her back and almost instantly she pops up onto my screen.

She's bursting with excitement. 'We did it. Well, Michelle did it. We don't need to wait until they return to the UK. If we ask Michelle to get copies of the marriage certificate, we can simply hand it over to the police. They'll have to investigate it and then close the case.'

I'm not so sure. 'Slow down. I know it's good news. But I'm worried that it will be too much for Max, at the moment. Think about it. Someone will have to warn him, before the police are brought into this, so that it doesn't come as a total shock to him. Nothing is certain until Aletta has been identified, what if it turns out not to be her? If our suspicions, and Michelle's research, is correct, he's lost Aletta for good and he may even wonder if he's the baby's father. It's a dilemma that could break his heart. I can't see Aletta, or her husband, accepting any form of contact from him. Everything was done in a very underhand, although I suspect quite legal, way and clearly Aletta wanted to sever all connections with her past life.

'Then there's Trista's part in all of this. She knew about the baby too and yet she chose not to tell either Max, or the police, about it. So it could be said that Aletta had already come forward, she just chose not to contact Max directly. What was Trista's motivation, though? In the will you said Max inherited everything?' I ask.

'Yes. And if he's survived by children, the estate goes to them. Oh, wow. Trista definitely knew what she was doing. She obviously thought Max was the father of Aletta's baby. I wonder if Aletta actually told her that?' Bella wonders.

I close my eyes and a sense of foreboding washes over me.

'She was punishing Aletta, while ensuring the business was in safe hands. Even if Max marries and has other children, Aletta's daughter would have a legitimate claim to the estate. Trista was simply cutting Aletta out of the will, not her entire blood line.'

Bella takes a sharp intake of breath.

'That's monstrous. Putting inheritance to one side, she has a granddaughter and why wouldn't she want to establish a relationship with her own flesh and blood? Family means everything and yet she can turn her back on her daughter and granddaughter as if she feels nothing. It looks as if Trista is simply trying to avoid another scandal rearing its head and further tarnishing the family's reputation. Or maybe this is all about money and the damage it could do in the future to the business? She really is the ice queen.'

The horror of the situation is overwhelming. What harm could we do by digging this up? Wouldn't time alone be a healer? Or is that wishful thinking, because it's an easy way out? If there are still those who believe Max had a hand in Aletta's disappearance then time won't help take that away. I have no choice but to voice another fear that has been going around and around in my head.

'What if Trista wasn't given a choice?'

Bella's face looks back at me, wearing a blank expression. 'What do you mean?'

'Aletta breaks the news to Trista that she's having a baby and she's in love with someone else. Trista knows that this would create yet another scandal, showing her daughter up in a very bad light. David Lancing has the money and the contacts to handle the disappearance. He's been divorced for a long time and Aletta is a beautiful younger woman. He does what he has to do to ensure their future happiness as a family. They give Trista an ultimatum. Cut all ties, or Aletta goes back with the baby and everyone is made aware of the truth in a very public way. Each of them has created a little chain of lies that implicates them in the wider scandal. It isn't until you stand back that you get a glimpse of the bigger picture and the damage they have done. Perhaps Trista couldn't face yet another trauma in her life and she, too, felt trapped by the lies she'd told.'

'Have they done anything illegal?' Bella is in shock and I feel exactly the same way. Our attempt at clearing Max's name has uncovered a monster that could potentially hurt everyone.

'I don't know, Bella. It's not fraud, nothing was stolen and it's not a crime to change your name by deed poll. In this case, it was essential if the plan was going to work. The only crime is the injustice to Max, as he's the only person in this sorry affair, who has been given no consideration whatsoever. He's also the only person who hasn't lied about anything.'

'Ellie, this is one big mess. I don't know what to say. I started all of this and now I know I can't handle it. What should we do?'

I don't mention anything about the contact I'm going to make with David's agent. The plan that has been formulating in my head isn't one in which Bella should be involved.

'If you step away now, then your name won't be linked to it in any way when the news gets out. You know I have Max's best interests at heart. I'll figure out the right way to handle this, I promise, so that our part doesn't become common knowledge. In the meantime keep this to yourself and, if you hear anything, I want you to respond in the same way as the people around you. Tell Piero you drew a blank. I know it's a lie, but it's the only way to protect you all. Focus on your future.'

I pause and then add, 'Eve will contact you tomorrow to commission two new pieces. I need Piero to drop everything and do this for me as a favour as quickly as possible. Cost is not a problem for the client who wants them, so I don't want him to think about giving us any sort of discount. This is going to give you both a nice little sum towards the wedding.'

Bella eyes well up.

'Ellie, I don't know what to say, other than thank you. Piero is working so hard, but he'll be thrilled to do this for you, and us. As for Max, I really do want it to be over before the strain gets too much for him. Will you tell him yourself?'

'There is one more thing I need to do first, but try to disconnect from this now. I won't let you know when the time is right for me to tell him. It's better that you have no knowledge whatsoever and continue as normal. Just handle whatever happens when that time comes. I'd love to hear all about the wedding plans, though, and I'm always here if you want to talk.'

She swipes her sleeve across her eyes.

'This was never going to end well, Bella, and I know that's not our fault. But Max's name deserves to be cleared so that he is free. Nothing at all may change about him working for the estate still, but that will be a decision for Max alone to make.'

Chapter 35

I slip into bed, feeling exhausted and anxious. I know what I have to do, but the next few days are going to be agonising.

Staring up at the ceiling I take long, slow breaths to calm my rapid heartbeat. The darkness clears a little and I'm there again, on the terrace with Max.

'You have to be strong, Max. What is coming will tear you apart and there's nothing anyone can do to change that. My heart bleeds for your pain and I wish I could take it away, but I can't.'

Sitting opposite me, I see that the table top is bare, with only the flickering candle between us. He places both hands on the table and reaches out to me. As my eyes fill with tears I reach out to him and our fingertips touch. There is a warmth that seems to grow from that small contact, although the rest of my body feels cold.

He doesn't appear to have heard my words.

'I know you can't be mine, Ellie. I know you have a

family and you love your husband. You can never be mine.'

Max isn't listening to me at all and in his head he's somewhere else. I'm frightened and the fear grows as the seconds pass. Something is wrong, very wrong. I'm not even sure it's about Aletta.

'It will be over soon, I promise,' I whisper into the stillness of the night.

I pull back and the next thing I hear is the alarm going off. I feel so tired, as if I haven't slept at all, and I know this can't go on for much longer. Even in my deepest sleep I can't seem to let go of my anxiety. I drew the line, but I'm going to have to step back over it for one last time. The thought sends goose bumps up my arms and I shiver.

As soon as I've dropped the girls off at school I head back home and ring Livvie.

'It would be easier to work from home today, is that OK with you? I have to track down this artist and that might take a while. I'll send the order details for the chandeliers across to Eve and I've already called in the favour with the craftsman.'

'You obviously didn't sleep well again, then. No problem at all. If you need me to do anything then give me a call.'

There's nothing I need from anyone now, as the last bit has to be down to me.

I'm staring at David Lancing's website and click on the contact page. There's an email address and a telephone number. I have no idea if it goes through to a gallery or his manager/agent, but I dial the number before I can change my mind.

'Good morning, this is Tom Preston, how can I help?'

'Hello. My name is Ellie Maddison and I'm one of the buyers for Bradley's Design Creative. I have a client who is very interested in buying one of Mr Lancing's paintings. The problem we have is one of timescale, as we are preparing for a magazine shoot in a few weeks' time. We feel that a David Lancing original is just the statement piece we are looking for and Richard Dale is a huge fan.'

Before I can go any further, I'm interrupted.

'Richard Dale, the TV chef?'

Yes. I have his attention.

'I've shown Richard the website and he's very excited. But there isn't anything on there that is big enough for the space we are hoping to fill. I wondered if David is displaying anywhere at the moment, or whether you have anything available immediately that isn't on the website?'

'I'm sure we can find something for you to look at. What sort of budget did you have in mind? Size is very relative to price.'

I don't give him a direct answer, to keep his interest piqued. 'Obviously Richard realises this is going to be an investment purchase. But it has to be the right piece.'

'Of course. We have something that hasn't been put on

the website yet and there are several pieces that David has in his studio at home. For an artist, everything is for sale at the right price.'

This guy is a good salesman and it's as I suspected.

'Is there any way I could talk to David himself? I think it would help steer us in the right direction if I describe the setting and the sort of impact Richard is hoping to achieve. I'm sure if we can come to an agreement, then David will be given a mention in the *Celebrity Style* magazine feature.'

I can imagine Tom Preston doing a fist pump in the air.

'I'm sure David would be delighted to talk to you. Give me an hour. David is on his way back from his holiday retreat and is due to land in the next hour. I'm sure, for something as special as this, there are a number of pieces he would be prepared to show you. I'll ring you in a little while. Thank you for your call, Ellie.'

'That would be amazing, thank you, Tom.'

That was unexpected; I thought Bella said they were due back at the end of August and not the beginning. What if I end up face to face with them? That wasn't my plan, which was to get David's number, ring to chat about the paintings and then find an excuse to ring again. If Aletta answers, I'm pretty sure I'd know who I was speaking to. Reeling, I put the phone down as my mobile begins to skitter across the desk top.

'Hello? Oh, Aunt Clare. How are you?'

'I'm fine. I was wondering how you were doing and if you wanted a chat. I'm not working tonight, if you're free.'

My head is buzzing and Aunt Clare will take one look at me and start worrying.

'I can't tonight, I'm afraid. We have a rush job on and I'm working day and night. Everything is fine, though.'

'Really? You're not just putting me off? I know you and I can hear that little undertone of stress in your voice.'

Now I understand how Hettie feels when she says one thing, but I'm reading something else entirely and it's so annoying you want to scream.

'It will be nice to chat, but I'll ring you next week when things will be calmer. We have a celebrity chef who enjoys a little drama and is giving me a major headache.'

'Oh, as long as it's only work-related stress and everything else is fine.'

'It is, and thanks. Next week, I promise.'

I put the phone down, feeling miserable. My life is suddenly all about being careful what I say, and to whom. I'm not that sort of person; yes, I may not tell people everything I'm thinking and feeling all the time, but I also don't usually lie, even little white ones like the one I told to Aunt Clare just now.

I feel horrible and I promise myself that when this is over I will tell her everything, in strictest confidence. I'm not telling lies to Tom Preston, I simply have a hidden agenda. If I can pull this off, then it will be Aletta who contacts the police. I have no idea if this constitutes some form of blackmail, but I intend to cross paths with her, somehow, and offer her two options. All I will be demanding from her is the truth.

The landline kicks into life and I pick up the receiver, rather hesitantly.

'Ellie, it's Tom. David would be delighted to meet you to discuss this further and can make himself available tomorrow. He has a number of pieces he can show you in his personal collection that are on display in his home. Would it be convenient to arrange an appointment some time tomorrow?'

I'm stunned. Just like that.

'Wonderful. I'm free all day.'

'Great. Shall we say noon? Email me via the website and I'll send you his address by return. It's been a pleasure talking to you.'

Tom is already counting his commission, no idea at all that Aletta is in for a big surprise from a total stranger.

'Thank you for making everything happen, Tom. The pleasure is all mine.'

I immediately dial Richard's number.

'I'm meeting with David tomorrow morning at his Knightsbridge home. He has a few pieces in his private collection that he's prepared to let me look at.'

'You really deliver, Ellie. I'm impressed.'

I have my fingers crossed Richard doesn't back out now, or think he can snap something up at a bargain price.

'It would be great if you could come along too, to meet him in person. It might help when it comes to negotiating a price. I did mention the upcoming magazine spread and indicated he would probably get a mention. I hope that wasn't over-stepping the mark, but it sharpened his interest.'

'Good move. A nice little incentive I'm sure he would appreciate. I'll rearrange a few things. What time?'

'Noon. As soon as I have the full address I'll email it over. See you tomorrow, Richard.'

'I hope you are getting a big bonus for this, Ellie.'

I'd smile, but this isn't about Livvie, Richard, or looking good, it's about Max.

~

It's been a long day. After the girls have their banter with Josh, I take the iPad up to the bedroom for our daily one-to-one.

'You look tired, Ellie. This is a real strain, isn't it? Hettie is growing and pushing the boundaries, and Rosie is starting to make herself heard too. Livvie is relying upon you way too much, in my opinion. And you are the person keeping everything together. You need a holiday or a break away. Maybe without the kids; just you and me. I don't want us to become distant in any way. I know there isn't much quality time during the week, and we're both tired when it comes to this point in the day. But you don't talk to me like you used to do, you know, about the small things.'

I try my best not to let a sigh escape, but it's hard. I need Josh to feel content at the moment and not add yet another person into the mix who wants something from me.

'I am tired, I admit that. Work is more than hectic, but it won't be forever. Please, don't worry about me. Very soon things will be back to normal. I just need you to understand that it takes a lot out of me to get through each day. I feel pulled in all directions and the best way you can help is to let me get on with it. Too much happens to tell you every little detail, of every day. Much in the same way that I only get an overview of your very separate life at work. The main thing is that everyone is happy and we don't have anything major to worry about.'

His face reflects sadness and concern.

'I do worry about you. I miss you like crazy. I miss lying next to you in bed. I worry it will be too much to cope with and what we have will fall apart.'

My heart feels so very heavy to hear him say that.

'I love you, Josh. This is us you are talking about. Together we can get through anything.'

'I know. I just need to keep hearing you say it. It reassures me. This isn't what we'd planned for our future, is it?'

'Family is everything, Josh, and the sacrifice is worth it. Start counting in terms of months before you can begin to look for something more local, then it doesn't seem quite so bad.'

I ring Livvie and tell her all about today's developments and she's delighted, even though it will mean another day out of the office. I booked the train tickets this afternoon and now all I have to do is select a suitable outfit. Tomorrow I need every little thing to be perfect and if fate is on my side, then it will all fall into place. Or, it will all go very badly wrong.

Chapter 36

The journey to London is uneventful, but in my head I'm going through every possible scenario. They've just come back from a long break away, so Aletta and her little daughter should be there too. Whether our paths will cross, that's something I can't control. But if it becomes apparent she's not there, then I'll have to prolong the meeting in the hope she will return.

It would be rude if David didn't introduce me to his wife, but it's fine to plan this all out in my head. The reality could be very different. Either way, I hope to walk away having satisfied an important client, at the very least. Well, I suppose I'm taking even that for granted. So instead I'll keep my fingers crossed.

~

When the front door opens onto the spacious hallway, the man before me extends his hand.

'I'm Tom, David's business manager. Very nice to meet you in person, Ellie.'

We shake and I step inside. It's Georgian splendour at its very best. All of the features have been retained, but the walls are merely a blank canvas to display David's artwork. And yet it doesn't overwhelm, it simply adds interest to spaciousness created by high ceilings and wide corridors. There is a distinctly feminine touch that softens the overall effect. It's definitely reflected in the clever colour choices and some of the decorative items.

I follow Tom along the hallway past several doors and out into a large glass atrium, beyond which I can see a much newer extension. I had no idea when I stood facing this impressive row of houses how much space there was behind them, assuming the gardens would be modest.

'Ellie Maddison, let me introduce you to David Lancing.'

David extends his hand, grasping mine quite gently, but then placing his other hand over the top of it. He holds that position for a few seconds, looking me in the eye and giving me a very genuine smile.

My first impression is that David has charm, instant appeal and an air of likeability. I was hoping to take an instant dislike to him, to make this a little easier. I can see why Aletta is attracted to him and why he is attracted to her.

'May I call you Ellie? You must call me David. An artist is always very grateful when someone of importance takes notice of their work. I'm very much looking forward to meeting Richard Dale, my wife and I really enjoy his programme.'

I nod and smile as he so easily defuses any awkwardness. 'Tom tells me that Richard will be joining us?'

'Yes, he'll be here very shortly.'

'Then perhaps we should sit and I'll organise some tea, or maybe you prefer coffee, like Tom here?

'Coffee would be lovely, that's very kind.'

I feel the part. Cool, professional and in control. But my heart is thudding in my chest. I swallow and take a seat on the grey linen-covered sofa, as indicated by David. He walks over to a console on the wall, presses a button and talks to someone in the kitchen.

'It won't be a moment,' he informs me, taking a seat opposite Tom.

'What a beautiful house, you have, David.'

He smiles and gives a little nod of acknowledgement. 'My wife has wonderful taste and she allows me to indulge my growing collection. Don't you, darling?'

The woman walking towards us with a tray is, without a doubt, Aletta Ormanni. I'm startled; I wasn't expecting to come face to face with her quite so quickly. The thudding of my heart increases ten-fold, until I remember that we have never met and to her I am a total stranger. There can be no recognition, or any reason for her to be suspicious about me.

'Vittoria, this is Ellie Maddison, thanks to whom you will very shortly be meeting your culinary hero, Chef Richard Dale.'

'He really is coming here? I'm so excited to meet him. And he's interested in David's work, that wonderful.' Her English is near-perfect, only the slightest hint of an accent that hardly registers on the ear; however, it gives her voice a very charming quality.

This wasn't at all what I expected from this young woman. She seems relaxed, happy and adoring of her husband. Aletta places the tray on the coffee table and walks across to shake my hand. Then she turns back to attend to the tray, placing cups in front of each of us in turn. She takes a seat next to David.

'Please help yourself to sugar. Art is a blessing, Ellie, isn't it? It lifts the spirits in much the same way that the chords of Puccini or Verdi can touch the soul. It takes us to a higher place.' Her smile is warm.

'My wife is of Italian descent and she has become my inspiration. Opera was never a favourite of mine, but I've come to appreciate there is a connection between the ear and eye, and that's the soul.'

A buzzer announces the arrival of Richard, just as my stomach begins to churn. Am I actually capable of doing what I came here to do?

A minute or so later a young woman appears, introducing

Richard. He strides across the room to shake hands vigorously with David, who is clearly delighted. He then shakes Tom's hand and turns to Vittoria.

'My wife, Vittoria. She is an avid fan. We both watch your programme and it has inspired her to venture into the kitchen. Much to the annoyance of our staff.'

Richard makes a big display of looking immensely flattered and taking Vittoria's hand. She blushes.

'Cooking is not a skill I have, unfortunately, but I've tried a few of your recipes. I don't flatter myself I can achieve the same result, but at least I've managed to surprise David.'

Everyone smiles, good-naturedly, while Vittoria pours out a coffee for Richard. He takes a seat next to me on the sofa and I think it's time I took the lead.

'Richard is renovating a beautiful Victorian property in Surrey. It has the most wonderful park-like grounds and the house looks out across a private lake. Inside, though, the inspiration is modern with a twist. A new interior inside a Victorian shell.'

All eyes are on me. I glance at Vittoria, who is listening with interest.

'We have a large wall facing the entrance to the house that is two storeys high. It was an earlier conversion when a sweeping staircase and galleried landing was added. The hallway itself isn't large, so it requires a feature; something big and bold, but a statement that also gives a hint to the style of the interior beyond. The heart of this wonderful building is twenty-first-century living. Richard, have I summed that up correctly?'

'Indeed. Much better than I could have done. I want something large, commanding and a talking point. It will be the focus, the welcome to my home and it has to reflect my personality.'

David is listening intently and nodding.

'I think I have a few pieces that might be of interest. I don't want to restrict you in terms of style, so let's have a walk around and you can look at my personal collection. I would be humbled to have one of my paintings in the home of such a celebrated and well-loved chef.'

We stand and the tour begins. First, David leads us into his studio. Tom insists on falling in behind Richard and me, leaving Vittoria to take the rear. The room is what you would expect of a working artist and it isn't particularly tidy. Several canvasses lean up against the wall, but most of them are only part-finished. The smell of the oil paint is heady, yet strangely compelling.

David leads us over to a large picture depicting a seascape. The piercing blue water is edged with almost jet-black rocks. Floating in the breeze is what looks like a piece of white muslin, or maybe a lace shawl, whisked away from a lady's shoulders by the wind.

It's time for me to take Tom to one side and get an idea

of the sort of cost involved. I don't want Richard to set his sights on something that will blow his budget.

'Amazing, isn't it, Tom?' I stand at his side, looking on. Vittoria is watching us and discreetly turns away. She idly straightens a pile of clean rags, obviously used for drying the brushes.

'What sort of price are we looking at for something of that size?'

'Around fifty thousand, maybe a little more. David's work is appreciating above market levels, so it's a good investment. The fact that this is Richard Dale will mean that David will, I'm sure, be prepared to entertain a little flexibility.'

'Excellent. I think this looks very promising, then.'

In fact, I'm relieved. I know that Richard's budget is around seventy-five thousand, so I can relax and leave the two of them to wander and confer. They are in deep conversation and I'd say that already we have a contender.

Now my heart is racing once more. I'm facing Vittoria and Tom has moved across to join in the general conversation, content that now it's simply down to finding the right piece.

'It's a great location. You must love living so close to the heart of the city.'

She smiles. 'I do. There 'eez no other place for me.'

It's the first time she has slipped and, aside from that,

it's only the way she rolls the letter *r* that gives a hint of an accent. With heavy blonde highlights and a chin-length cut, her style is very chic and she could easily be French, or even Spanish.

My heart starts pounding and I almost falter, but then I think of Max and it gives me courage.

'It's wrong to hide like this, Aletta.'

The shock of my words are reflected in her face as the colour abruptly drains away. She grabs onto the workbench to steady herself.

'Why are you here?'

'To buy a painting, but I recognised you.'

'But I don't know you. How can you know me?'

'I have visited Villa Rosso.'

She looks around at her husband, but they are all in deep conversation, about to head back out of the studio to look at the next painting.

'We can't talk here.' She whispers, panic mounting in her voice.

'I know.' I take a slip of paper out of my pocket and hand it to her. 'Here's my number.'

She reluctantly takes it from my hand and I hurry to catch up with the others, hoping my momentary absence hasn't been noticed.

~

I phone Livvie from the train.

'How did it go? Come on, tell me.' She sounds as if she's expecting bad news.

'We have a painting. Fifty-five thousand pounds and the artist is delighted. Richard is ecstatic and Tom is going to arrange a little flurry of publicity. David is going to unveil the piece at Richard's housewarming party. In tandem with the magazine spread, I think this is a win-win situation. But I feel totally drained.'

'Poor you. I can imagine the tension. I can't believe you pulled this off. I mean, how on earth did you discover David and his hyper-realism? Now you've raised his name and I've checked him out, I can't believe I hadn't heard of him before. But then art has never been my thing.'

Awkward.

'Just research on artists in general.' Another little white lie. It occurs to me how easily a lie slips between one's lips and maybe we all fool ourselves that the lie we are going to tell will do no harm.

'Well done you. Have a relaxing evening and I'll see you tomorrow.'

My evening is going to be anything but relaxing.

Chapter 37

Keep calm, Ellie. Focus on dinner. I look over my shoulder at Josh, chatting away to the girls. Rosie has a problem with her maths homework and Hettie thinks it's funny because Josh, too, is struggling.

'You did go to school, Dad, didn't you? I mean this isn't rocket science.'

I laugh at the tone of her voice. This is my normality. Visiting Knightsbridge today, Richard's house in Surrey, Villa Rosso – they are all alternative realities to me. Different aspects of this world, like parallel planes. Will Aletta ring tonight? If she does I imagine it will be from fear of losing what she has rather than from a guilty conscience over what she's done.

'Dinner is ready, ladies. Have you finished with Dad?'

They both blow him air kisses and sit at the table so that I can head off for some quiet time with Josh.

We talk as I walk.

'How did your trip to London, go?'

'It was a success and Livvie was pleased. It's a big problem solved and the end of the job is in sight. Virtually everything, except two chandeliers, is ready and waiting for the team. Once the painters have finished, the last bit happens relatively quickly. Although it always astounds me how long it takes to unpack the items and have things mounted on walls.'

'You love what you do and I'm glad of that. I hope you never think we've held you back, Ellie. You know, stopped you developing your full potential. But when Rosie is a little older and Hettie has more freedom, you could chase that dream if you wanted to. I hate to think that because of the nature of my job, it always has first priority.'

'There must be a weird collection of thoughts running around inside your head, Josh. Teamwork is about giving and taking. Besides, I have everything I want right here.'

'What if Livvie offered you a partnership?'

I lean in to scrutinise his face.

'Have you been talking about me behind my back, Josh Maddison?'

'I spoke to Livvie to enquire how her mum was doing and your name happened to crop up. She was sounding me out before approaching you.'

'Oh, but in the first place you were checking up on me.'

'Don't be cross. You know I've been worried.'

'So what did you say to her?'

'That I would never stand in your way, even if it meant I had to change jobs sooner rather than later, as we'd planned. I mean, would the idea excite you? I want you to feel confident that you can grab what comes your way and not feel you have to rule things out because everything falls on your shoulders. I mean, it does at the moment, but we could change that. If that's what you want.'

I love you so much, Josh. I wish our life was simpler right now. I wish I could fix everything for everyone and wake up each day safe in the knowledge that I'd made a difference.

'My answer right now would be *no*. Not because we couldn't make it work, but because I don't want that work-life balance to push me more in one direction than the other until the girls are a little older. In a couple of years' time you'll be settled and, hopefully, back home for good. I know Livvie is impressed when I rise to the challenge, but the cost is great. I end up in these situations and I might look confident, but inside I feel like a fraud and that at some point it will be discovered. I walk away in a cold sweat, grateful when it's over and where's the joy in that? Yes, I've enjoyed the additional responsibility that has come my way but I want to grow my confidence over time. If I take on too much, too quickly, I will feel out of my depth. The truth is that Livvie needs to take on an experienced partner now, and I need to do what is best for us and the girls. Livvie is quite a force and can be very demanding at times. I fear I'd end up letting her down. But if an opportunity comes up in the future, then I'll feel better placed to grab it and run with it.'

'Okay, if you are sure. But I'm proud of you, lady. If someone you love asked you to move a mountain, you'd try, wouldn't you?'

I can't answer that; it's too close to the bone right now and my throat has closed over.

He smiles. 'See you later, alligator.'

I make an enormous effort to sound normal. 'In a while, crocodile.'

~

I'm in the study. My mobile phone is in the centre of the desk and I'm sitting in darkness, watching the digital clock glowing red like a demon's eyes.

I pull the iPad out of the drawer. I always put it away the minute I finish talking to Josh. If I leave it within reach, I can't stop myself from checking in case Max has sent a message. There's nothing new and I don't know whether that's a good thing or something to worry about.

There's a buzz and the phone lights up, the vibration making it look as if it's alive.

I clear my throat, press the button and raise it to my ear.

'Ellie Maddison?' Aletta's voice gives away no hint of emotion.

'Yes.'

'I thought maybe this was a trap and you hadn't come into our home to buy anything at all. But I was wrong. I can't remember you from the villa, but then there were so many guests. And it wasn't a happy place for me.'

My head is starting to ache and I wish I'd bought some water upstairs with me. My mouth feels dry.

'I'm sorry about that. I recognised you immediately, but the name made me hesitate for a moment.'

'Yes. Things have changed. You said it's wrong to hide. What did you mean?'

I breathe out quietly and then take a deep breath in.

'I've been to Italy recently and the effects of your disappearance still have a very real impact. Even as a visitor, it became very clear that it continues to hang over everyone. Such a shocking incident has divided opinion in the local community. There is persistent gossip and a few insist on believing that Max Ormanni is responsible for you going missing. If it carries on much longer, the police could reopen the case and cause major problems for Max.'

She gasps.

'They think I'm dead?'

'I know very little, but I believe some do think that, yes.

When people go missing anything is possible. I was there to tour some of the local workshops and the consequences of this unsolved case extends way beyond the Ormanni family.'

'I … I had no choice in the matter. It was wrong, I know, but I had to escape. I did contact my mother, who told me that the scandal had killed my father and broken his heart. I did not find out until several months after his death. I wanted to go back to explain then, but my mother would have nothing to do with me. She said she had no daughter.'

'And now you have a daughter, too.'

'She represents my new life. Free of the Ormannis. Everyone believed my father loved me, but that wasn't the case. What he truly wanted was a son and I was only ever a disappointment to him. So I did everything he demanded of me, but even then it wasn't enough. I did the only thing I could do and that was to give him Max in my place.'

An awful silence hangs between us. The truth is even uglier than I could have anticipated.

'What do you expect me to do?' She sounds fearful, a half-sob catching in her throat.

'There is an innocent man whom some believe may have committed an awful deed. You need to be aware of the full impact of your decision upon the people you left behind. Your new life is at the cost of someone else's happiness and that's bad karma. Maybe it's time to put it right, Aletta, so that you can continue with your new life with nothing on your conscience.'

There's no response and I let the moments pass in silence.

'This has been our worst fear, continually over-shadowing our happiness. If I promise I will face the consequences, will you vow not to get involved? If you, as a third party, go to the police, or the press, then all of our lives will be ruined, forever. My husband doesn't deserve that, neither does my daughter.'

'Nor Max,' I add firmly.

Her appeal sounds genuine enough, convincing me this is no empty promise. I find it totally shocking, though, that she isn't doing this first and foremost to right the incredible wrong she has done Max. The result will be the same, but she acts as if she did Max a favour when she left. Is that what happens when one lie turns into two, then three and it all becomes so complicated the truth is difficult to see?

'I have no intention whatsoever of exposing you, or hurting your family in any way. I was simply in the wrong place at the wrong time. You would have done the same if the situation had been reversed. You have wronged a good man and left him struggling with an impossible burden, because he feels he has no other option than to shoulder the responsibility. I think he believes that you left because you felt he took your rightful place within the family. He was simply trying to please you and only ended up driving you away. It's better to face this now than always live in fear of the truth being discovered. Imagine what your daughter would think if this came out many years down the road, Aletta.'

'You have my word on this and thank you for your silence. But I wish our paths hadn't crossed,' she whispers.

The line goes dead and I realise that the darkness has enveloped me in an uncomfortable and eerie way. My inner voice is trying to be positive and tell me that this is the best resolution and the least damaging for everyone. The last piece in the puzzle is Max. Should I warn him? Should I re-establish contact, ready to be there to hold him together? I know that's not what Josh would expect of me if he was in command of all of the facts.

Livvie would tell me it was time to walk away, I know that. I could talk to Aunt Clare, but this has gone so much further than I had anticipated. How can I explain this need to right a wrong after the advice she gave me? I feel as if I'm in a state of shock, numb is the word that comes to mind. I'm so exhausted, both mentally and physically, that I couldn't repeat the whole story to someone else even if I wanted to.

Why don't I feel happy? Relieved? Like a weight has been lifted from me?

Instead I feel that I may have done Max some harm.

Can you harness good karma and send it to someone

in need? If that's possible then, please, enough pain has been suffered and it's time for the healing to begin. Just let the path be smooth and the wounds heal quickly.

Be strong Max. I need you to be strong.

But in my dreams that night his eyes stare directly into mine, as if he's looking into my soul.

'I never really knew what true love was, but I do now. I'm not sure I can carry on without you, Ellie.'

'Please don't say that, Max. It isn't true. Your life has been on hold for so long, you've lost sight of how wonderful it can be. Look at Piero and Bella. Wonderful things happen every single day. I want that for you, but you have to want it for yourself.'

I want it for you, too, because you are in my heart, whether that's right or not. This isn't about choices. For me, it's simply a fact I can no longer deny.

He shakes his head. 'I can't let you go. But I wish I could.'

'It's time for you to live again, Max, but in the real world. Aletta is alive and has a husband. There is a child.'

'A child?'

'A little girl. The news will come to you soon, but I want you to be prepared.'

'The sins of the father should not be visited upon their children.'

It's a saying I recognise, based on a quote from the Bible, I think.

It's the last thing I remember, but the words echo around and around in my head. Does it count as an affair when nothing physical has occurred between two people and the passion is only in your head and your heart?

PRESENT DAY: ONE MONTH AFTER OUR NINETEENTH WEDDING ANNIVERSARY

Chapter 38

Ever since Livvie threw our anniversary party I can't seem to shake off the memory of what I saw in that crystal ball.

Bella's latest email is open in front of me and I can feel the turmoil everyone is going through at Villa Rosso.

Dear Ellie

It's been a little while, but times flies at the moment. Most of us have had a flu virus that's going around and now Max has it. The doctor says with the stress he's been under he has to take a week off to rest. Can you imagine Max taking a little time off? But in a way I'm rather glad as Luca is managing reasonably well and Trista has no choice but to work with him. It's about time Max realised he can take some time for himself and he doesn't have to feel he's letting anyone down.

Since the news broke, Trista is still acting as if she's the innocent party. The family don't know all of the facts, but they believe Aletta met someone in England and fell in love. I don't think anyone knows about the baby. It goes without saying that everyone is feeling very sorry for Trista, all over again. If only they knew she pushed her own daughter away.

But there's something else and there's no easy way to break this news to you, other than to simply say it. Max's legal representative has been here quite a bit and I overhead them talking about a DNA test. Max is the father of Aletta's baby. I'm the only one Max has told, at the moment. He will be flying to the UK very soon to meet his daughter. Talks are on-going over the custody arrangements and Trista even admitted she knew very early on that Max was the father. He can't wait to meet her, Ellie, and although the situation isn't the best, it's given him something to hold onto. Aletta could never come back here after what's happened, so he has to be patient for a while longer. At least Aletta isn't fighting him on that, probably out of guilt, or fear about bad press and the impact it could have on her husband. Maybe you will get to meet up with him again when he flies over to the UK and I know that would make him very happy.

There is quite a bit of gossip going around, still, but the tension has gone. We all feel indebted to Max in some way or other, for his strength and his loyalty. We *continue to thrive because of him and the personal sacrifice he chose to make.*

Piero and I have decided to delay the wedding until things have returned to normal. Well, the new normal, once Max has begun his life of freedom. It's hard to imagine him not living and breathing work, every waking hour, but also having a life of his own. He said that the people here kept him going and he'll never walk away from us. However, he will move out of the villa at some point and he seems excited about the prospect of putting down some roots of his own.

I asked him to give me away and I could see it meant a lot to him.

I hope things are going well with you and your family are all behaving themselves. You are the person who keeps everyone going in your world and it was wonderful to see first-hand how much they adore you. I hope, one day, that Piero and I can have a family and will be just as happy as you and Josh.

Try not to worry about things at this end. You did everything in your power to help and I feel awful that I'm the only one who knows, and can thank you for what you did.

Goodbye for now and I'll email in a couple of weeks' time to give you an update on Max.

B x

I'm glad Bella knows. I visit Max every night now in my dreams and have done for quite a while. Aletta lied when registering the birth of baby Elouise and she gave David's name as the father. She knew a DNA test would prove that not to be the case, because she'd already had one done. She'd told Max that she had wanted to make sure before she began her married life with David. When the results were confirmed that he wasn't the father, she admitted she was shocked. But he told her it didn't make any difference and she said she loved him even more because of that. Obviously, she has to face the consequences of giving false information when registering the birth.

I wondered how Max felt when he heard that as, to me, it sounded hurtful in the worst possible way. Aletta might be in love with David in a way she never was with Max, but this showed she, too, had that ice-cold side to her nature. But as she already knew the truth she had no option other than to acknowledge that Max had a right to be a part of his daughter's life. Somehow they have to make that work.

I know he can't wait to meet his little daughter for the first time and will be frustrated not to be heading off on a plane straight away. But a short rest will recharge his batteries and give him the strength to face Aletta once more. That first meeting will be the worst and I wish I could be there for him, but it isn't my place.

Sadly, what could have been a true fairy-tale ending to a dark story has turned into a bit of a nightmare, as each country has its own custody laws. But if the courts rule that he can have shared custody of his daughter then she could, perhaps, take regular holidays with him once their relationship has been allowed to blossom. That's something Aletta and David will have no control over, and for Max it's a reason to make a new life.

After Aletta had called me that night, I did a little more digging into David's background. It turned out that his first wife had died of cancer a little over ten years' ago and left him alone and devastated. They had no children and his name was never linked to any other women, as far as I could tell. Maybe Aletta and David were destined to be together and he's the one man who can bring out the best in her. I hope so, for little Elouise's sake.

Me? I still feel trapped by the glass wall.

How would I describe it? Like an ice-cold splinter in my heart, chilling my soul and freezing the essence of me. I'm suspended in time, trying hard to establish a sense of what's real. The glass wall isn't fragile; it's tougher than steel and just as impervious. Yet I'm able to glide through it as easily and naturally as taking a single step forward. My day is full of the blessings in my life, but when I lie down to sleep it's as if I leave this world behind. I simply take that step and then, there I am, standing on the other side and experiencing a different reality with Max. Of course, that's an analogy – or maybe I'm romanticising something that has never been real to me. My life is split into two; two lives that run in parallel and only cross over in my dreams. In this world I adore Josh and my girls absolutely; in that world Max is my soul mate and what I feel for him is unreserved love. A love that isn't new, but seems to have existed forever.

Is it possible to have two soul mates? Ironically, I don't know the answer to that question. I do know that I have a charmed life with a man I love and a passion that is fierce. My life seems perfect, and yet, what lies behind the glass wall is a mirror. A life with a different man: my other soul mate. I'm torn – with guilt and longing; longing for a normal life with my husband and wonderful girls, but unable to let go of either of the two men who make me feel complete. One in my day-to-day life and one in my dreams.

What I didn't understand before fate made me cross that divide was that a heart can be split into two halves and each half can have a perfect, life-changing love.

All I can do is let fate play out and hope that once Max has begun his new life I can slip away, content in the knowledge that he is happy. And, I hope that I will have played some small part in that. Only then, I believe, will the glass wall finally shatter and I will begin to feel whole again. I have to prepare Max for that, as gently as I can.

But everything is looking so hopeful now and he has the best reason in the world to start living again. How easy it will be for me to let him go, I have no idea. I seem to keep finding excuses to hang on, wanting just one more brief moment together and it's never enough.

~

'There's a chill in the air tonight.' Max slips off his jacket and places it around my shoulders. We're on the terrace, sitting at our usual table. The glow of the candlelight creates little flickers of shadow on his face.

'I welcome the breeze, it's been hot today.'

Our fingertips touch.

'Max, things are moving forward. You will soon get to hold your daughter in your arms. But you do know we can't have a life together, don't you?'

His frowns deepens and he extends his hand to cover mine.

'But you are the one for me, Ellie. I wasn't grieving for the loss of Aletta, but for the emptiness in my heart. I long to see my daughter, but you, too, have given me something that was missing in my life.'

It's like talking to a very young child who is listening to a string of words that they can't comprehend. The words are empty of meaning.

He puts up his hand to stop me speaking.

'Close your eyes. Please, just humour me for a few minutes. I want to take you on a little trip. Can you feel the sand beneath your feet?'

It takes a few moments, but then I wiggle my toes and I can feel it.

'Now you can open your eyes.'

The sweeping, panoramic view of a bay fills my entire line of vision and when I look down I see the soft, white sand beneath my feet. The air is still, the crystal-clear waters stretching as far as the eye can see, shimmering like ripples on a sheet of glass.

'It's beautiful, Max. Where are we?'

'Sapri. This is the Gulf of Policastro. Cicero called it "a small gem of the southern sea" and I think he was right.'

I spin around, taking in the wide promenade that is packed with bustling bars and restaurants. It's so full of life and I feel drawn to it. Beyond that, a small town is set against the backdrop of green hills and a majestic mountain range, like dark sentinels, stationed there to protect the bay. There's a sense of elegance to the scene in front of me.

Max clasps my hand in his and we stroll contentedly along the beach.

'This is where I come when I want to get away from it all. I love the olive groves and the sweeping planes surrounding Castrovillari. But here I can disconnect and simply enjoy a very different sort of beauty.'

He continues to draw me away from the sounds of the people milling around, and we head out towards the water's edge. The water laps gently as it travels further up the beach, creating little crests of turbulent white foam. Then the ebb once again drags the flow back down, with a soft whooshing sound. We stand here for a while, fascinated by the almost rhythmic sounds of the sea. It's powerful, yet calming.

I close my eyes, struggling to let go of the moment and yet conscious that this isn't real.

When I re-open them, I can't stop the tears from flowing down my cheeks. It's so hard to encourage him to seek out someone else. A part of me longs to be the one by Max's side, the one whose face he kisses. And the person lying next to him each night. But every single fibre of my being knows it's what I'm supposed to do. Whether I have the strength to do it, I simply don't know.

'It will be even more beautiful when you are here with the person you are destined to be with forever, Max. You know that person cannot be me.'

'But you are here, now. Why can't you simply stay?'

'You know why, Max. People are only meant to live one life at a time, not two. This is the time for me to be with Josh, Hettie and Rosie.'

'But I need you, too.'

'You have to do this for me. Let me go, so you can learn to live again in the real world. Fate will take us both where we are destined to go and trying to cling onto something not meant for us won't change a thing.'

His face looks bereft, as if he's watching everything he so badly wants, slip away from him. It breaks my heart. But it has to be done.

Chapter 39

The hammering sound coming through the wall is beginning to grate on my nerves. For the next couple of days I'm working from home while the guys are here to knock down the wall between Rosie's room and the guest bedroom. I remind myself that it's going to make her one very happy young lady and it's important that we acknowledge her growing needs.

Lack of sleep, general anxiety that never seems to wane, and the disruption to the house is extremely taxing.

An incoming message pings on my phone. It's from Josh.

How's it coming along?

Good. Noisy. Just stopping to make them a cup of tea.

I was thinking about a holiday. Just the two of us. Belated anniversary present. What do you think?

My body slumps as I don't have the capacity at the moment to plan anything. Just getting through each day is a trial. Josh has great ideas, but I'm the one who makes them happen. I know he means well and that he's concerned I need a break. I do, but not at this precise moment and not something that will be another drain on my time.

Once the house is straight again we'll talk about it.

Great. See you later, alligator. Love you! J x

In a while, crocodile. xx

I'm going through the motions at the moment, living from day to day. Somehow I have to take back control. The doorbell chimes and I wonder if it's a delivery of building supplies, although the guys didn't say they were expecting anything.

When I open the door it's Aunt Clare.

'Have you been avoiding me?' She launches herself inside and throws her arms around me. 'You look awful, don't you ever sleep?'

'Thanks, exactly what I needed to hear, today of all days. I'm about to put the kettle on for the workers.'

Now they are sawing and I grit my teeth as I lead Aunt Clare into the kitchen, shutting the door behind us.

'They're working overhead, in Rosie's room, so we might have to talk a little bit louder.'

She nods.

I prepare their tray and two mugs for us.

'How's the love life coming along?' I ask. She looks amazing, the best I've seen her look for a long time. There's a buzz about her and she's in a good place. I'm happy for her, because she's had her share of dark times.

'Well, it's not all about work, any more, that's for sure. I'm doing the work/life juggling thing and having a ball. How you fit that in alongside coping with two teenagers, I don't know. Mind you, mine might have left home a long time ago, but at some point they will probably be dropping off grandchildren for me to look after. Imagine that!'

'You're a nurse. If you can cope with a job like that, you can cope with anything. I'll just take this upstairs – make yourself comfortable.'

I leave the tray on a little table on the landing and pop my head around the door.

'Looking good, guys,' I smile. Rosie will be thrilled, but already the dust is circulating throughout the house and it's yet another task I'm going to have to add to my 'to do' list. It won't be a dust-and-vacuum job, but a complete top-to-bottom exercise.

When I go back downstairs, Aunt Clare has settled herself

on the sofa and I sit next to her, flopping down and forgetting she has a hot coffee in her hands.

'Whoops, sorry. Here's a tissue. I can't ever remember feeling as depleted as this before.'

She sweeps her eyes over my face.

'Maybe you are a little anaemic. You should pop to the doctors for a blood test. You are rather pale. Perhaps you need a dose of sunshine.'

I scoot back a little further and let my body go limp.

'Have you been talking to Josh? He texted me only a couple of minutes ago to say we need a break away, just the two of us.'

'Great idea, why not?'

'Because I'd have to make all the arrangements and until the house is straight I can't even think about organising it.'

She frowns. 'That's not like you. I can take a few days off work and come to stay here with the girls. I'd enjoy that.'

'Thanks, we'll probably take you up on that. I feel Josh and I need some alone-time together. We rarely get a date night since he changed jobs.'

'Things still aren't back to normal with you, then? I thought Italy was all behind you now?'

I lower my head, staring down into the coffee mug in my hands. I made the mistake of telling her everything. It was cathartic and afterwards I felt lighter, the burden of guilt wasn't so heavy on my shoulders. But I also made her a promise.

'I've tried everything, even sleeping tablets left over from when Josh struggled during that nightmare at his old firm. Look in my desk drawer, you'll find a stack of meditation CDs. I've even been to yoga. It's there, it's constantly there and I can't hide from it.'

'Ellie, I told you, mental health is as serious as something going wrong physically with your body. If your leg hurts, you go to the doctor to get it checked out. If you aren't getting enough proper rest, and I mean uninterrupted sleep, then it affects your mind and your body. You're always on the internet, type in sleep deprivation and see for yourself. At the anniversary party Josh barely took his eyes off you and when you were out of sight, he was uneasy. We're all worried about you right now, including the girls.'

I'm so stupid. Josh asked her to come and he must have texted me because he was checking I was here.

'Okay, I'll make an appointment. But what the hell do I say? How do I explain what's going on? It sounds completely crazy.'

'Tell him about your dreams and explain how exhausted you feel. Keep it simple, don't complicate it. It could be a hormonal imbalance upsetting the chemistry of the body, for instance.'

Or he could say that I'm mentally unbalanced. There's a medical term for those who talk to people who aren't really there. Aunt Clare is well aware of that.

'Promise me. I'm serious this time, Ellie. Please promise me you'll make that appointment.'

I nod and she changes the subject, asking about Hettie and Alex. That's Josh's next biggest concern and in a way that adds to my anxiety. He's talking to Aunt Clare about it because he has to talk to someone and he doesn't want to add to my worries.

Reluctantly I accept that I can't avoid making that appointment any longer.

As we sit and chat. She's doing her best to make me laugh. Nursing has a funnier side and I appreciate her attempts to lighten my mood.

'Are you still getting those cluster migraines?'

I nod, wondering how she can tell.

'I thought so. You've just turned a very strange colour. Nausea?'

It comes in waves and the coffee was a big mistake. I should have had water.

'How would you like a couple of hours on your own, to relax? What if, after Dawn drops the girls back home, I stay and take them out for pizza? You can have a few hours of peace and quiet. I'm sure the guys upstairs will be quitting soon. Have a long soak in the tub and whatever work you haven't done can wait until tomorrow. You need this, Ellie, so don't refuse a helping hand when it's offered.'

'You've become my substitute mum,' I admit, acknowledging the increasingly important role she plays in my life. My mum would have looked at me and known exactly what I needed in much the same way.

'Sometimes you have to learn to take a little, Ellie. Being a giver is a wonderful thing, but accepting a little help at the right time keeps things ticking over. I'll make sure the girls get to bed afterwards and I'll pop in to tell you when I'm off home, so you can lock the door behind me.'

'You're an angel and I will make that phone call.'

Chapter 40

The girls are delighted to find Aunt Clare here and the thought of a mid-week treat sends them scurrying to change out of their school uniforms. The builders leave at four-thirty and in less than an hour the house is empty and silence reigns. I still haven't moved from the sofa, as the pain above my right temple makes any movement a stomach-churning one. Aunt Clare left a glass of water and my migraine tablets on the coffee table and I know that if I don't take them soon this will develop into a full-blown attack.

I ease myself forward very slowly, grab the tablets and the glass, and then gently lower myself back against the cushions.

As I take a mouthful of water to swill down the tablets, I look around the room. Even when the girls and Josh aren't here, it's full of them. If I concentrate hard enough I can visualise them, sitting around the table, laughing and joking.

After a short while the nausea begins to subside once more and very gently I ease myself up off of the sofa and head upstairs to run a bath.

I place the iPad on the windowsill next to the tub, ready for when Josh makes contact. But as I lie back and the fragrance of the lemongrass bath salts begin to soothe my pulsing headache, I reach across and turn on the iPad to message him.

Hi Josh, the girls are out with Aunt Clare. I have a migraine and I'm having a soak in the bath, but after-wards I need to lie down on the bed for a while. Will text you later. Miss you, xx

I know I've let things get on top of me and I think I'm a little run down. I'm no good to anyone like this and I need to start taking better care of myself.

The iPad lights up and I reach out for it, visualising the worried look Josh will have on his face. I didn't mean for him to worry, but I really do need to lie here quietly for a bit. Steadying it on the edge of bath, and clicking the accept call button, it isn't him.

Bella's face appears on the screen and her face is rigid, like a mask. But it's the look in her eyes that frightens me.

'What is it? What's wrong?' The words catch in my throat.

'He's dead, Ellie. Max is dead.'

The sound in my ears is like a loud drumming. I'm sitting here amidst the bubbles and listening to a sound that is threatening to drown out her words.

A tear rolls down her cheek and a stab of severe pain hits me in the chest. And then I finally understand. I've felt this pain before. This isn't the first time I've lost Max and the first time it left a scar so deep that my soul has never recovered. When, or where, we lived our life together I have no idea, but I now understand the saying that *true love never dies.* Clearly, you can have two soul mates, just not in the same reality. My head feels so heavy, even heavier than my heart.

'I have to go. I'm sorry.' My voice is barely audible as I replace the iPad on the windowsill, watching the action as if it has nothing whatsoever to do with me.

Tears fill my eyes and a scream works its way up from the pit of my stomach, but my throat has constricted and it can't escape. I choke it back down, wondering if this is simply a bad dream. Am I imagining this?

'Max can't be gone.' My whisper echoes around the bathroom and I swipe angrily at the tears as they track down my face and plop into the water. I wrap my arms around my knees, rocking back and forth for comfort.

'You were nearly there, Max. How could you give up when you could have had a life full of happiness?' I throw the words out into the hollow emptiness of the room.

I think about the fact that his precious little daughter

will never know her biological father now and it breaks my heart. He was a special man, who cared about something more than just himself. All of the people whose lives he touched, and the difference he made, is his legacy. Fate reached out to me to help him because our link transcended time. Just as my love for Josh will go on forever, too. If the soul lives on, then so can enduring love.

I'm not sure how much time passes. I wipe my eyes with the palms of my hands, the chill that has settled on my skin making me tremble. Easing myself out of the bath, my eyes are watery still and I can't find the towel, so I wrap my dressing gown around me. Half-stumbling out of the bathroom, something isn't right and I don't know what. Where is everyone?

As I walk across the landing I look behind me and see my footsteps imprinted in a thin film of dust covering the wooden floor. Did I do that? The drumming in my head won't allow me to think and I need to lie down.

Max is dead. Did Bella say that, or was it a dream?

If I take some painkillers and maybe a couple of Josh's old sleeping pills too, then maybe this drumming will stop and I can lie down for a while. When I wake up I'll be able to think straight. The water slides down my throat and feels so good.

There was something I had to do, but I can't seem to remember it. Did I take some tablets? Maybe I should take a couple more painkillers, just to be sure. If only the drumming would stop.

My eyes need to rest, they are so heavy. Was it Max? Did he need me?

'Ellie, Ellie, I'm waiting for you.'

Max's words are heavy with anguish and seem to float around me.

'I'm alone. I need to know you are here. I can't see you.' He calls to me, but the room is empty and he isn't here.

'I'm with you, Max. You have nothing to fear.'

But Bella said Max was gone. Behind closed eyes there is nothing, except a black void filled with Max's voice.

'Whenever you think about me, I'll be here.' I gently reassure him, wishing I could see his face.

Random and disorganised thoughts begin to whirl around inside my head, making me feel dizzy. The drumming is getting louder. It makes the blood pound in my ears. Did I take some tablets? Which ones and how many? I can't remember.

Sadness grips me and I call out. 'Josh, Hettie, Rosie ... where are you?'

I feel myself falling, down and down in a gentle motion that seems to go on forever.

~

Everything hurts. My eyes won't open and when I try to lift my hand nothing happens. I want to move, but I can't. Nothing seems to work.

I hear a sound, or maybe it's a voice, I can't be sure, because the ability to concentrate is not within my grasp. There's hollowness around me, like an echo that goes on forever. Even my thoughts travel through the hollow space, like ripples in the water, before coming back to me again.

Maybe the echo is actually inside my head. I'm tired and I don't want to think, so I stop thinking and it feels good. Sleep tries to claim me, but suddenly that elusive thought comes back once more. 'Josh, don't let me go.'

Something touches my hand and I feel as if I've broken into a million tiny pieces. I'm travelling through the hollow space full of echoes and I think I can hear Josh's voice.

Chapter 41

'I'm here.'

My eyelids flutter, but I can't seem to open them. As awareness sweeps over me, I begin to panic. Why does everything hurt? I try to lift my body up off the bed a little, to ease the stiffness in my back. Why am I in bed? Was I sleeping?

'Gently, gently.'

The words wash over me, familiar and soothing.

'It's Josh. I'm here, Ellie.'

As if someone has just woken up my body, sensations begin to kick in as the blood starts to flow. Suddenly I'm conscious of my hands, then my arms and this peculiar sensation continues on around my body, until everything suddenly feels connected correctly. It's a strange feeling. Why would I feel disconnected? I try to stretch my back again, arching it slightly against the hard surface of the bed. Something touches my shoulder.

'Don't try to move too quickly, Ellie. Just relax and let yourself wake up gradually.'

'Have I been asleep?'

'Yes, you've been asleep.'

'Am I okay? I can't seem to open my eyes. Can you hold my hand?'

Josh places both of his hands around mine and I realise he's hunched over, his cheek resting against my skin.

'I'm going to wipe your eyes, Ellie. Just lie still.' It's a voice I don't know and I wonder what's happening. Josh squeezes my hand, encouragingly.

The coolness of the wipe against my eyelids is refreshing and gradually I feel them ungluing as if they were stuck. But as I open my eyes fully, everything is hazy and I realise the lights around me are so very bright that I have to squeeze my lids shut again.

'The light hurts, Josh. I can't stand the light.'

Immediately the brightness dims and I open my eyes again, searching for him.

'Here I am. Give me your hand again. You're in hospital, Ellie, but you are going to be okay. You're going to get well, my darling.' A sob catches in his throat and suddenly he leans over me. His arms are so gentle and warm as they surround me; all of my anxiety begins to slip away.

'Where are the girls?' Fear grips me once more and I try to lever myself up.

'Sshh, lie back. The girls are fine. You'll see them very soon. Can you remember what happened?'

As my eyes begin to adjust, things start to come into focus. We're in a small room and we're alone. I turn my head and Josh looks at me.

'I thought I'd lost you,' he whispers. 'But you came back.'

'I chose you, Josh. I couldn't let go.'

He doesn't seem to understand, but as he smiles at me there are tears in his eyes. I so badly want to stay awake, but tiredness overcomes me once again.

'Stay with me,' I call out to him and he increases the grip on my hand.

'I'll be here when you wake up, Ellie. I'm not going anywhere.'

~

'A week? I've lost a week of my life just lying in this bed?'

Josh is trying his best to encourage me to eat something, as he explains what happened.

'Clare and the girls came back home and you were on the bed, fast asleep. She made them some hot chocolate and they said goodnight. Clare went in to let you know the girls were safely tucked up in bed, when she saw the empty bottle on the floor and a few sleeping tablets scattered on the bedside table. She couldn't rouse you and called an ambulance.'

Tablets? 'Why was I taking tablets?'

Josh edges his seat a little closer to the bed.

'You had a migraine, do you remember? When Clare left with the girls she put your medication on the coffee table. You took your tablets and then went upstairs. You had a bath and you sent me a message to say you were going to lie down. Is it coming back to you, now?'

It's all hazy. Why was I crying in the bath? And then I remember. Poor Max, my poor love. I turn my head to look at Josh. I chose you, my darling. You and the girls. Max will understand.

'A little. Why was the bottle on the floor?'

Josh has a pained look on his face.

'We think you wanted to take two painkillers, as you usually do. But something happened, maybe you fell asleep and forgot what you'd taken and you took some more. We're not sure how many.'

He thinks I took an overdose on purpose. I reach out and grab his hand, unable to stop myself bursting into tears.

'I wasn't trying to escape, Josh. If I took more than I should have done it was a mistake. Please believe me when I say I would never leave you and the girls. Ever.'

He pushes away the tray in front of me and comes to sit beside me on the bed.

'Thank God, Ellie. I thought I'd let you down. I thought we'd put you through too much. I need you: we need you.

Nothing is the same without you, Ellie, and the girls have been distraught.'

He kisses my forehead, his tears soft and warm against my skin.

'We're so lucky, Josh. Fate pulled me back when it could so easily have taken me away.'

My heart grieves for Max, but I'm where I belong. I know he's finally gone, not because I can remember Bella's words, but because the link between us has been severed. As it was meant to be.

Chapter 42

The wind whips my hair from beneath my hat, as the cold, salty spray begins to sting my face. The girls are striding ahead, eager to traverse the sandy beach and begin the walk from Caswell Bay along the coastal path to Langland Bay.

Josh and I walk hand in hand, content to pace ourselves for the two-mile trek along a stunning part of the Gower coast.

'Careful on the steps up near the top, girls. The rain will make them slippery.' My voice carries on the wind and fortunately it's in their direction. Hettie looks back and acknowledges my warning.

'I'm glad we decided to get away for a week. It's not quite the rest I wanted for you, but the fresh air will do you good.'

I smile, knowing full well what he means. Renting one of the apartments that sit on the edge of the sandy beach here at Caswell Bay takes us back to our honeymoon. He wanted this trip to be just the two of us, but after what we've all been through I didn't want to leave the girls at home.

I feel as if I have taken back control of my life. Each day I savour the normality of it. The fact that I could so easily have lost it is still shocking to me. If Aunt Clare had left me to sleep and let herself out that night, it would all have been over. The hospital pumped out my stomach and then it was a waiting game. Anything could have happened, but I was spared.

Now I'm here, alive and well, tasting the saltiness in the air and seeing my girls letting off steam. And Josh, holding my hand and stealing a kiss or a hug at every opportunity.

As we leave the sand behind us and begin the climb on the first leg of the walk, the view out across the bay is stunning. The low sun has turned the pale-grey water into a liquid silvery gold. So bright that it hurts the eyes as the light skims and bounces across the uneven surface.

Overhead, despite the light rain mixed with the spray from the heavy waves, the seagulls wheel and dive, their raucous call grating on our ears.

'Do you remember?' Josh asks, tweaking my hand in his.

'Yes. We did this walk every morning and every evening. There's something special about watching the sun rise and set when the only thing standing in the way is the ocean. It's magical, Josh, isn't it? And now we're here with our beautiful girls.'

We hasten our steps, wanting to catch up so we can all walk together.

'I wish we could bring Alex here,' Hettie turns towards us, the hair that has escaped her hood falling in straggles around her face.

'We will,' Josh promises.

'Even though it's your special place? I mean, look how long it took you to bring us here,' Rosie adds, sounding mildly peeved.

'We weren't keeping it to ourselves, darlings. It was always something we meant to do. And in future we'll make more time for trips like this.'

'Can we sit on the seat – that one over there?'

As we mount the sweeping steps that take us up to the highest part of the walk, I nod my head. 'It's rather windy, so let's walk over there together.'

We link arms at the very top, edging forward towards the bench. The only one that is so close to the edge and looks out across both bays.

Rosie and Hettie let out little shrieks of laughter as the wind tries its best to push us back towards the path.

'Keep going, we're nearly there,' Josh shouts, his words

obscured by the swooshing of the water below us.

We press ahead and eventually we're there, all four of us staring out to sea.

'Okay. One thing you'd like us all to do this year. Hettie first.'

Josh turns towards her. She laughs and then puts on her thinking face.

'We should go to a concert. But I get to choose which one.'

'You next, Rosie.'

Rosie is untangling her hair and trying to push her hat back on. I take off my gloves and manage to catch most of it, twisting it into a ponytail as she forces the hat down over her ears.

'I want to get a kitten.'

Josh and I exchange glances.

'That's not really something to do together, Rosie,' Hettie levels at her. 'But I second that.'

I roll my eyes at Josh and he raises his eyebrows, shrugging his shoulders.

'Mum next.'

'No, you next, Josh. I'm still thinking.'

'Well, I'd like us to fly to Italy for a holiday.'

My heart skips a beat and I look at Josh. His eyes reflect a loving smile and I relax as I continue to look at him.

'What? It's an experience I think we should all share.'

The girls do a high-five.

I scan the horizon as I filter my thoughts. I have no regrets about Italy and I know we will have a wonderful time there.

'Come on, Mum. You have to choose something.'

'Well, I'd like us to do a family run.'

Three sets of eyes peer at me, as if I've lost my mind.

'I'd like us to raise money for the hospital.'

'I'm in,' Hettie calls out, having to turn her head sideways to avoid the buffeting wind.

'Me, too,' Rosie chimes in, standing up and spinning around to face me. The wind presses her forward and I laugh as she half-stumbles into my arms.

Josh nods his head in agreement and when I look at him I can see his emotions, mapped out so clearly on his face.

This is my life; this is exactly where I'm supposed to be at this moment in time. I will no longer take anything for granted. I will strive to live in the moment and enjoy every single day of the rest of my life with Josh and the girls, knowing I have been truly blessed.

Epilogue

Max:

True love is such a powerful emotion that it never dies, even with the passing of time. And many, many years had passed before I was to meet once more the woman with whom my heart was inextricably linked. How I wish those memories were clear to me when I first saw Ellie on the terrace that day. Instead, I simply knew that she had been sent for a reason and that was to help not just me but a whole community of people. As a stranger, she was no stranger to me, or I to her. She was our guardian angel. We both knew that, but our minds simply could not comprehend it. How can you love someone you don't even know? Until you realise we can only see what we are supposed to see at any given time.

I understand now that she could not, and would not, be unfaithful to her husband. Not because she was self-righteous, but because she was in love with him. And it was their time, not ours.

I had no idea that I had a congenital heart condition. Or that fate had, in fact, been smiling down upon me, because timing is everything. In allowing me to meet Ellie once more, it was simply taking me towards another part of my destiny. A destiny that would always be linked to her, because the day I died, the part of her that is mine came with me this time. It allowed her to be free to finally live her life in peace, as it was intended. And that is *our* ongoing destiny.

As for my darling little daughter, I will always walk alongside her and guide her footsteps as best I can. Aletta will make a good mother and will ensure that history doesn't repeat itself because of what we've all been through.

I turn my head to smile at Ellie as we walk across the terrace, past the sweet-smelling oleanders and head out towards the olive groves. Every day is special and Ellie has given my life a meaning again, as she did once before, a very long time ago.

As we walk along, hand in hand, Ellie leans into me.

'Fate had a plan for us, after all,' she whispers. And for that I'm eternally grateful.

Acknowledgements

The main thank you has to go to the very beautiful town of Castrovillari, in Southern Italy. While the story and all of the incidents, people and places used are purely fictional, the setting is very real; as was the worst Italian olive harvest on record, in 2014. It was, however, the key to the story I wanted to tell. The setting had to have a magical feel, a sense of paradise: for that reason, it will always hold a very special place in my heart.

Hugs to my awesome editor Charlotte Ledger, for her guidance in helping me to make this story come alive on the page; also for her overall support and for being a listening ear. You are a star!

As usual, no book is ever written without there being a long list of people to thank in getting the book out there, publicising it and, of course, the kindness of reader/reviewers. You continue to delight, amaze and astound me with your generosity and support; it's truly humbling. Without your kindness, I wouldn't be able to indulge myself in my guilty pleasure ... writing.

A virtual hug to the lovely Shona Lawrence for the cover quote – one to treasure! And a special shout out to wonderful reviewers Kate, Shaz, Suze, Anniek, Nikki, Shona and Kaisha for their amazing support in spreading the word. I am honoured to count you as my dear friends.

Feeling blessed and sending much love to you all, Linn x

Printed by RR Donnelley at Glasgow, UK